S0-ARM-575

FIRE

IN THE

SEA

BUSSELTON SENIOR HIGH SCHOOL

LIBRARY

Myke Bartlett was born in Perth. He is a journalist and a film reviewer. He currently lives in Melbourne with his wife and a Boston Terrier called Moxy.

mykebartlett.com

Teaching notes available at textpublishing.com.au/resources

FIRE IN THE SEA

MYKE BARTLETT

BUSSELTON SENIOR HIGH SCHOOL

X 41017.01

F
BAR

LIBRARY

TEXT PUBLISHING MELBOURNE AUSTRALIA

textpublishing.com.au
mykebartlett.com

The Text Publishing Company
Swann House
22 William Street
Melbourne Victoria 3000
Australia

Copyright © Myke Bartlett 2012

All rights reserved. Without limiting the rights under copyright above, no part of this publication shall be reproduced, stored in or introduced into a retrieval system, or transmitted in any form or by any means (electronic, mechanical, photocopying, recording or otherwise), without the prior permission of both the copyright owner and the publisher of this book.

First published by The Text Publishing Company, 2012

Design by W H Chong
Typeset by J & M Typesetting
Printed and bound in Australia by Griffin Press

National Library of Australia Cataloguing-in-Publication entry
Author: Bartlett, Myke.
Title: Fire in the sea / Myke Bartlett.
ISBN: 9781921922749 (pbk.)
9781921921513 (ebook : epub)
Target Audience: For secondary school age.
Dewey Number: A823.4

FSC
www.fsc.org
MIX
Paper from
responsible sources
FSC® C009448

The paper this book is printed on is certified against the Forest Stewardship Council® Standards. Griffin Press holds FSC chain of custody certification SGS-COC-005088. FSC promotes environmentally responsible, socially beneficial and economically viable management of the world's forests.

For my grandparents Joan and Bart, an inspiration

PART ONE

THE
BOY
WHO
CAME
BACK

1
SOMETHING IN THE WATER

Somewhere there were fires burning. Black smoke rose to the east behind the grey hills, then slumped west over the Perth suburban plain, the breezeless air taking it nowhere. Ash dusted squat brown houses and dry-grass yards, where dogs sneezed beside blackened barbecues.

The sea breeze had switched off three weeks ago, as summer tightened over the city. Only twice since then had Sadie Miller seen even as much as a white cloud. Nothing ever stirred, ever changed, ever happened.

'Okay,' Heather was saying. 'Shuffle the pack and try to focus your energy into it. Think about any questions you want answered.'

Sadie blinked, looking at the oversized cards in her hands. Her cousin had been pestering her about a tarot reading since the holidays started, but it had taken a month of boredom for Sadie to crack.

'You know it's not normal, talking to stationery.'

'C'mon Sadie, you agreed.'

It was an afternoon like any other. The four of them, lazing on the terraces at Cottesloe beach. Kimberley arranged on a carefully laid-out towel, touching up her lip gloss. Her twin Heather, twenty-two minutes younger and twelve times as serious, turning over tarot cards. Tom sitting away from them, staring out across the glaring white sand.

Sadie had tried finding refuge in her book, but the heat boiled any meaning out of the words.

'Okay,' she said. 'I'm thinking.'

It wasn't just boredom. Sadie did have questions she wanted answered. So she willed magic into the pack and, under instruction, split it into three parts. With some attempt at ceremony, Heather turned the first card over. It was a picture of the Earth. Heather consulted her book to find out what this meant. The next card was the Knight of Cups. Again, the book came out. Sadie began to lose interest. There was some excitement—from Heather, at least—when a card predicted romance. Tom shifted on his towel and Sadie made sure she didn't notice.

Then, inevitably, there was the death card. That one, Sadie thought, needed no research. Heather dropped her practised boredom, her hands twisting in jerky circles. 'Um. That's a really good card to get, seriously. It means change. Things are going to, like, totally change for you. Maybe—' She stopped talking, realising what she had said. 'I mean, you know…'

Sadie did know, and it wasn't the future she was thinking about. It was six years since things changed, like, totally. Six years since she woke up in hospital, with her parents gone. And every day she missed them more, not less.

'It's all just fairy dust and voodoo anyway,' she said. 'You know these cards are coated in plastic. Very mystical.' She was joking, wanting to break any tension, but as she stood up, she accidentally scattered the cards with her foot. Now it looked like she was having a go.

'You're so bloody sure about everything, aren't you?' Heather plugged in one then the other of her earbuds and sank back behind tightly-folded arms.

Kimberley raised a plastic bottle of pink liquid to her glossy lips and sighed with purpose. She was never less than immaculate, her blonde hair untousled by salt or sweat. It seemed she might have something to contribute, but instead she declared:

'Raspberry water is my life. It literally is.'

Sadie grabbed her mask and snorkel from beside her towel and pulled her dress off over her head.

'If anyone wants me, I'll be underwater,' she said.

Sadie clambered down the salty rocks on the south side of the rocky groyne, keeping clear of the fishing lines and the purple crabs skittering between barnacles. She tightened the strap on her mask and dived in. A shallow reef jutted out a small distance from the shore, then dropped away into sudden depths. Sadie swam along its bony edge, where ribbons of kelp rose up from the dark water. Small silver fish sparked about her. The voices of the fishermen above dissolved beneath the comforting rumble of breakers.

Here she was, at last, herself. Here there was no one to offend. One more year of school and she would be gone. To Oxford. Melbourne. Anywhere. She drifted happily in her solitude.

A large shadow shifted in the kelp, startling her. Instantly, it was gone. Sadie broke the surface, nearly choking on the water in her snorkel, and looked around for a diver's flag.

Something brushed against her legs and she ducked again. A lithe, dark form retreated into the depths. Way too fast for a diver.

Sadie, you idiot.

Sunset was feeding time, everyone knew that. It was less than six months since the last surfer had been taken by a white pointer. She could see the headline now: *Sadie Miller. Shark Victim.*

The shadow buckled and turned back towards her. She swam frantically back to the groyne. It buzzed past her, so close that she was spun sideways in its wake. Ahead, she could see Tom climbing down the rocks to the water. He had seen her panic. Everyone had.

Then she was skinning her knees on the rocks. Tom was grasping her hand and yanking her out of the water.

'You okay? What happened?'

Sadie snatched back her hand, getting to her feet and tearing off her mask.

'Nothing, I'm fine. I'm an idiot. I'm fine.'

There was no sign of anything in the water. But Sadie was haunted by a glimpse of that shadowy thing. Something fast and sleek, but not a shark. Something with arms and legs.

As always, they stayed late. Kimberley refused to budge from the grass until the last of the good-looking boys had gone.

They waited half an hour for Aunt Margot in her BMW. Above, the bright car-park lights snared small galaxies of insects. As Margot leaned over to open the passenger door, her daughters whinged at her for being late and cool air spilled out of the car.

'Need a lift, sweetie?' she trilled.

'I've got my bike,' Sadie said, nodding at the ruby-red three-speed leaning against her hip.

Kimberley pulled the passenger door shut, leaving Sadie and Tom watching the tail-lights as the car pulled away.

'I'll drive you home,' Tom said, nodding at his

Land Rover.

'I've got my bike, idiot.'

Tom nodded. Sadie sighed.

'Tom, I just called you an idiot. Come on, give me something, please.'

'What d'you mean?'

'I mean, you know, punch back occasionally. Show some signs of life.'

Tom said nothing.

'You can put your bike in the back.'

She wheeled her bike in Tom's direction, then released her grip on the handlebars so that he had to dart forward and catch it.

'You put it in the back,' she said, waiting. For something, anything. But he only nodded, already leading the bike away. She followed him, furious. She wasn't sure where this sudden fire had come from. It wasn't Tom's fault, not really. Sometimes it felt like anger was always there, simmering in her boots. Waiting for the smallest excuse to rise up and consume her.

Tom didn't start the engine. He turned the stereo on, filling the cabin with hip-hop: angry, jangling rhymes about life in the ghetto. Sadie opened the glove box and started pulling out CDs.

'Why do you listen to this crap?'

'I like it.'

He stared at his knuckles on the steering wheel,

willing himself to say more. To lean across to Sadie in the passenger seat. But the distance from his seat to hers was wider than the parking space. She was watching the sea and the lights of Fremantle Harbour. Darkness stretched on forever. He knew what she was thinking. Anything worth doing or worth seeing was happening somewhere else.

He just needed a chance. A chance to be noticed.

Sadie punched him lightly on his left shoulder, then rubbed the wound and let her hand drift down to his.

'Sorry,' she said. 'I was being a bitch.'

The funny thing was, he didn't want her to apologise. An apology was worse than a putdown. 'It's cool.'

'No it isn't. You're my best friend.'

Sometimes, he thought, being friends felt a whole lot like nothing. His fingers meshed with hers on the wheel. He could pull her in and kiss her. She would be surprised, in the moment, but then it would make sense. She would see him, would feel it too.

But she was already easing her hand away and looking out through the windscreen.

'Hey, check that for an outfit.'

An old man walked along the pavement towards them. He wore a soft cap pulled down over a head of thick white hair, a blue paisley silk scarf and a suede vest buttoned over a long-sleeved shirt. The leather strap of a beige canvas satchel was pulled tight across his chest.

'That look would totally suit you Tom. I'm serious. No more baggy jeans.'

The man paused at the edge of the terraces, turned and looked out to sea. He seemed transfixed by the twin lighthouses on the invisible horizon.

Then, suddenly, there were two other figures on the grass. Neither Sadie nor Tom saw them arrive—they were, at once, just *there*. One knocked the man to his knees. The other grabbed him by the throat. Choking him.

'Hey!' Sadie was shouting. 'Do something!'

It took Tom a moment to realise she was talking to him. 'Right, yeah, sure.' He fumbled with the car keys. Sadie threw her door open and ran towards the commotion.

'Hey! Hey!'

The figures on the grass turned to look at her, casual as anything, and it occurred to her that she was running towards danger, instead of chasing it away. But she kept going.

Behind her, an engine roared. Tom's Land Rover jerked forwards and its lights snapped to high-beam.

Now Sadie could see the attackers. There was something not right about their faces, something withered and horrible. Something demonic. She wondered if they were wearing masks.

Recoiling from the light, the attackers reeled away down the terraces in impossible arcs, crossing ten metres of sand in two or three bounds, like flickering shadows. Almost immediately, they were in the black water, gone.

When Sadie reached the old man, he was lying face down. She turned him over. There were vivid red welts around his throat. His pale blue eyes looked back at her. He was trying to speak.

'Wa-watch out…' he croaked. He was English, Sadie realised, and she thought of her grandfather.

'Watch out for what?' she asked.

'F-f-for m-m-men w-with w-w-wet sh-shoes.'

He must be delirious, she thought. Tom was standing by the car, hands in pockets.

'What are you doing, Tom?' Sadie shouted. 'Call an ambulance!'

2
MR FREEMAN

By the time the ambulance arrived, Sadie might have been frantic if Tom hadn't beaten her to it. While he paced and swore and clenched his fists with such energy, Sadie felt herself grow calmer. Remembering her first-aid classes, she rolled the old man on his side and checked his pulse. His breathing was ragged and irregular.

The paramedics loaded him into the ambulance and Sadie jumped in too, yelling at Tom to follow in the Land Rover.

'Name?' One of the paramedics had a clipboard.

'Sadie. Sadie Miller.'

He frowned. 'He doesn't look like a Sadie to me.'

'Oh. I don't know his name.'

'You just jump in an ambulance with any old sick bloke?'

'I guess so. I didn't really think about it.'

The paramedic whistled. 'A regular Florence bloody Nightingale.'

Fremantle Hospital was a collection of brick buildings at the edge of the harbour town, beside a football oval and an old jail. On arriving, the man was taken away and two nurses tried to make Sadie sign a small library of forms. When she said she was sixteen, they asked about speaking to her parents. Sadie wished them luck. Her parents had been dead six years but, now she thought about it, her cousin was pretty good with the tarot cards. Maybe she could dig out a ouija board?

The nurses looked embarrassed. There were things Sadie knew she shouldn't joke about. But they were the things she most needed to joke about. That was what got her through.

A policeman had questions too. He was Sergeant Bradbury, a large forty-something-year-old man with a thick red moustache and a button popped from the belly of his shirt.

'Did you get a good look at these attackers?'

'No, well, sort of. They were tall. And thin. But they were wearing masks, I think.'

'What sort of masks?'

'I'm not sure. They were kind of like skulls, or maybe demons.'

'Demons, right. Let's leave that. Did you see where they went?'

'Um, yeah. They went into the sea.'

The policeman paused. 'They went swimming?'

Sadie's mouth dried up. She realised it didn't make any sense. Why didn't the attackers just run off up the bike path? Why attack the old man in the first place? And what about that shadow by the reef? She had seen something, there was no getting away from that. Was that just coincidence?

'So, we're looking for three demons who like a midnight swim.' Bradbury put his book away. 'Not a great help.'

When Sadie phoned home, Nan answered, sounding half asleep. The television was on in the background and Sadie could picture the two of them dozing off in their armchairs after the first evening bulletin.

'I'll get Grandpa to come and get you.'

'Tom's here Nan, it's fine. He can drop me home.'

She could hear her grandmother relax. 'We'll wait up.'

Sadie sat in the waiting room beside a man holding a bloodied napkin to his forehead. One of his eyes had disappeared behind a puffy, purple bruise. Across from her, a worried-looking mother held a crying baby. There was no air-conditioning, or it was broken, and the stagnant harbour air filled the room with a warm stickiness. Walls and foreheads gleamed.

It was the first time Sadie had been inside a hospital since the accident. Did that explain the rumbling nausea in her gut? The bad electricity in her fingertips? There was a strange magnetism shifting in these walls, drawing her in unwanted directions.

After a while, Tom stood up and said he was going for coffee. Soon after that, he came back empty handed and asked Sadie if she had any change. He was still wearing his board shorts.

Before she could answer, a man in a blue three-piece suit tapped her on the shoulder. He was short and almost bald, with a crimson cravat tucked neatly under his chin.

'Do excuse me, it's Miss Miller, isn't it?' he asked. He had an English accent, like the man at the beach.

'Sadie, yes. Who are you?'

'Apologies. Terribly rude of me.' He stuffed a damp handkerchief in his breast pocket and crammed his greasy palm against Sadie's. 'Horace Frobisher. I'm Mr Freeman's lawyer.'

'Is that his name, the old man?'

'Hmm? Yes. I don't suppose he said anything to you, when you were with him?'

Bradbury had asked the same question. Sadie felt even more ridiculous answering it this time. 'He said I shouldn't trust men with wet shoes.'

'Ha.' Frobisher laughed brightly and, Sadie thought, unconvincingly. 'How strange. Most unusual.' He noticed Tom standing by, still waiting for change. 'You are?'

'Tom Fitzgerald.'

'Hmm. Not important.' The lawyer blinked and

turned his attention to his leather satchel. After some jostling, he extracted a business card, a fountain pen and a small, hardbound address book. He gave each one to Sadie in rapid succession. 'Write down your phone number, will you? Mine is on the card.'

'Why do you want my number? I didn't do anything.'

'How modest. Mr Freeman was very grateful for your actions and, I can assure you, you'll be handsomely rewarded.' He was still fossicking about in his satchel. When this proved fruitless, he patted all of his pockets before finally finding his handkerchief. He mopped again at his shiny forehead.

'What do you mean, *rewarded*?' Sadie asked. 'I didn't do anything.'

'Just your name and number. Under M, ideally.'

Sadie scrawled her details on a page cluttered with addresses. 'Is he okay?'

'Hmm?'

'Mr Freeman. Is he going to be okay?'

'Oh. Didn't I say? He died ten minutes ago.' The lawyer's voice and manner were all business. He took back his address book and put them in his satchel. 'I'll be in touch.' He doffed his handkerchief as if it were a hat and left.

Sadie didn't see where he went. She could hear Tom saying her name but she wasn't listening. Her throat was tight and, although she couldn't be sure why, she felt guilty. She knew nothing about this man and now she never would. Did he have a family, a wife?

Somewhere out there, she thought, someone would be waiting up for him.

3
SOME GREAT REWARD

Uncharacteristically, Sadie's grandmother let her sleep in. Any other morning, Ida would have knocked on the door at nine and then again at nine-fifteen and finally, at nine-thirty, would have come in and told her to stop wasting a beautiful day. She was a small, determined English woman who had never quite lost the bedside manner of a wartime nurse. Today, Ida woke Sadie only by accident, holding a conversation at the front door.

'Is your granddaughter at home?' a man's voice asked.

Sadie peered down the hall. Ida had the front door barely open. 'I'm afraid she's not available.'

One of the two men stepped into view. He was young and clean cut, with a name badge pinned to his suit jacket. Sadie recognised him as one of the God squad that was forever cycling around town. She was grateful to her grandmother for fending them off. She'd been snared on the doorstep before. Sometimes she wondered if they sniffed her out, these religious types. Perhaps they caught an irresistible whiff of grief.

'We're setting up a new youth club. We're even hoping to put together a netball team.'

'I'm not sure she would be terribly keen.'

The second man appeared from behind the door. He was pretty much identical to the first, except for his blond hair. 'We're committed to local young folk,' he said. 'Where does she like to hang out? Perhaps she'd prefer a film night?'

Ida's smile tightened into a polite, but firm line. 'Thank you, but no.'

'Perhaps we'll come back another time.'

'Well, I don't know about that.'

The door clicked shut.

Pushy, Sadie thought, *even for door knockers.*

Turning back into the house, Ida saw her granddaughter peering out and gave her a smile.

'I've just made a pot,' she mouthed, in case the God squad were still listening. 'Grandpa's in the garden.'

Sadie never had to ask where her grandfather was; the information was always offered. She wondered sometimes if Ida was simply keen to reassure her she hadn't been abandoned. Not again.

Opening the blinds, Sadie could see him with a shovel, digging up the lawn near the chicken coop. He was a tall, wiry man with a crest of white hair, as vigorous at eighty-nine as he had been at fifty. He said it was the tai chi classes he took three times a week on the Fremantle esplanade.

Ida called out to Stan that Sadie was awake. Stan stopped digging out a patch of weeds, rubbed sweat and grit from his forehead, and waved.

Sadie waved back, thinking of old Mr Freeman dying alone.

Her parents had died together. Sometimes that was a comfort. They had been driving back from Christmas in the hills. The roads were steep and winding, shining with a rare summer shower. One minute Sadie was dozing in the back seat and the next she was woken in hospital by her grandmother.

Since then, grief had always been with her, waiting for Sadie to think, say or hear the wrong thing. A remark, a tarot card—everything was booby-trapped, capable of setting her aflame.

Still, she didn't hide from it. She wanted to prove that she was strong enough to cope. So she studied hard and made no excuses, for herself or anyone else. She read her father's history books and wore her mother's dresses. Sometimes, a dress would release a trapped ghost of her mother's perfume, or the grain of a dog-eared page would remind her of hiding under her father's desk. In these bubbles of lost times, she was as close to them as she ever would be again.

'Global bloody warming,' her grandpa said, washing his hands at the kitchen sink.

Sadie was reading the paper at the table, halfway through a triangle of buttered toast. She looked up, mouth full.

'The television was saying this morning that everything's getting cooler. Ask me, they should be spending more time out of their air-conditioned studio. Bloody stinking. Sixteenth day with no wind, I make it. Incredible. Those fires are still going too. Could smell them, wind or no wind. Still, some bugger will put them out, the days will cool and then we'll all forget again, won't we. When there's no panic, everything seems too difficult, doesn't it. More tea?'

Stan had never done small talk. His conversations followed the headlines he stuck on the fridge—injustices and crusades: clippings of wars in Afghanistan and Iraq, Vietnam and Japan, mushroom clouds and detention camps. He had arrived in Perth fifty years ago, tired of post-war London, and had been arguing ever since. The house was full of old pamphlets, windows marked with faded stickers for women's rights, Korean flags and anti-nuclear marches. One of Sadie's earliest memories was holding his hand at a protest rally. How proud she had felt, standing up for something, even if she wasn't sure what it was.

Cold water hissed in the kettle as Stan frowned across at her. 'Your nan says there were some nutters at the door, asking for you. We're not losing you to some cult, are we?'

Sadie mimed affront. 'No way, the great spaghetti monster in the sky would never forgive me.'

'Quite right.' He gave her a wink. 'It would take a lot for you to disappoint me Sadie, but that might just do it.'

Never, Sadie thought. 'Is this a good time to mention my new tattoo?'

Stan's laugh rattled the spices in the pantry. The kettle began to murmur. Sadie realised her grandfather was watching her.

'That was a brave thing you did last night,' he said.

Sadie couldn't quite look at him. 'I didn't do anything, not really.'

'It gives me hope, you know. That this world has people like you in it. People who do what's right.' He jabbed a finger at the newspaper, at a picture of some politician. 'Shame it's also full of idiots like him. Have you read that yet?'

Sadie shook her head, listening. She was glad to move on to a conversation that wasn't about last night.

An hour passed over the morning paper and then there was an empty afternoon in front of her. She wasn't sure she could stand another day with her cousins. Before she realised it, Sadie was staring at the wall, thinking of last night. Of the lithe figures standing over Mr Freeman. And the demonic masks they wore.

There was still no breeze. The beach was infested with tourists dragging themselves from their towels to the surfless sea. Swinging her leg off her bike, Sadie looked out towards the horizon, where a convoy of cargo ships waited. It had occurred to her that there might have been a small boat moored a short distance off shore. The assailants might have swum out there. Now, in the glare of the afternoon sun, it seemed unlikely. She would have seen a boat in the moonlight, seen the attackers come up for air.

But what other explanation was there?

Sitting in the patchy shade of a Norfolk pine, Sadie wondered if she had just imagined the whole thing.

When she got home, there was a car she didn't recognise in the drive. An old grey Jaguar. Her grandparents were both in the lounge, as was Mr Frobisher who was sitting in Ida's armchair, sipping tea. He was wearing the suit he had worn the previous night and he looked just as overheated. Stan sat in his own armchair, frowning. No one was saying anything.

'This man tells me you've met. He says he's a lawyer,' Stan said.

Frobisher stood up, brandishing a manila folder. 'This is a will, made last night by Mr Jacob Freeman in the minutes before his death.' He proceeded to rattle off the names of witnesses and legal jargon that Stan, Ida and Sadie ignored. They were waiting for the point.

Frobisher opened the folder and held it out to Sadie. She wasn't sure if she should take it.

'You'll notice your name and address. Mr Freeman was most insistent.'

Ida put a hand lightly on Stan's arm and smiled at the lawyer. 'Has he left Sadie something, Mr Frobisher?'

Sadie read the document in front of her. She found her own name and kept skipping between it and the man's name, trying to make the connection. *Jacob Leonard Freeman. Sadie Veronica Miller.*

'No,' she said. She felt at once strangely weightless and incredibly heavy. 'He's left me everything.'

'What?' Stan was on his feet.

'Conditionally,' Frobisher said quickly, mopping his brow as he peered up at the sinewy man standing over him. His manner had been officious and, Sadie thought, somewhat superior. Now, in the shadow of her grandfather, Frobisher seemed suddenly small.

'And what does that mean, conditionally?' Stan demanded.

'Mr Freeman has no known family. He has been estranged from all his relatives for at least fifty years. As far as we know, there are no living descendants. However, should any next-of-kin make themselves known, the inheritance will pass to them.'

'Ridiculous. That makes no sense whatsoever.'

'Mr Miller—'

'Mr Greene. Stanley Greene. Sadie has her father's name. Don't go jumping to conclusions unless you want to look like an idiot.'

'Stan,' Ida said again, calmly but with enough force to make him sit down.

The lawyer continued: 'If no family member makes a claim within the next twelve months, all belongings will pass to Miss Miller in perpetuity.'

'Why not wait twelve months then?' Stan asked. 'Why tell her now? In three weeks, she'll have school to worry about. Exams.'

Frobisher seemed tired of questions. He snapped the latches shut on his satchel. 'There are responsibilities attached. Mr Freeman didn't want to leave his house or belongings unattended. It's all in the documentation. Now, if you'll excuse me.'

Without waiting to be excused, Frobisher left. He barely looked at Stan, but Ida saw him to the door.

Sadie was staring at the will, waiting for it to make sense, and then she saw the address: *1 Ocean Street, Cottesloe*. A house. Right on the coast. She had a feeling she knew exactly which house it was.

It seemed impossible. She looked at her grandfather. 'He left me his house,' she said.

Stan stood up and snatched the will off her. 'You don't need this,' he said, carrying it away to the study. 'None of it.'

4
OCEAN STREET

It was possibly the biggest and certainly the oldest house in Cottesloe. Three storeys of worn limestone and greying timbers. In front of it there was nothing but a vacant lot, the coastal road and then endless sea.

Every other house on the steep street was immaculately maintained but this one had been decaying for decades. Long, brown grass grew in patches behind a half-collapsed picket fence. Every window was coated with dust, and leaves from several seasons past stuffed the sagging gutters.

Sadie had been right about which house it was. She had often stopped her bike on the beachside path to admire its sagging grandeur. Now she stood on the pavement with her grandparents, pulling at the strap of her mother's handbag, and waiting for Frobisher. She wondered if he was late, or if there were legal complications. Part of her hoped there were, that all of this would come to nothing.

Stan had one foot on the first of three steps that led to a short garden path. He stared up at the house as if staring it down. Ida looked from his back to Sadie and smiled. Sadie couldn't quite manage to smile back.

There had been no relatives at the funeral that afternoon. It was held at a squat brick crematorium on the outskirts of Fremantle. The director, a tall man in a narrow suit, read through the service with care. There were no eulogies. Frobisher had hurried in at the last minute, sweating in a black suit and already looking at his watch.

Now he arrived at Ocean Street in a taxi, carrying his satchel and a large brown paper bag.

'Good good, you found the place,' he said, pushing past Stan to make his way up the crumbling brick path. He shoved his satchel in an armpit while he checked through a dozen keys. He tried each one in the door, with diminishing patience, then tried each again, with more effort. Finally, the lock crunched and he shoved the door open onto a dark, cool hallway.

Sadie waited.

Ida frowned. 'Sadie?'

'If we're going in, we're going in,' Stan said.

Sadie wasn't sure why she felt so hesitant, as if crossing the doorstep was going to change something.

'Sadie?'

She turned to her grandmother. It wasn't the moment,

she decided, for opening up. She puffed out her chest. 'If anyone finds any coins down the back of any armchairs, they're mine, okay?'

Off the hallway was a large living room with burgundy drapes, a Persian rug, an armchair and a broad oak desk. Two walls were lined with bookshelves, the others crammed with paintings and old photographs. In a gilt frame was a painting of a young woman in old-fashioned dress, buttoned up to the chin. She was quite beautiful, Sadie thought, with her dark eyes glaring across the room.

Next there was a dining room adjoining a kitchen. A half-drunk cup of tea was left on the bench.

On the second floor there were six bedrooms, only two with beds. Of the rest, three were empty and the other was a junk room, its tall shelves piled with odds and ends. There were six filing cabinets, drawers open and contents spilling onto the floor. The bathroom had a clawfoot bath and the wall tiles were yellowed like a smoker's teeth. There was a single toothbrush in a glass by the basin.

These small signs of the former occupant upset Sadie. One day, would a stranger be poking through her things, knowing nothing of their significance?

In each room, Ida would coo twice: once at the size and once at the condition. Stan would note some design or structural flaw—damp perhaps, or subsidence—and shake his head. To Sadie, the house was a curiosity, but it didn't quite seem real.

The attic was better kept than any of the other rooms, although a similar number of pictures cluttered the walls. Stan peered intently at black-and-white portraits of fighter squadrons, perhaps thinking he might recognise a face. A number of the portraits were of the ancient Greeks, and there were busts of heroes and gods and monsters on the mantelpiece. Sadie recognised Zeus, Kronus and Poseidon.

Beside these, balanced on the corner of the ledge, was a dark wooden box that might have been a cigar case. The grain felt warmer than Sadie expected in this cold house. With half-hearted interest, she lifted it and attempted to prise the lid loose. When it refused to budge, she put it back on the shelf.

Sadie.

'Sorry Nan?'

Ida shook her head. 'I didn't say anything, love.'

Strange. Sadie thought she had heard her name, as clear as a tap on the shoulder. She turned, ready to accuse a suit of armour standing dusty in a corner. Mounted on a wall were swords of all kinds—cutlasses, broadswords, scimitars, katanas. Beside these were parchment maps of worlds that no longer existed. Monsters no longer waited in unknown seas. Other shelves were filled with clocks and strange artefacts.

'It's like a museum,' Sadie said, 'of weird and useless things.'

'Well, useless or not, they're all yours,' Ida reminded her.

Stan didn't look away from the photo in front of him.

'I don't want them,' Sadie said.

But then she looked out on the Indian Ocean stretching before her from Fremantle Harbour to Scarborough Beach. The sunset had painted a prizewinning blaze of orange and pink across the well-hazed blue.

She couldn't help herself. A little thrill ran through her. A spark of happiness. Something was finally happening to her.

Then she heard Frobisher yelling.

Sadie sprinted down two flights of stairs and found the lawyer on the other side of the rear screen door. He had gone out into the backyard, where a dog had found him and sunk its teeth into his arm. It was a tan and white bulldog, with a face like an unmade bed.

'Bloody thing! Down! Get down!'

Sadie pulled open kitchen drawers one after another until she found a rolling pin. No sooner had she opened the back door than the dog released its grip on Frobisher and went for her instead. As its mouth opened for her bare arm, Sadie shoved the rolling pin in. The beast bit down on the end and pulled.

'Sit you stupid thing!' Sadie commanded. 'Sit!'

Her boots were beginning to slide, along with the straw doormat on the veranda.

'You're wasting your time,' Frobisher shouted. 'He was the only one it ever listened to. The thing's a menace. Should be destroyed.' He held up his ragged sleeve. 'This suit was tailored by Anderson and Sheppard!' he barked. The dog's growls and huffing were becoming increasingly aggressive. But it soon tired of its tug of war, let go of the rolling pin and went for Sadie's legs.

She gasped and reached behind her for the door handle, but her hand instead snatched at her grandpa's shirt buttons. Stan shoved Sadie against the screen door and slapped the dog hard across its snout. It fled whimpering under the house.

'Get inside,' Stan ordered.

Granddaughter and lawyer obeyed.

In the dining room, Frobisher laid the contents of the brown paper bag across the dusty table. They were the clothes Mr Freeman had been wearing: a long-sleeved grandfather shirt, a pair of beige chinos, a brown suede waistcoat and a leather cap. A canvas satchel on a leather strap held a wallet, house keys and glasses case. Tucked into a pocket was a still-ticking ancient watch, its face hidden behind a leather hood. Tangled about the hood was a chain with a brass talisman—a small, tarnished disc, engraved with a sickle. Each item seemed only to draw attention to what, who, was missing.

'This should all go to charity,' Stan said. 'Give it to someone who needs it. You could sleep twenty people in this place. There are people out there spending nights on park benches.'

'It's not for us to say Stan,' Ida said quietly. 'It's Sadie's place.'

Sadie was about to disagree, but then Frobisher pulled the last item from his bag. It was an earthenware urn.

'What's that?'

The lawyer blinked, surprised she had to ask. 'It's Mr Freeman.'

He cleared his throat, resting one hand on the urn's lid. 'I am obliged to point out clause 2.2 in the documents I supplied yesterday. Miss Miller is not permitted to sell or otherwise dispose of any articles from, and including, these premises. Not until the twelve month caretaker period has elapsed.'

'She's not after money, if that's what you're thinking.'

'*Stan*.' Ida's tone was forceful enough to cause her husband to step back.

'As noted in clause 3.4, there is a substantial amount of money in a savings account, to which Miss Miller will gain access after the twelve months. If she has proved satisfactory in her role.'

Stan's forehead creased. 'Role? What role?'

'Miss Miller will be required to protect the house and its contents.'

'You want a fifteen-year-old girl to fight off burglars?'

'She's sixteen,' Ida reminded him, gently tapping Sadie's shoulder. 'What do you want to do, Sadie love?'

'Um,' Sadie looked to her grandfather, but he wouldn't meet her gaze. Instead she asked the lawyer: 'What would I actually have to do, as caretaker?'

Frobisher stared at a point just below a decorative cornice, as if his lines were written there. 'Ideally, you,' he paused, glancing reluctantly at Stan and Ida, 'and your family would move in here, immediately.'

'Not going to happen,' Stan snapped. 'Sadie has a home.'

'Mr Freeman has—had—a lot of valuables. Some of them are very…unusual.'

Sadie swallowed hard. 'Grandpa, please.'

Stan ignored her, pressing in on Frobisher. 'She has exams. She's going to university.'

'Those are the conditions of the will,' Frobisher said calmly, picking up his leather satchel. 'Good afternoon.'

The front door key had been left on a ring with several others on Mr Freeman's folded clothes. Sadie went to pick it up, but her grandfather swept the belongings from the table and shoved them back in their paper bag.

'When you're eighteen, you can make your own decisions. For now, these stay with me.'

Taking the keys, he dumped the bag on top of the kitchen cabinet, where he intended it to stay.

Sadie hadn't thought she wanted the house, not

really. Now she felt a strange duty to Mr Freeman and, even more than that, she didn't like having a decision taken from her. She was ready to argue with her grandfather, but Ida's look told her it wasn't the time.

That evening there was an argument like never before. Stan refused to discuss the matter of the keys and Sadie refused to let it drop. But for all her shouting and demands and attempts to sound reasonable, Stan wouldn't budge.

'I don't want you going anywhere near that house,' he said.

Sadie slammed three doors on the way to her room. One of them hadn't been shut in years and she pulled her shoulder. It was still aching an hour later as she lay on her bed, staring furiously at the wall. Ida came in and sat on the edge of the mattress behind her. She placed a cup of tea on the bedside table.

'He worries about you Sadie, love. He and I aren't going to be around forever—'

'Don't say that,' Sadie snapped.

'Well, it's true. We're not immortal—'

'I don't want to hear it.' Sadie's eyes burned.

'Family has always been the most important thing to him. He'd do anything to protect us.'

Sadie didn't say anything. She was too angry to see any good intentions on the part of her grandfather.

She slept lightly. Her stomach was rumbling and empty. Around midnight she realised she was awake, staring at the ceiling. The window was open, to tempt in a breeze. In the garden someone was scratching about. Was it Stan? Was he also sleepless and miserable?

Sadie went to the window and pressed her nose to the flywire. She caught the sweet, meaty scent of over-ripe figs and almost called out to her grandfather, but she remembered her grudge and kept silent.

She heard breathing—heaving and snorting like a wild animal. Something was clawing at the dirt and ripping up the veggie patch. Squinting into the darkness, she tried to find a shape among the shadows.

Then the thing moved into moonlight.

It was a man, stripped to the waist and hunched over on all fours. Sadie eased herself away from the window, intending to make a quiet path to the phone and call the police. But then the man stood up.

He was at least seven foot tall and as broad as a body-builder, his arms as thick as legs, his legs as thick as pylons. But Sadie was looking at his head. It was too wide, even for such broad shoulders. And above each oversized ear, was a horn. *Horns.* The half-naked stranger in her backyard had horns.

Sadie screamed.

The horned man startled, echoed her scream in a bellow, stamped his feet and then tore off, shredding the garden and crashing through the timber fence.

Sadie's bedroom door burst open and Stan hurried in, tying up his dressing gown.

'Sadie? Are you all right?'

'There was a man,' she said, 'in the backyard.'

Stan peered out through the flywire. 'Well, there isn't now.'

He smiled at her. Then, remembering his bad mood, his head lowered and he closed the door behind him without another word.

Sadie stayed awake, her eyes darting from one shadow to another, but the man with horns didn't come back.

5
THE INTRUDER

There was no conversation over breakfast. Stan was in the garden, tutting over destroyed carrots and hammering chipboard over the hole in the fence. Last night's visitor had torn through the vegetables, but nobody seemed to want to talk about it. Sadie ate her toast and pretended to read the newspaper. Then she wheeled her bike out of the garage and rode off to meet the others at the beach.

The scene on the terraces was the same, from a distance, but it felt more uncomfortable than ever.

Every hour or so, Tom stood up and announced his intention to swim. For five minutes he would splash about in the low surf, then resume his position, hugging his knees on the sand. Throughout the afternoon, Sadie could feel him looking to her for some contact or connection, but she couldn't bring herself to offer it. Instead she turned pages without reading them and every so often threw the book on the grass and dropped back on her elbows.

'What is wrong with you, anyway?'

Sadie sat up. Kimberley was peering at her over the top of her designer sunglasses.

'Sorry?'

Kimberley nodded at Heather. 'I mean, *she* does the whole emo thing, but it's like a fashion statement. With you, it's like a sickness and, seriously, I don't want to catch it.'

It occurred to Sadie that her cousin was asking after her health.

'You actually want to know?'

'I want you to get over it, so if that's what it takes, yeah.'

Sadie thought she would want to say nothing. But it was such an odd experience, having her cousin interested in her, that she found she wasn't quite ready to brush her off. Maybe she did need to talk things through and, in the absence of a girlfriend, maybe Kimberley would do. So she told her cousin about the old man, how she and Tom had run to his rescue. How he had died. She told her about Frobisher and about the house on the beach. About the view from the attic room. About her grandfather taking the keys and the argument that followed.

Kimberley was indignant.

'No way. The old man gave you that house. Grandpa has no right to take it off you.'

'Yeah, well, I said that. It didn't do any good.'

'Let's just go.' Kimberley was already putting on her

sandals. 'We could totally have a protest or something. You know, occupy the place. What's Grandpa going to do, call the cops?'

Even Heather was listening now. She had unplugged a single earbud and tinny music buzzed at her throat.

This talk of injustice and rebellion excited something in Sadie. Maybe she did need to take a stand. Most days she despised Kimberley for caring more about shoes than rising sea levels, but today Sadie needed a bit of selfishness.

'It's not even that I want the house,' she said. 'But Mr Freeman gave it to me for a reason. Looking after it is the right thing to do.'

It was only a kilometre to the house, if that. Maybe she could do this. But the stark sunlight burned these thoughts out of her.

'Thing is, Grandpa's got the key.'

'*A* key.'

Everyone looked at Tom, surprised.

'I mean, it won't be the only key,' he continued. 'You know what old people are like. Bet there's one under a pot plant somewhere. Or a doormat maybe.'

Sadie nodded with growing enthusiasm. 'There was a doormat. On the back veranda.'

'I'll drive,' Tom said.

~

In the evening half-light, the house had a morose aspect, as if judging Sadie for disobeying Stan.

Kimberley peered out through the windscreen. 'That is a seriously ancient house. It's like five hundred years old.'

Sadie peered over her cousin's shoulder from the back seat.

'Wow. Remind me how much your parents pay in school fees?'

Kimberley rolled her eyes. 'Don't get all superior and snarky, geek girl. I'm just saying it's old, that's all.'

Heather hadn't said a word. Occasionally she coughed in Sadie's direction, to remind her that they still weren't speaking.

'If I was a vampire, that's the sort of house I'd live in,' she said now.

Kimberley scoffed at her sister in the rear-view mirror. 'What d'you mean, *if*?'

Tom opened his door and put his shoulders back. 'I'll go round the back. See if that key's there.'

'Watch out for the dog,' Sadie said. 'He doesn't play well with others.'

There was a narrow, overgrown path up the left side of the house, where ivy tangled around a locked wooden gate. Tom strode through the long grass like some old explorer.

'I so reckon it's haunted,' Kimberley said, wiggling

her fingers as if playing a ghostly organ. 'Heather could make some friends, finally.'

'I *have* friends.'

'You so do not.'

'I so *do*.' Heather sniffed, peering out her window. 'Anyway, you shouldn't make fun of ghosts. They could be listening.'

Just then, a light went on in a second floor window. Kimberley squealed.

'Spooky!'

'It's Tom,' Sadie said.

Heather shook her head. 'Uh-uh.'

Tom was still beside the house, just through the gate.

Another squeal from the passenger seat. 'Double spooky!'

Sadie opened her door.

'What are you doing?' Kimberley asked.

'I'm supposed to be looking after the place. Maybe it's time I started.'

The front door was unlocked. Trust Tom not to try it, Sadie thought. The thing was, she clearly remembered Stan checking the handle when he shut up the house. Someone else had reopened it. Looking back to Tom's car, she noted her cousins had wound up their windows, and pressed themselves invisible against their seats. She was on her own.

She put one foot down on the hall floorboards. Nothing creaked and no one came running. But there was someone in the house, that was certain. Someone was moving about and muttering upstairs. Something thudded and something else crashed.

Okay, Sadie thought, *feeling a bit less brave now.*

The front room was in complete disarray. Books had been pulled from shelves and scattered across a rug. Various ornaments had toppled onto cushions, if they were lucky, and onto floorboards if they weren't.

Sadie remembered the figure in the garden last night, remembered his horns. From the stand by the front door, she grabbed the old man's walking stick and, brandishing it like a baseballer, began a slow climb up the stairs.

Sadie Miller. Armed vigilante.

The first step creaked and she froze. The clatter and cursing from above continued. The second step sighed and Sadie stopped again. Something glass shattered overhead.

On the first floor landing, she waited. The intruder was in the attic. The door was wide open and various artefacts rolled out. Was she really going to do this? She lowered the walking stick, wishing she'd brought her mobile with her. She should have called the police. Why didn't she just call the police?

Something else shattered and Sadie lifted the stick again. She climbed the rest of the stairs with slow, deliberate steps, but, on reaching the second floor, a floorboard groaned, and she flattened herself to the wall, listening. There was no longer any noise coming from the attic. Whoever was in there had heard her. The light went off, plunging the corridor into darkness. Her palms were sweaty on the walking stick. She edged along the wall towards the doorway.

There was a sudden movement in the shadows and Sadie's legs were swept out from under her. She landed heavily on her back, the air thumped from her chest. The walking stick flew out of her reach. Before she could be sure what was happening, there was someone astride her, bare knees either side of her waist. A blade, cold and sharp, was at her throat.

'Where is it?' a man's voice hissed.

Sadie had always imagined that on the edge of death she would cling to dignity. Now, any idea of dignity deserted her. 'Don't hurt me, please.'

'Answer me quickly and I'll let you live. Where's the relic?'

'The what?'

'You broke in here. I know what you were looking for.'

'I didn't break in. The front door was open. You're the one who broke in.'

Sadie felt the blade shift. Her attacker's hand flicked out to the hallway light switch, and she blinked against the sudden glare. Straddling her hips, a sword in his right hand, was the most gorgeous boy she had ever seen. There was a moment of sudden heat in a cold place in her chest. She felt embarrassed and exposed.

The boy was naked, except for a pair of cotton boxer shorts. Water glistened in his long dark hair and there were traces of shaving foam on his square jaw. Shadows sculpted the tight muscles of his arms.

It took Sadie a moment to remember he had a sword at her throat.

'I know you,' he said.

Sadie was as irritated at herself as she was at her attacker. 'There's no money in the house, if that's what you're after, or drugs.'

The boy frowned. 'Drugs?'

He was about her age, Sadie thought, maybe a year older. She felt her fear ebbing. 'You were having a shower. Not really normal behaviour for a burglar, is it? So it's a drug thing, right? Unless it's a perv thing. You break into other people's showers—that is a bit pervy.'

'You're rambling.' The boy glared down at her, with his head tilted as if he needed a better angle from which to understand her. 'You looked different last time I saw you. Younger.'

Sadie blinked. 'Younger? This *so* is a drug thing.

What are you on?'

'It was you. You were there, the night I died.' The boy sniffed the air, nostrils flaring like a wild thing. 'Is that perfume?'

'What? Stop smelling me, please.' Sitting on her, with an alarmingly casual air, the boy was clearly crazy. Gorgeous, almost naked and crazy. 'I've called the police,' she said.

'Why on earth would you do that?'

'I saw the light on from outside. We thought the place was being burgled. Of course I called the police.'

'Burgled? And how exactly does a man burgle his own house? Oh.' He stood up and the blade finally dropped from Sadie's throat. 'It isn't my house,' he said. 'It's your house, isn't it.'

Sadie smiled, clambering upright with her back to the wall. 'That's right, this was all just a simple misunderstanding. We all get our houses mixed up sometimes. And you're still saying you're not high?'

'Frobisher has transferred the deeds to you, as caretaker.'

Sadie's wide eyes blinked. 'What did you say?'

'It's what he does, when I die. I'm getting better at it, but there's still no saying where I'll end up. It takes a while to get back from a mud hut in the Kalahari, believe me.' All of this he said without even the hint of a smile. His blue eyes were steady.

'Hang on, slow down, rewind. You know Frobisher, the lawyer?'

The boy nodded. 'Of course. His family has always looked after my affairs. It took a great deal of convincing to bring them out here.'

There was something not quite right about the way he spoke, Sadie thought. He sounded like an old film, the sort her grandmother loved and her grandpa scoffed at—a fighter pilot keeping a stiff upper lip on a train station platform. It wasn't a way of talking that matched an athletic boy in boxer shorts.

'Why are you talking like that?'

'Talking like what?'

'Like, I don't know. Like it's fifty years ago.'

The boy frowned again. It seemed to be his default expression—brow lowered, as if there was always something very serious just out of sight ahead of him. He put the sword down and held his hand out to shake hers. 'Jacob Freeman.'

'Piss off.'

'Charming.'

'That's not even funny.'

The boy snatched back his hand. 'Regardless, it's my name. I suppose yours is too much to ask?'

'Sadie Miller.'

'Of course. You're protecting the relic. It's why I left you the house.'

'*Mr Freeman* left me this house. And nobody said anything about a relic. What relic?'

'A box, a wooden box, containing something terribly dangerous.'

'Frobisher didn't say anything,' Sadie began, but she was already looking to the mantelpiece, at the empty space between the busts of gods and monsters.

'But you came in anyway, alone. To confront a burglar. To protect this house?'

'I guess so.'

Then, at last, there was the barest hint of a smile. 'Impressive.'

Before Sadie could say anything else, the dog began barking downstairs. Jacob's shoulders tensed.

'Did you really call the police?

Sadie shook her head.

'Friends of yours then?'

'Tom. He was going around the back to look for a spare key.'

Jacob ran for the stairs.

The dog had Tom on his back on the dry grass, grasping his right forearm in its slobbery maw. Each seemed to be growling at the other.

'Kingsley!'

Jacob threw open the screen door and strode out onto

the veranda. The dog relaxed its jaw and ran across the yard and up the back steps. Reaching Jacob's bare feet, it paused, sniffed each one, and then licked his hand.

'He's very loyal,' Jacob explained. 'And excessively defensive. He doesn't take well to strangers.' He cupped the dog's crumpled face in both hands and ruffled his ears. 'Kingsley, this is Miss Sadie Miller. Say hello to her.'

The dog dropped both paws from Jacob's knees and, without looking up, offered one to Sadie.

'Kingsley?' Sadie asked, lightly shaking the paw.

'I always call my dogs Kingsley. It avoids confusion.'

'You get confused?'

He nodded, looking for Sadie's gaze. 'I suppose you don't believe a word I've said.'

'Did you expect me to?'

'I suppose not. But you're clever.' He glanced at Tom, who was brushing dirt and grass from his bare knees. 'Come and see me here tomorrow,' he said quietly to Sadie. 'We'll go to Frobisher together and he'll explain everything.'

'My grandparents,' Sadie began, but Tom was already at the steps. He frowned at the half-naked stranger.

'Who's this?'

Jacob lifted his chin. 'I'm—'

'This is Jake,' Sadie said quickly. 'He's a distant relative…of the old man.'

She wondered why she had come so quickly to the

boy's defence. Who was she protecting?

'I thought the old bloke didn't have any family,' Tom said, holding out his hand to Jacob.

Jacob didn't move. 'You were wrong.'

Tom looked to Sadie and withdrew his hand. 'You okay with this, Sades?'

Sadie considered, while Jacob waited patiently for her answer. Could any of this be true? It was a ridiculous story, so why tell it? And then there was ferocious Kingsley, lying blissfully on his back while his belly was being rubbed.

'We'll go see the lawyer,' she said. 'First thing in the morning.'

6
DEATH AND THE DALAI LAMA

Early the next morning, Sadie wheeled her bike across the small front yard and waved to Ida on the veranda. She was off to the beach, as far as anyone was concerned. Even as the gate closed behind her, she expected to hear her grandfather call out, demanding proof of her destination.

Maybe it was paranoia that made her notice the two suited cyclists who hurriedly swung their well-polished shoes over the crossbars on their bikes.

It was the same pair who had accosted Ida on the doorstep. They built up speed along the narrow street. At the stop sign, Sadie considered waiting to let them pass, just to prove to herself that they weren't following her.

But something made her turn right, hurry downhill in the wrong direction and quickly pull left into Gill Street.

Gill Street ran nowhere. It was a short sprint of squat houses and dry grass. Sadie waited at the next intersection, as if checking for traffic. Sure enough, the God squad came around the corner behind her.

Miming forgetfulness, as if she had only now remembered where she was going, Sadie turned left again and headed back uphill. She moved slowly, waiting to see if the men followed.

They waited at the kerb behind her, seeming to look for traffic. After a brief discussion, they pedalled away in the opposite direction.

Sadie smiled. She was ridiculous. As if anyone would be stalking her.

Jacob was waiting for her on the front step, dressed in the old man's clothes. He had clearly found the paper bag in the kitchen. The hooded watch was on his wrist and the talisman around his neck. It wasn't nine and the ride over had been gentle, but Sadie's skin was glistening. In cap, trousers, waistcoat and shirt, he had to be boiling.

'You can't wear those,' Sadie told him, parking her bike.

Jacob didn't blink, or smirk. 'Why ever not?'

'You'll, well, you look a bit, well, gay, that's all.'

'And gay is a bad thing?'

'No, of course not. It's just—' The earnest stare had Sadie disappointed in herself. 'I don't even mean gay, not really. Look, all my, well, okay, so none of my friends are gay. As far as I know. But I'd be very happy if they were.

I mean, not more happy than I am now, I wouldn't prefer them that way or anything, I just mean we wouldn't stop being friends if, well—' Sadie caught the tip of her tripping tongue and began again. 'Why, are you gay?'

Jacob frowned, glanced down at himself, and seemed to give the matter some consideration. 'I don't think so, no.'

'It's cool if you are. All I meant was, people around here will think you're a bit odd, going out like that.'

'Rubbish. I'll wear what I like.'

'Okay, the thing is, you just can't. Not around here. People can be a bit, well, limited? Judgmental.'

'I can see that.'

'I don't mean me. That stuff doesn't even fit you.'

This was true. The shirt was too tight, the trousers ankle-high and the waistcoat snug about the ribs. Jake attempted to fasten the top button, but gave up. 'What should I be wearing then?'

'I don't know, I'm not exactly Miss Fashionista myself. But—' Sadie's shoulders surrendered. 'Just, please, at least lose the cap, Jake.'

'My name's Jacob.'

'I'm not calling you that. Nobody's called Jacob.'

'To be honest, I'd prefer you called me Mr Freeman.'

'Shut up now, Jake.'

~

Jake got rid of the cap and, after some negotiation, unbuttoned his collar. Ten minutes later, Sadie waited beside him on the highway for a bus. A Commodore screamed past, heavy bass threatening to fracture the windscreen. Some idiot wound down the back window and stuck his head out.

'FAAAAGGOTTT!'

Jake frowned, as if puzzled by the brake lights. Sadie said nothing.

To Sadie, Fremantle was an appealing blend of the flash and the feral. Graceful sandstone houses nestled their two-tone tin roofs against decaying council flats of pebble-dash and concrete. The sea breeze was cool on the back of a dress damp with sweat and, most seductively, there was the constant movement of the docks. Fremantle was the edge of the world, where vast vessels visited from far better places.

Today there was no breeze, and the stench of a docked sheep ship draped itself across the town. Sadie followed Jake towards the dead end of High Street, where paint peeled from forgotten shops. The sun was prickling her bare shoulders and searing the pavement.

Across the road a strange-looking bloke in a long military coat kept to the shade of the Army Surplus shop-front. There were always a few crazies about—overdressed and underwashed, seeming to inhabit a different, cooler planet.

Jake had stopped. He was looking up at a dusty sign above a warped, flaking door. *The Law Offices of Horace Frobisher*, it read, *First Floor*. Jake went up, three stairs at a time, threw open the frosted door that topped them and called for the lawyer.

By the time Sadie had caught up, Frobisher's flushed and shiny head was peering around the door.

'Make an appointment,' the lawyer snapped. 'This isn't one of your drop-in centres. We *charge*.' Then he saw Sadie, standing with her arms tightly folded, and he straightened up. 'Oh,' he said, mopping away with his handkerchief. 'My word.' He wasn't looking at Sadie anymore. The young man in the borrowed clothes had his full attention.

Jake had lifted the brass talisman from beneath the front of his shirt and was letting it catch the light.

'Mr Freeman?' Frobisher asked. 'My word. Is it you?' He was mopping twice as hard now. Any moment, Sadie thought, he would pause and wring a bucket of sweat from that rag.

'The girl called in sick,' he said, wincing in the direction of the empty desk. 'Ordinarily, there would have been someone to meet you. I'm not accustomed, I mean, I have people to do these things for me.'

He was nervous, Sadie realised. Perhaps even scared.

Wondering why, she looked to Jake. He was smiling serenely.

'Calm down Frobisher,' Jake said. 'I'm sure my business remains in safe hands. You've done well this time.'

Sadie realised Jake was looking at her.

Frobisher bowed with what was either forced humility or genuine gratitude. 'After all these years, I would hope I knew my business,' he said. His eyes flickered towards Sadie. 'I presume you've come to resolve property rights.'

Jake nodded. 'In a moment. First, tell her who I am.'

The lawyer cleared his throat. 'Surely not?'

'Tell her everything.'

'Everything? My word.' Frobisher sank into his absent secretary's seat. 'W-well then.'

Sadie stepped forward. 'Okay, look, you said I was the caretaker. You said I had to look after the house and all its belongings, yeah? Well, that's why I'm here, isn't it? You told me to watch out and I did. Last night, I went round there and found this idiot pulling the place to pieces.'

'Right, yes. Of course. What you need to realise, well. The thing is, Miss Miller…'

'Yeah, yeah, I know. He's been reincarnated. Like the Dalai Lama.'

Sadie enjoyed Frobisher's blinking astonishment. 'I'm sorry?'

'That's what you're going to try to tell me, yeah? Reincarnation. The Dalai Lama carks it and his mind, spirit, soul, whatever, gets handed on to someone else. Then the poor monks have to go looking for him.'

Jake looked at her, as if seeing her properly for the first time. A smile felt its way onto his face.

The lawyer didn't smile. 'Well, Miss Miller, you do seem very well informed. I'm not sure there's much more I can tell you.'

'You reckon? Why not try convincing me that that's the same man over there, the one who died last week on Cottesloe beach.'

The lawyer nodded, straightening up in his seat as if taking his place in court. 'My family has been his lawyers for two centuries. We ease the transition. These days there's an interminable amount of paperwork…'

Sadie persisted. 'Okay, fine, whatever. Is it him though? Actually him?'

'That is Mr Jacob Leonard Freeman, the same man who bequeathed his estate to you less than a week ago. I'm surprised to see him again so soon. It can take months. I was expecting to be arranging passports and plane tickets.' He frowned, looking to Jake. 'I imagine I'll still need to. You'll be moving on, if they've found you.'

Jake was looking at his watch, allowing it to hold his attention.

'I can have you in Rio by the end of the week,'

Frobisher continued. 'Unless,' a note of hope rang, 'you'd prefer somewhere cooler? We've never done Toronto. I hear it's something to be seen at this time of year. The streets all ice and snow.'

Jake was staring at Sadie, so intently that she worried she'd blush. 'Well,' he said. 'It's certainly too dangerous to stay here.' His square chin lifted and he went to lean on the edge of the desk with both hands. Finding the edge lower than expected, he fell forward. 'But we have a problem. The relic's gone. Stolen.'

The lawyer edged his squint towards Sadie. 'You think the girl took it?'

'No. I want to speak to Vincent.'

'Wait there a moment,' the lawyer said and disappeared into his office.

There was an assuredness, an authority to Jake's movements that was, well, Sadie wasn't sure what it was.

'So how old are you then anyway, eighteen?' she asked. 'Nineteen?'

He held out his hands before him, turning them over. 'You tell me. All I know is, I feel like I belong in my skin again. It's been a long time.'

'Okay, whatever. The thing is, it doesn't make any sense. The old man only died last week. How can you be here, that age, this week?'

Jake nodded. That smile again flickered. 'You know about the Dalai Lama. Well, he's rarely found as an infant, is he? The spirit can move backwards, forwards, sideways even.'

'You don't even sound like you believe that.'

'Nevertheless, here I am.'

'Okay, whatever. You're not the Dalai Lama. What's so special about you?'

Frobisher returned from his office with the small black address book he had carried at the hospital. 'Most of your squadron have kept themselves close by. But I've seen neither hide nor hair of Vincent for some years.' After an extended search through his secretary's drawers, Frobisher located a Post-It note and a pen. 'He was running a secondhand bookshop in the city. Rather grotty little place—last I heard, it closed down.'

'Patrick might have seen him,' Jake suggested. 'He had more patience than the rest of us.'

The lawyer nodded, flipping pages in his book. 'Of course. Exactly what I was about to suggest. Patrick runs a newsagency now.'

He gave Jake the address, then, without looking at Sadie, handed her a stapled wad of forms. 'I'll need your signature,' he said. 'To transfer the deeds and other property. As you're under eighteen, I'll also need that of your legal guardian. I trust this won't be an issue?'

Sadie thought of her grandfather. She wondered what he would think if he saw her here. Something about Frobisher had rubbed him up the wrong way and she wasn't sure it was just his manner. In any case, that wasn't why she hesitated now. This was all too quick, with too many gaps in the story. She folded her arms more tightly, refusing the forms.

'Why exactly do you need me to sign? I was just the caretaker, he's the rightful owner.'

'I'm sure you can understand that might be difficult to establish, legally.'

Sadie smiled. 'Yeah, right. So maybe we should just wait a bit. Until everything's established, I mean.'

'Now, listen to me, young lady.'

Jake stepped forward. 'Wait, Frobisher.'

The lawyer's face burned. 'I've never seen such insolence. She had one simple job to do and—'

'Frobisher, don't rush her.'

'*Don't rush her?*' Sadie repeated. Something about Jake's worried tone and the slight edginess in the way he held out his hands crystallised her suspicion. She felt, at last, that she understood what was happening. This was all a performance—they were in on it together, playing out some elaborate scheme that would only make sense when it was far too late.

'This is all a con.'

Jake blinked. 'I'm sorry?'

'I'm such an idiot. You two are no better than all those Nigerian princes sending out spam emails.'

Jake straightened up, as if slapped. 'Nigerian princes?'

'Did he even die, the old man? Or was that just part of the scam? Come to think of it, I don't even know if those were real policemen. I mean, who has a moustache like that, seriously.'

'Sadie,' Jake said, 'shut up and sit down. You're not making any sense.'

His irritation merely strengthened Sadie's conviction. 'Bullshit. I finally *am* making sense of all of this.'

Now the lawyer took his turn, attempting to corral her back into their well-rehearsed scene. 'Listen, Miss Miller, I know this must all seem strange—'

'It's supposed to seem strange,' Sadie snapped. 'That's how these scams work, isn't it? You offer something too good to be true, something unbelievable but irresistible. You make someone feel that, just for them, just this time, it could all be real. Money, a house, a handsome prince.'

Jake's eyebrows lifted. 'Handsome?'

'Shut up, Jake. I don't know why you chose me, what you even wanted from me, but you can forget it. Find someone more gullible next time.'

Jake was nodding. Again, he seemed impressed. 'Very clever.'

'I said shut up.' Sadie pulled her handbag up to her shoulder in a gesture of self-righteousness, then left them standing there as if struggling to remember their lines.

She stomped down the stairs, then came to a halt on the scorched pavement. Even after the stifling air of the lawyer's office, the heat outside was a cruel surprise. She reached into her handbag for her sunglasses and her anger caught up with her.

She had been so stupid, she could see that now. How easily she had allowed herself to forget being sensible and hope that life might somehow have secrets, that it might excite her.

Sadie turned south and collided with a man in a long military coat.

Even before she saw him properly, she knew it was the man she had seen outside the Army Surplus shop. A foul stench rose off him and choked the dry air from the back of her throat. Base and sulphurous, it was the same rotten-egg stink the sea breeze chased in from the dog beach, from a thick reef of rotting seaweed.

The smell was the first thing Sadie noticed. The next thing was the man's skin—his flesh was puckered and blue, in parts translucent, with dark twitching veins. At that point, she might have whimpered. She saw his salt-knotted hair, his scratched, grubby sunglasses, his stained, ill-fitting clothes. Then, most frightening of all, she saw his shoes.

The man took a step closer and his soles squelched.

Sadie thought of Mr Freeman's final words.

Watch out for men with wet shoes.

She tried to turn and run, but found herself going nowhere. She watched, transfixed, as the man opened his mouth and began to sing.

7
WET SHOES

It was music, Sadie was sure, but she'd never heard such sweet sounds before. There were voices working as all the instruments of an orchestra, summoned up from this greasy man's throat. At times, he might have been sere-nading softly in her ear, at other times singing from some immeasurable distance.

He was heading for the harbour and she was following. She could feel the searing sun, but she couldn't move into the shade. People passed and she could do nothing more than smile. Her voice was trapped some-where behind her heart, somewhere she couldn't reach it. Her feet lifted and fell, moved by someone else, listening to the song that called from everywhere and nowhere, calling her to the sea.

They crossed the railway tracks. The toe of Sadie's left boot snagged on a rail and twisted her ankle, but that wasn't enough to stop her. She wanted to stop and she didn't want to stop. Wanted to scream and wanted only to walk on towards the water.

There were few people around. The markets in the old wharf sheds were closed and the harbour workers were busy elsewhere. Across the deep green water, cranes lifted containers from ship to crowded dockyard.

The man in the overcoat walked a metre ahead of her. His head was bent forward and his shoulders hunched, as if he was attempting to hide from the sun. Sadie didn't ever see him move; he was simply somewhere else whenever she blinked.

Soon they would be at the wharf's edge and she knew what would happen then. She would follow the man into the water. Part of her wanted it, knew that it was right. Whenever she doubted it, the music was there to reassure her. *Everything is as it should be. A wonderful place awaits.*

Sadie held her breath. It was all she could do to stop herself from being drawn onwards. If she could hold her breath long enough, maybe she would just drop where she was, unconscious but safe. Yet each time she tried, her lungs would panic at the last instant and pull her back.

Four more steps. Three. Two. The toes of her boots were on the raised wooden edge of the pier. The man stood by, watching, as she teetered. She stared down at the dark green water. Low waves washed against the barnacled timber posts. Sun glittered irresistibly.

And then she was leaning over the edge. She wanted to scream and to flail, but her arms stayed by her sides, and her tongue was still behind tight lips. *Welcome home*, the music told her. She could smell the fresh salt, feel the cool salve of the water on her skin. She fell, almost gladly.

A strong hand snatched at her dress and pulled her back, swinging her around onto the pier. It was Jake, shining with sweat, breathless and snarling. He wasn't looking at her, even as he let go. He glared at the man who had lured her to a drowning, the man with wet shoes. The man who was no longer singing.

'She has nothing to do with this,' Jake spat.

The man smiled. His teeth were jagged shards, his voice a salty gargle. 'She brought you to the water.'

Then three figures shot up, one after another from the harbour depths. They rose ten metres in the air, trailing saltwater, and then dropped onto the wharf. Their hair was knotted and foul and their faces warped and discoloured. They wore tight-fitting, tarnished armour: chain-mail vests stained with verdigris, and heavy bracelets on bony wrists. Helmets sculpted into sinister scowls masked their eyes, exaggerating their brows into curled horns. One carried a double-bladed axe, one had a sword strung from his rotting leather belt, and the third gripped a trident.

Sadie sat on the pier, dazed and squinting at the figures. Jake's body was rigid. He held a fist to his chest, and his other hand stretched towards the figure that was shrugging off his overcoat.

'This is a warning,' Jake said. 'I'm not looking for a fight. Leave now and I won't hurt you.'

One of the new arrivals stepped forward and pulled his sword from his belt. The blade was dull and mottled. He took a swing at Jake.

Sadie tried to cry out a warning, but it snagged at the back of her throat. Her body was slowly waking up and returning to her, but she felt heavy and sluggish.

Jake barely moved. The sword sliced towards his left arm and he stepped aside. It swung again and he caught the blade neatly between his palms.

'I don't want to fight you,' he said.

The man bared ragged teeth and howled, spraying Jake with salt water and spittle. Still gripping the blade, Jake pulled the sword and its wielder forward in a sharp movement. The figure stumbled and fell. Jake raised his left arm and brought his elbow down twice, hard, on the man's spine. There was a swift, almost casual, violence to the movement. Sadie flinched at the crack of breaking bone. The man's limp body fell heavily to the ground.

Another of the men was already on Jake's back. Jake was thrown to his knees. He yelped in pain, then grabbed the wrists that were either side of his neck and lifted his attacker up and over his head, bringing him down head-first with another horrible crack. The man writhed a moment, then his tense frame slackened and the trident clattered on the tarmac.

The last man was taller than the others, and broader. A thick, dark beard obscured much of his square face. He paced around Jake, blue fingers tight around the handle of his axe.

Then the bearded man stopped. He let his axe fall and his shoulders relax. For a moment, Sadie thought the fight was over. The man's head went back, as if to laugh, then his chin dropped forwards sharply and he vomited a fierce jet of water that blasted Jake three metres back. Instantly, the man was over him, lifting his axe high while Jake spluttered.

The weapon swung down, sparking on bitumen, as Jake slid through the man's legs and leapt to his feet. His foot lashed out at his attacker's legs and the man went down. Then Jake was on the man's back, a bloodied knee in his spine and a hand holding his hair. Almost gleefully, he cracked the man's forehead against the edge of the pier. Once, twice, three times. There was blood. Four times.

'Stop! Please, stop!'

Sadie had found her voice. She was on her feet, directly behind Jake.

'Stop. Seriously, stop. You'll kill him.'

Jake's eyes were wild, hungry. But Sadie's protest stalled him. He looked up and across at the man in the overcoat and sunglasses. 'Consider this just retaliation,' he said.

'Just?' The man lifted his sunglasses, revealing a pair

of soft-boiled eyes. 'What would we know of justice?'

Jake stood up, leaving the large man unconscious on the wharf. His chin fell and he stared, suddenly appalled. Any argument went out of him. 'There's nothing I can do about that. I'm sorry.'

'She is waiting for you. In the water. Always, she waits for you. For you to bring her what is hers. How much longer must she wait?'

'Lysandra knows I can never give it to her. Open that box and she'll bring down the sky. This world will burn.'

'If that is the price of life, then let the sky fall.' His bile-coloured lips peeled back on glassy teeth. And then the man and his unconscious compatriots were gone, leaving nothing on the pier but bloody water, a crumpled overcoat and a pair of scratched sunglasses.

Jake stood on the edge of the wharf. He was fighting for breath. His knuckles were torn, his knees gashed and his shirt ripped. One of his shoes had been lost over the edge of the pier. He looked to the water, as if wondering where it had gone. Sadie could see the scattered sunlight reflected in his eyes. But there was something else there too, something dark.

'Who were they?' She barely got the words out. She had seen fights before, outside beachfront pubs. Drunken idiots shoving each other about until friend or bouncer pulled them apart. But this was different.

'We call them the Drowners,' said Jake, 'although it's

a name I never liked. They were like you once, but they dreamed of being Gods. Now they're damned to spend eternity in the depths.'

'Like you?'

'I'm sorry?'

Sadie was feeling woozy, but she held onto the conversation. 'You said like you, like me. As if you're something else.'

Turning back from the water, Jake straightened his shoulders, bracing himself. 'You asked what was so special about me.' His firm gaze met Sadie's. 'I'm an envoy, from the Gods.'

'Yeah right.'

'The Gods were never that good at dealing with mortals. We bridge the gap. I live in a human body, but I'm immortal.'

'Shut up.'

'It's the truth.'

'But you've got a whole new body. Where did that come from?'

'Immortality is the Gods' gift to their servants.'

'Don't be stupid. There are no Gods.'

'Yes there are. They once walked among you. If the relic is opened, they'll come back. And they'll be angry.'

'The relic.' Sadie felt her sarcasm fade. She remembered holding the box in the attic that first evening at Ocean Street and hearing her name called from nowhere.

'You said there was something inside it. Something dangerous.'

Jake nodded. 'A demon,' he said simply. 'One with the power to bring any dream to life. A power humanity was never supposed to have. And the Gods will do anything to keep it from you.'

'Okay. You had a demon, in a box, in your house.'

'For safekeeping. The demon is a weapon, its power a threat to the Gods' sovereignty. If any human dare use it again, the Gods won't take any risks. They'll destroy you. All seven billion of you.'

He was so earnest, so insistent, it was hard for Sadie to keep him at a sane distance. She shook her head, as if to shake off his words. 'No. This isn't true. None of it.'

'It's why I've been hiding away here. The relic has to stay hidden. For all our sakes.'

'No, no. This is crazy. You're crazy.'

'It's a lot to take in, I understand. We'll take a cab back to Ocean Street.'

That was the last thing she wanted. She found herself staring at the blood on the pier, and then on Jake's knuckles. There was blood on her dress, she realised. She didn't know whose it was. Wiping at the stain, she saw her hands were shaking. She wanted to go home, to apologise to Grandpa and have Nan put the kettle on. She wanted to wrap herself up and forget the last few days.

'No, no. No no no. You can have the house back. Everything.'

Jake raised an eyebrow. 'I was under the impression you thought we were trying to con you.'

'I don't care,' Sadie said, trying to hold her voice firm. 'I'll sign whatever you want me to. I don't want anything to do with this.'

'As you wish.'

They walked together back to Frobisher's office. Jake was lopsided with his one bare foot. Every few steps he would look across at Sadie and frown. Occasionally, he touched her elbow or shoulder, but she shrugged him off. She wanted to push him out of her life and to be glad he was gone.

The door at the top of the office stairs was open. Maybe she knew then that something was wrong, that her old life was gone forever.

Frobisher was face down on the carpet with one hand outstretched, as if trying to drag himself to safety. There was a ragged, bloodied hole in the right shoulder of his jacket and another, tidier one, in the back of his head. Dark blood pooled around him.

Jake ran into the back room, but found it empty. Hurrying back, he said something, but Sadie wasn't listening. She was trying not to look at the lawyer's face.

He was dead. Really dead. Half an hour ago she had been arguing with him, now there was a hole in his head.

A hole in his head. Dead.

Sadie thought of another scene. A scene she was sure she didn't even remember: lights flashing red and blue in bitumen puddles, someone she didn't know whispering reassurance, a blue blanket around her shoulders, consciousness coming in fits and starts. And there, in the front seat, with the broken glass, then on a stretcher, then being zipped forever into nothingness—

Sadie's throat tightened. She thought she was going to faint.

Jake slapped her. She blinked and slapped him back. That flash of anger felt good.

'Listen,' he said, not even wincing. 'You need to be sensible.'

From the street outside, the sounds of a siren and car doors slamming.

'Who did this?' Sadie hardly recognised her own voice.

'It's not important. Sadie—'

'He was your lawyer. Your friend. He's dead and you're not even surprised.'

'Sadie—'

A terrible thought occurred to her. 'I left you alone with him. You did this.'

'Don't be absurd. Why would I kill the one man who can help me?' There were footsteps on the stairs. Two, maybe three, pairs of heavy boots. Jake spoke quickly.

'That'll be the police. Tell them you just walked in. They can't find me here. Not now.' He leaned in, without warning, and kissed the cheek he had just slapped. 'You'll be fine. I'll find you.'

Then he was at the window, pulling it open and kicking away the flywire.

'You can't just leave,' Sadie hissed. 'He's *dead*.'

Without another word, Jake followed the flyscreen down to the car park. It was at least a four-metre drop, but he hit the ground and was gone.

8
BLOOD

First through the door was the same policeman Sadie had seen the night the old man died. He strode in, ignoring her, and went straight to the body. His lips were pursed and he looked tired, as if he was thinking about having to tidy up.

'You make the call?' he asked.

'I'm sorry?'

'Did you phone the police?' A young constable had appeared at the top of the stairs. She had sandy hair, chafed cheeks and thick, rimless glasses. 'I'm Constable Williams, this is Sergeant Bradbury. Did you call us?'

'No. I only just got here,' Sadie said, a little too quickly. She was trying not to look at the lawyer's body, but felt her eyes pulled to his wounds. She wondered if that made her look guilty. She wondered if she felt guilty. 'Is he dead?'

Bradbury snorted. 'Big hole in the back of his head. Yeah, I'd say he's dead.'

Sadie nodded, too dazed to respond to the snark in his voice. Trying to look anywhere but the body, she noticed a photograph on the lawyer's desk. He probably had a wife, she thought. Maybe a family. Soon, someone would receive a phone call, not knowing someone had pulled a thread that would unravel their world.

Williams put her hand on Sadie's shoulder. 'It must have been a shock,' she said. 'What were you doing here?'

'Oh.' Sadie couldn't tell them, not really. She saw her explanations play out and backed away from them, embarrassed. 'It was a family thing. Nothing important.'

Bradbury glared at her. 'Is that blood on your dress?'

Sadie had forgotten the blood and had to fight the urge to clap a hand down over it. She wondered if she should tell them about Jake, about the fight at the harbour. And how she had been hypnotised by a man with wet shoes. No, she would only sound crazy.

'Maybe it's sauce,' she mumbled. It sounded like a terrible excuse.

'Seen you before, haven't I?'

'She was at the hospital,' Williams put in. 'A couple of nights back. That's right, isn't it?'

Sadie nodded. Was that enough to incriminate her? Two dead men inside a week?

'Right.' Bradbury nodded. 'The old man had been mugged. You said they swam out to sea.'

'They did.'

'You make a habit of hanging around crime scenes?'

'No, I just—' No matter what Sadie said, she sounded guilty. She would need to give them the truth, or some of it, at least. 'Actually, that's why I'm here. Mr Freeman left me something in his will. Frobisher,' she pointed to the man on the floor, 'was his lawyer.'

Her explanation dried at the back of her throat, as she realised Bradbury was looking at the window, at a scuff mark left by Jake's shoe.

'You were alone in here?' he asked Sadie.

Now was her chance. Her knees sagged with relief. She could tell them about Jake, about everything. Let the police sort it out. She could just return home, resume her quiet life. So why was she already nodding?

'Yes, just me. Here I am, alone.'

She didn't trust them, she realised. She couldn't believe all the stuff Jake had said, but she'd seen things the police wouldn't understand. Chances were Frobisher's killer was skulking about the bottom of the harbour.

Bradbury pointed at the scuff mark. 'Someone's gone out the window.'

'The murderer, maybe?' Sadie said.

Bradbury turned sharply. He glared at her for what felt like a minute, while she tried to hold her hands still.

'Get her out of here,' he said to Williams, who was already reaching for Sadie's shoulder.

Detectives arrived in well-pressed suits, followed by

men in white coveralls. Bradbury compared notes, then came to join Sadie and Constable Williams in the police car. Sadie waited for the inquisition to recommence. But when Bradbury slammed the driver's door behind him, he didn't say anything. Williams asked for Sadie's address and they drove her home in silence. It was only as the constable came around to open Sadie's door for her that Bradbury looked up in the rear-view.

'Just know this,' he said. 'I'm watching you. If you're connected to this, then I'm gonna bring you in.'

Sadie nodded, but she was barely listening. The drive home had passed in a daze.

Going into the house, she heard the front door click closed behind her and heard her grandmother call from the kitchen, but it felt like all of these things were happening somewhere else. She stood at the foot of her bed and she fell face first onto the doona. She had been holding herself together until this moment, she realised. Telling herself she just needed to make it this far.

Fall apart when you're safe, when you're alone.

She didn't cry. She stared at the wall. At the harbour waters offering a welcome. Stared at Jake breaking bones on the quay. At the hole in Frobisher's head. And at blue and red lights flashing in a puddle.

9
THE QUIET LIFE

When Tom came in the next day, Sadie was pressed into the far corner of her bed, wearing her striped cotton pyjamas, even though it was late afternoon. She had *The Odyssey* open in front of her, but was staring out the window.

'Hey.' Tom closed the door behind him. 'You okay?'

Sadie barely looked across at him. She had been expecting him, she realised. She had wanted him to call. But now he was here she wasn't sure what she wanted to say to him.

'I heard what happened,' he said, 'with the police.'

'Nothing happened. They gave me a lift home, that's all. Grandpa made a big fuss over nothing.'

'Kim said you'd been arrested.'

'Kim says walnuts give you warts.'

Half a minute passed.

'So?' he prompted.

'I don't want to talk about it.'

'Okay.' Tom nodded and glanced about the room

for a clue. The furniture was Sadie's grandparents, but everything else was Sadie—an eclectic collection of books, op-shop knick-knacks, CDs and, in the corner of the room, a shop mannequin wearing one of her mother's dresses and a straw hat. On the walls, there was a large, dog-eared photo of Bob Dylan, another of Nick Cave, and tour posters for The Triffids and Okkervil River.

'Is that it?' Sadie was staring at him, her arms tightly folded.

'What?'

'You're not going to try a bit harder?'

'Harder?'

'Tom, if a girl tells you she doesn't want to talk about something, it means she wants you to make more of an effort asking.'

Tom bit his lip and sank his shoulders.

'Was it something to do with the old bloke?'

Sadie flinched and then nodded. 'Kind of. But it's complicated.'

'And that boy at the house? Jake?'

A funny sort of smile bent Sadie's lips. She really didn't want to be talking about Jake. 'Kind of.'

'Have you been hanging out with him?' The question burst from him so quickly that both of them winced.

'The lawyer is dead.'

'What?'

'The lawyer who arranged everything. The one who

gave me the house. We went to his office and he was dead. Shot.'

'No way. You saw him?'

'Yeah. The thing is, that's not all. There were these, well, I don't know what they were. These people. In the harbour.'

'At the harbour?'

'No. *In* the harbour—they came out of the water. At least, I think they did. The whole thing's seriously weird. It was like I'd been drugged. But Jake fought them.'

'He got into a fight?'

'Yeah. Well, no. The thing is, they sort of attacked me. Oh, look, it sounds so stupid. I don't know exactly what happened, but he fought them off.'

'Why did they attack you?'

'I don't know. I think they wanted him. I thought he was going to kill them right there.'

'So he's a psycho? You're not going to see him again?' Tom wanted this to be a statement.

'I don't know. But it's all connected with him, it has to be. Whoever killed Mr Frobisher, they did it because of him.'

'Yeah, but it's not your problem, is it?'

'Isn't it? I feel like it is. Aren't you curious?'

Tom shrugged. 'It's nothing to do with me.'

Sadie pulled her knees up and looked out the window. There was no breeze, but Tom felt something shift in the room. That conversation was over and he couldn't help feeling he'd somehow disappointed her. He studied his shoes, twice tweaking the laces. 'So, are you grounded or what?'

'Who said I was grounded?'

'Guess.'

'Grandpa was pretty angry,' Sadie admitted. 'But Nan talked him down. We've sort of agreed that I won't go anywhere until the weekend. You know, to show I can be trusted, something like that.'

'Right.'

Tom glanced again around the room. It suddenly seemed smaller and uncomfortably intimate. Sometimes he would give anything to be alone with Sadie, but other times the air pulled tight. Today, more than ever, he felt a new distance between them. Something kept pulling her away, into unexpected silences.

Still, by the time he left, she seemed more like her old self.

'We'll go for a swim tomorrow,' she said at the screen door.

'Okay, cool.' He turned to go, but she put out a hand, just fleetingly, to his elbow, and it was enough to turn him back.

'Thanks for coming around,' she said.

Tom stood a moment longer on the doormat. There was eye contact and this long, electric second opened before him. Magnetism was at work, he could feel it. He was going to kiss her. Maybe just a peck, maybe just a friendly kiss, maybe more. It felt right. The other night would have been bad timing. But now, now—

'Okay, bye then!'

Sadie snapped the screen door shut and disappeared away up the hall.

They were friends. It was nothing.

It was a twenty-minute walk home, but Tom was in no hurry. He was already an hour late for dinner.

Around the corner from Sadie's, he left the street and took himself down the sandy laneways that cut through the leafy residential blocks. It was his favourite way to walk. Through loose palings and wire fencing, he could see into expansive backyards and through living room windows. Swimming pools, tennis courts, lawns large enough for a footy match. As he walked, he rehearsed conversations he knew he would never have. He talked, Sadie listened; he held her chin and they leaned towards each other.

He was lost in an imagined scene, when he heard the beast. A loud snort and a grunt. He stopped and looked behind him. Without streetlights or moonlight it was hard to see anything, but he could discern a dark shape there, a large dog maybe, snuffling and snorting in the dirt.

Each step felt clumsy as he moved on, as if his feet were in more of a hurry than the rest of him. He heard the animal bound after him. He stopped again, and turned.

It was less than ten metres away, too large and too heavy to be a dog. Horns jutted from the sides of its broad, dark head. It was a bull, a large, black bull.

He didn't run, not straight away. He remembered warnings about running from bulls. If anything, he should run at it, yelling furiously to scare it away. Right now, that didn't feel like a good idea.

Tom backed away, facing the beast. It stayed where it was, pawing the ground, its fierce breath shifting dirt and dry grass. Tom tripped, but managed to keep himself upright. When he had put twenty metres between himself and the animal, he turned and ran for his life.

The beast gave chase. Tom was a good runner, but he could hear it gaining on him. He emerged from the laneway onto a well-lit, narrow street. He considered turning left or right, but ended up running straight on, into the next lane. He was looking for a fence he could jump, but they were all too high.

Tom realised the bull was no longer following. It had stopped at the end of the previous lane. He could see it shuffling about in the shadows.

He laughed, with relief. The creature was scared of the light. He should tell someone, but who? He was about to call triple zero when he saw the bull emerge, hesitant, into the light.

Tom almost dropped the phone.

It was walking on its hind legs.

No, he realised, it was *running* on its hind legs. Running towards him, each stride covering two metres.

Tom ran, terror burning at the back of his throat. Too soon, he could hear the beast, whatever it was, close behind him. He could smell its rancid, sweaty animalism. Then he could feel its hot breath on his back and then—

Tom dived left, and the beast charged on, barely missing him. He felt it pass, carried on by its own momentum, a solid mass of muscle sucking the hot night air behind it.

There was a second laneway here, running towards the Cottesloe town centre. Tom raised himself on grazed knees, limped a bit and then sprinted on. He had barely started before he heard the beast behind him, its hooves tearing chunks from the dry earth.

The lights of the shopping centre car park were at the lane's end, a hundred metres ahead of him. Tom pushed himself, ignoring his screaming muscles. Each breath felt like broken glass in his chest, but all that mattered was he was in front. There was the finish line! There was light, and safety!

His right foot went down and collided with the concrete lid of a storm drain. His ankle twisted and his knee gave way. The beast was on him. A new, sharp pain scalded his left side, just beneath the ribs, and he was lifted up and thrown into the air, crashing through the brittle branches of an overhanging peppermint tree.

He slammed against cold concrete, and sprawled in the car park beside a badly parked Volvo. The voices of Saturday shoppers and the rattle of supermarket trolleys surrounded him—so ordinary, so reassuring. He was back in the light.

He clutched at his side with a grazed hand and found his T-shirt wet. The beast had gored him. He could hear someone nearby calling an ambulance.

Fighting for breath, he stared at the laneway's end, where the dark path was marked off by three steel bollards. The beast was there, lurking in the patchy night, out of reach of the bright car-park lights. It had the body of a man—matted with dark hair, but human—and a rotting chamois was tied on a rope around its waist, as some small gesture of modesty. But the head! The horns! It might have been a mask, but Tom knew it wasn't. He had glimpsed the spittle on those black lips, had seen snot and steam jet from those huge nostrils.

Tom wasn't sure he believed in God. But now, here in a supermarket car park, he was sure he had just met the devil.

10
STRANGE CURRENTS

That night, Sadie dreamed of Frobisher. There was no escaping him. Several times she woke, frightened by every shadow on her ceiling, but then fell back into the same nightmare. He was dead, staring at nothing. Sometimes he sat up and spoke to her.

'I blame you,' he said.

Jake was there too, running away. She wanted to tear at him, to pull him back, to shout at him, to bite him, to slap him—but also to embrace him and cling to him as if he was the single still point in this madness. Strange currents stirred in her blood.

Sometime after midnight, Sadie was woken by heavy breathing. There was an animal outside her window. The night was absolutely still. The dry heat wrapped itself around her as she took careful steps to the flyscreen.

The moon was high and almost full, and the garden looked sharp in the silver light. A figure was rustling in the shadows under the fig tree. Sadie thought about calling for her grandpa—whatever had torn a hole in his fence had come back—but she wanted to see it for herself.

She had fallen asleep reading, clutching *The Odyssey* to her chest. It was still in her hand now, raised like a weapon. She lowered herself onto the sofa beneath the window and then slowly lifted her head to peer out. Two large paws slapped down on the window sill and she jerked back in fright.

'Kingsley, get down.'

The bulldog dropped back down between lavender bushes, then sighed and swaggered over to his master's feet. Jake stepped out into the moonlight, sniffing at a large, ripe fig.

'The fruit of paradise,' he said. 'I might take a few for breakfast, if your parents don't mind. Fresh figs, yoghurt, Turkish coffee. I got quite a taste for it back in Constantinople.'

'My parents won't mind,' Sadie told him, wishing he'd lower his voice. 'They're dead.'

'Oh.' Jake stopped, his lips pursed in concern. 'Who killed them?'

It wasn't the question Sadie was expecting. 'Nobody. It was an accident. Six years ago.'

Jake nodded. 'Good.'

'Good?'

'I was worried you'd had an extremely bad day. Are you all right?'

'It was six years ago.'

'Forgive me, I meant with what happened yesterday. Did the police give you a hard time?'

'Not really. No thanks to you.'

Jake nodded again, resigned to any blame, if not actually apologetic. He was looking at the book Sadie was still wielding. She let it drop. 'The thing is, I owe you an explanation or two. I wondered if you might like a midnight stroll.'

'I can't. I'm grounded.'

'I thought you said your parents were dead.'

'You think I was making that up? I live with my grandparents.'

'I see.' He jerked a thumb towards Kingsley. 'I brought a chaperone, if you're worried about your virtue.'

Sadie wasn't worried about her virtue, but about her grandpa. She'd had a taste of his disappointment and didn't want another. But there were things she needed to talk to Jake about. Things she could talk about with nobody else.

'I keep seeing him lying there. Frobisher.'

'You've never seen death before?'

Again, Jake's blunt response surprised her. 'No, I don't think so. I don't remember. I hope not.' She moved closer to the flyscreen. 'It wasn't just some random walking in off the street, was it. It's something to do with you and that box of yours.'

'Everything centres on the relic. We need to find it

before anyone else does. Before more people die.'

'You don't seem upset. Frobisher was your friend, wasn't he? He was murdered.'

'Frobisher's dead. There's seven billion people out there who aren't. What might happen to them worries me more.'

Sadie knew what she should do. She should close the window, return to bed and forget all about Jake. But she also knew what she had to do. Her fingertips, pressed at the flywire, were tingling with static. Tom was wrong, this *was* her problem. 'These explanations of yours—I want the truth.'

Jake put his hand on his heart. 'The whole truth, et cetera.'

'Give me five minutes to pull some clothes on.'

Jake and Kingsley waited at the corner of her street.

'May I ask you a question?' he asked when Sadie arrived.

'*You may*. But you need to stop talking like that. It makes you sound like a dork.'

'I see. Why is there a hole in your back fence?'

'Oh, that. Funny, it was probably a mate of yours.'

'What was?'

'There was something in the garden, the other night. I thought it was some kind of animal, but then it looked more like a man. Except—and if you laugh at this I'm going straight back to bed—except he had horns.'

Jake didn't laugh.

'You don't believe me,' Sadie said, 'after all the garbage you expect me to swallow.'

Crossing the road outside the closed corner shop, she noticed Jake seemed to be studying her. She adjusted her dress, in case it was tucked into her undies.

'You were reading *The Odyssey*,' he said. 'That's not normal bedtime reading, is it?'

At first, Sadie thought she would say nothing. She never talked about these things, not with Tom, not with anyone. But there was safety with a stranger, there was space, so she answered. 'My dad was a professor of ancient history.'

Jake nodded and, perhaps, understood more than she wanted him to.

'That creature you saw,' he said, as they reached the next corner. 'It was the Minotaur.'

Sadie laughed, but not for long. 'Don't be stupid.'

'It was the Minotaur,' he insisted, with the same ridiculous earnestness. 'It's the Drowners' pet. Their slave, to be more accurate.'

'Yeah, right, the Minotaur. You seriously expect me to believe that?'

'Let's hope you never have to.'

They crossed the railway line and followed pavements

uphill, towards the coast. Soon, the golf course spread out alongside them and, beyond that, the sea. Twin lighthouses winked at either end of Rottnest Island.

'You know, I had decided I wasn't going to see you again,' Sadie said.

Jake glanced sideways at her. Maybe he was no more convinced than she was.

'And I'm still not sure I was wrong. Can you blame me, after yesterday?'

Jake frowned. 'I'm sorry you had to see Frobisher dead. And I'm sorry I had to leave you there. If the police had found me, there would have been trouble. I've no papers, no passport, no way of proving who I am.'

'Yeah, I get that, but that wasn't why.' Sadie paused. 'Those men at the harbour. You would have killed them, if I hadn't been there.'

He listened, considered, and then nodded, apparently unrepentant. 'I'm a warrior. I was born a warrior. I've spent countless lives fighting.'

'Stop saying things like that. I don't want to hear things like that. Just say normal things. Real things.'

'I'm telling you the truth, Sadie. And I think you know it.'

'Right, the truth. So you've killed people. There's a murderer on the loose and you're telling me you're a killer. That's really putting my mind at ease.'

'I've killed,' Jake said, explaining nothing. He turned

off the path, blithely walking through an open gate, into the Cottesloe civic centre. Seeing Sadie wasn't following, he turned back.

'What's the matter?'

'You can't just say something like that and expect everything to be okay.'

'You wanted honesty.'

'Honesty's one thing, being a psycho is another.'

The civic centre had once been the home of someone important, although Sadie had never been interested enough to remember who. It was an impressive white, Spanish-style villa with a terracotta tile roof. Even more impressive were the grounds—several levels of parks and gardens and playgrounds, surrounded by grey stone walls. To Sadie, it had always been a safe place. When she was a young girl, she had played there. Tonight it felt like a trap, its dark places concealing unknown terrors. She thought of that beast in her backyard. She thought of muggers and murderers. She thought of the strange boy beside her.

'You said you were a killer.'

Jake held up his left wrist, showing her the leather hood of his watch. 'I fought in the Great War,' he said quietly. 'I'd always been a soldier but I'd never seen anything like it. Such appalling bloodshed. Then, twenty years later, it began again. Great cities burned in an instant.' He breathed in sharply, as if surfacing from a memory. 'After that, I'd had enough of fighting. Enough of death. So I came here, to the end of the world. I hid, and I kept the relic safe.'

Bored with this conversation, Kingsley lay down on the grass inside the gate.

'Who were you hiding from? Those Drowners?'

'Yes. Lysandra.' Just saying the name seemed to cost him something.

'So who was she—*is* she?'

A sour smile arrived at the corners of Jake's mouth. 'The Drowners were once a great civilisation. The Gods blessed them, and their empire spread out across the seas. Lysandra was their priestess, but she became tired of worshipping Gods. She dreamed of making herself a God. She craved immortality and she found a creature powerful enough to give it to her.'

'The demon.'

'Indeed. A forbidden creature. Lysandra summoned it and challenged the Gods' rule.' He smiled, although nothing was funny. 'You can imagine their outrage. A human rising up against them, a servant reaching for her master's crown. As a warning to the rest of you, the Gods sank Lysandra's city beneath the sea, cursing her and her people to the depths, forever. Their immortality became a living death. That's what the Drowners are—immortal souls bound to rotting bodies.'

Sadie shuddered. 'Nice.'

'The demon was trapped in a box and the Gods

exiled themselves to the heavens. They swore that if the demon's power was ever used again, they would return. And their vengeance would be terrible.'

'On the Drowners, you mean?'

'On all of you.'

'How is that fair?'

'Why should it be fair? You know your history.' He tapped the hood of his watch. 'In 1914, one Yugoslav shot an Austrian and all of Europe caught fire. If anyone, Drowner or human, asks that demon for anything, the Gods will set the whole planet ablaze.'

'And that's what Lysandra wants?

'She wants the demon's power. If she sets it free, it will choose a new master. It will lift the curse and grant her immortality. She'll have the power she needs to take on the Gods—to have her revenge.'

'Which would be bad news for the rest of us?'

'It would be the end of the world.'

'No, but seriously?'

Jake tugged the talisman from his open collar. 'Gods' truth.'

He walked through the gate again. Sadie followed a small way behind. But at the very edge of the streetlight she grabbed his elbow.

'Why did you come for me, tonight? I've already said you could have the house back.'

'I need your help.' Jake straightened his shoulders,

preparing to own up. 'This afternoon I went to see Patrick. He hasn't heard from Vincent in a year.' He withdrew a dog-eared business card from his waistcoat pocket. 'But he did give me this.'

Sadie took the card. *Lost Treasures Found*, it read. There was no address, not even a phone number. 'Not very helpful.'

'That's what I thought. But there's some sort of code on the back. I've seen similar codes all over the place, on billboards, in newspapers. Means nothing to me. I didn't know who else to ask.'

Sadie turned the card over, then shook her head. 'This is why you came to find me?'

Jake nodded. 'It's essential I find Vincent.'

'Because you think he killed Frobisher?'

'I think whoever killed Frobisher wanted to know where I was. They wanted to find the relic. But I think Vincent already knew exactly where the relic was.'

Sadie understood. 'Okay, you think he stole it. Why?'

'He was there when Lysandra first summoned the demon. He showed her how it was done.'

'And now he wants to give it back to her?'

'I think so. We have to find him, quickly.'

Sadie saw herself standing there, on the edge of darkness. She could hear the surf on an empty beach. The ordinary world was calling her. Somewhere nearby, a car horn sounded long and low, like a warning.

She was still holding Jake's elbow. She looked at the card once more in the last of the streetlight, then flicked it at him. 'That isn't a code. It's a website, for a shop. There's bound to be a street address.'

'Remarkable.' Jake turned the card over again. 'So what is a website?'

Sadie laughed, ignoring his hurt look. 'I keep forgetting. Last week, you were like, what, eighty?'

'Sadie, I'm thousands of years old. Eight thousand, at least.'

She stuck out her tongue. 'That's *gross*.'

'Is it?'

'A bit, yeah. I mean...' Sadie couldn't explain herself. She couldn't tell Jake that it was hard to think the good-looking boy before her was, until a few days ago, a wrinkled old man, that he was older than her grandparents.

Jake noticed her nose crinkle. 'There were legends about my people once. Your ancestors called us the Old Ones. But when you live forever you don't grow old, not really.'

'Yeah, sure. But everyone else does. I mean, whoa, eight thousand years. I'm sixteen—to me eight weeks is forever. And, you know, what do I look like to you? A fruit fly? Blink and I'll be dead.' She watched him a moment, but he didn't disagree.

'I know all about death,' he said, and pressed on into the dark grounds.

Sadie went with him. A winding path led around to a wide concrete stage where wedding parties often posed for photographs. Jake stood before it, arms folded, like some night watchman. His jaw was set and his brow lowered. He stared out to sea as if waiting for bad news.

'What's it like?' Sadie asked, not quite looking at him. 'Dying, I mean?'

'At its best, quick,' Jake said. He almost said nothing more, staring into darkness. Sadie could sense a sudden tension, a sudden anger. But perhaps he remembered he had promised honesty, even if it was a question he'd never thought about answering. His shoulders relaxed. 'Sometimes it's a heaviness, your body filling with cold water. Other times, it's a surrender. Like you just give yourself up to the sky, like it's the easiest thing you've ever done.'

'And afterwards?' Sadie's throat was tight. She had always thought she knew the answer to this question. For the first time, she was hoping to be proved wrong.

Jake gave her a soft smile. 'I don't know, Sadie. I come back.'

She nodded, shrugging like it was nothing, but her gut felt hollow. 'Always? You and your mates don't ever die? Not really?'

Jake lifted the talisman from the front of his shirt. 'This marks me as a servant of the Gods. As long as I wear it, I'll always come back.'

'Good for you. So you don't die. You don't get old.' Sadie looked down at the dog by his feet, the dog with the same name as countless dogs before him. She saw herself, staring at a dog, standing on grass she'd played on as a child. 'No. Seriously, what is wrong with me? Demons, Gods. A magic box. I mean, I've never even read *Lord of the Rings*. I hate all that stuff.'

Jake held out his hand. 'Do you want proof?'

His hand, when Sadie took it, was cool, despite the hot night. He led her off the stage and around to a small rose garden, where a dozen bushes were in bloom. The heat of the last fortnight had singed leaves and wilted petals, but a few buds still held a crisp shape. Studying each bush in turn, Jake picked a rosebud and gave it to Sadie.

'A gift of my gift. Each of my people has a particular talent. This is mine.'

'Stealing roses?'

'Don't put it in water, don't care for it. Just keep it somewhere safe. It won't wither, or die. It will stay perfect forever.'

'Oh, it's plastic?'

Jake gave her a stern look. 'Sometimes, Sadie, it's okay to be impressed.'

He snatched the rose back off her and threw it hard against the nearest wall. Kingsley pounced, snatched it from the grass and dropped it by Sadie's boots. It was still immaculate.

'Okay then,' she admitted. 'That is a pretty cool party trick.'

Jake put a hand on each of her shoulders and looked for her eyes. 'I've been hiding from the world too long, Sadie. I need your help to find the relic, before it's too late.'

'Me, or anyone under sixty?'

'You, Sadie. I trust you. Will you help?'

While Sadie was still thinking of something to say, her phone buzzed inside her bag with a message. She checked the time—almost two a.m.—and panicked. Had her grandparents woken to find her gone? With some relief she saw the message was from Tom.

In hospital. No stress.

Sadie called him straight back and he answered in a whisper.

'I don't think I'm supposed to be using this here.'

'What are you doing in hospital?'

Tom told her, calmly, about the attack, with assurance that everything was fine. Sadie was not reassured.

'You were gored by a bull and you're telling me you're fine?'

Jake snatched her phone off her. 'You said you saw something in your garden. With horns, yes?'

'Yes. Give me my phone back.'

'And now your friend has been gored by a bull.'

'You're not going to start talking about the Minotaur again?'

'Did it draw blood?'

'He's in hospital. What do you think?'

'Right then.' Jake put the phone to his ear. 'Tom, this is Jake. Shut up. We're coming to get you. Right now.' Taking the phone from his ear, his expression was grim but determined. 'We need a taxi. Your friend is in mortal danger,' he told Sadie. Then, looking at the phone in his hand, he frowned. 'How exactly do I make this thing hang up?'

11
THE HUNTER

The taxi driver hadn't wanted to let Kingsley anywhere near his back seat. In the end, Jake convinced him the dog was only going a few blocks south and that he'd pay to clean any drool from the upholstery. At the corner of Ocean Street, the taxi paused, a back door opened, and Kingsley jumped out.

'Home, boy,' Jake said, and the dog strutted away towards the old house.

As the taxi pulled away from the kerb, Jake sat forward, on the edge of his seat, as if hoping to spur the driver on.

'The Minotaur goes ashore whenever the Drowners are near land,' he said, nodding to Sadie. The moon was bright and low over the black ocean, laying a glimmering path from the horizon. 'Sometimes at its masters' bidding, sometimes to feed.'

'I wish you'd stop saying Minotaur,' Sadie said.

'Once it has a scent, once it's tasted blood, it never

abandons the hunt.'

'You mean it's hunting Tom?'

'When it finds him, it'll feed,' Jake said. 'Turn right here.'

'I know where I'm going, mate,' the driver complained.

Sadie put her hand on Jake's elbow. 'Tom's really being hunted by the Minotaur? I mean, really?'

'I'm afraid so. Now turn left.'

The driver whistled through his teeth. 'Listen, mate—you wanna drive?'

The hospital reception was airless and over-lit, painting sick skin on the cheeks of every visitor. A harassed-looking nurse directed them upstairs to a small ward on the fifth floor. Tom was on a bed in hospital pyjamas. His bloodied T-shirt was neatly folded on the cabinet beside him.

'Mum wanted to chuck that out.' Tom said. 'What's he doing here?'

Jake was standing back by the door and peering left and right along the corridor.

This was awkward. Sadie hadn't meant Tom to know she was on a midnight stroll with another boy. There was something about Jake, she realised, that made her forget everything else.

'Oh, we're totally dating, didn't I tell you?' Sadie

blurted, already wincing. That had definitely sounded funnier in her head. 'No, look, it's a bit complicated, okay?'

Jake stepped forward as if he was making a diagnosis. 'Tom, we need to get you out of here, now.'

'I can't,' Tom said. He didn't want to look at Jake. 'I've got stitches. They want to keep me in overnight. They're worried about infection.'

'Infection's the least of your worries. If it makes you feel better, I have some rudimentary medical training.'

'Yeah right.' Tom looked at Sadie. 'What's he talking about?'

'Okay, look, I know how stupid this is going to sound, and I'm not saying I buy any of it,' she said, 'but come with us. The thing is, that thing that attacked you tonight, well, it's going to come looking for you. And, sort of, um, eat you.'

'Eat me?' Tom sat up on his bed, winced in pain, and then lay down again. Sadie thought he was about to laugh, or accuse her of losing it, but instead he gestured for her to come closer and whispered through clenched teeth. 'Sades, I saw it. I know what it is.'

'You do?'

'You're right. It sounds stupid.' Tom's eyes were wide. 'It's the devil.'

'It's not the devil,' Jake said, bluntly. 'The devil's just an idea. Ideas don't tear you open with their horns and feast on your gizzards.'

A nurse appeared at the door, looking irritable. 'What's going on here? People are trying to sleep. Your brother here—'

'Brother?' That word seemed to hurt Tom more than the stitches in his side. It had been a necessary lie on Sadie's part, otherwise the nurse would have had them wait downstairs until morning.

'—needs rest. Everyone here needs rest. We don't want the patients disturbed.'

At that moment, a loud alarm sounded and Sadie nearly left her boots. She had still been hoping this was all nonsense, but now the last of that hope left her, leaving a rising, breathless horror in its place. Every patient in the ward sat up, one clapping bandaged hands to bandaged ears. The nurse frowned, then turned and hurried off down the corridor. Jake went after her. Sadie smiled apologetically at Tom and followed.

'You don't need to be so rude to Tom,' she said, matching Jake's stride.

Irritation twitched in Jake's right cheek. 'Is that important right now?'

'He's my friend. It's not his fault he doesn't understand what's going on. I don't understand what's going on.'

The nurse was using a wall phone, but seemed to be having trouble hearing. She put the phone down and turned, bewildered, to find Jake in her way.

'It's here, isn't it?' he said.

'Someone broke a window downstairs and some people are hurt. That's all I know,' she said.

Jake grabbed the woman by the shoulders. 'You need to get everyone out of here. Now. Nobody is safe.'

The nurse remained calm. 'Please take your hands off me. I know you're upset about your friend, but there's nothing for you to worry about.'

'Listen to me, you stupid—'

Somewhere nearby, a scream. A long, shrill, terrible wail. Then silence.

Jake forgot about the nurse and ran back up the corridor. Sadie didn't hesitate to run after him.

'On your feet,' Jake said, snatching up Tom's belongings. 'It's here.'

'No way.' Tom looked at Sadie. She nodded.

Clinging to his bloodied T-shirt and grubby sneakers, Tom limped down the corridor with an arm around Jake's shoulders. Sadie felt the sense of panic in the nursing staff as they hurried from ward to ward. The alarm was still ringing, but no one seemed to know what it meant.

'We'll take him back to Ocean Street,' Jake told her, punching the button for the lift. 'I can look after him there.'

'What if the Minotaur comes knocking?'

'I said, I can look after him there.'

'What?' Tom shook his head, confused. 'What d'you mean, Minotaur?'

Sadie decided it would be best if she didn't use that word again.

The lift bell rang and the doors opened onto a gruesome scene. A doctor lay on the floor. His crumpled white coat was soaked with blood and gore. He was dead. Sadie felt her throat tighten.

Standing over the body was a tall, dark figure whose head pushed at the plastic casing of the fluorescent tube above him. He might have made an imposing statue with his thick legs cast from bronze. Every muscle was clearly sculpted, from the broad biceps to his calves. Sparse hair embellished his weight-lifter's chest. A heavy, rusted lock hung from a chain around his neck. His feet were bare and blackened, the skin thick and crusted, and long, dark nails curled from his gnarled hands.

Still, nobody was looking at his hands. All eyes were on the matted fur of his head, the exposed and bloodied teeth, and the horns. The head of a bull, the body of a man, the teeth of a lion.

'It's the Minotaur,' Sadie murmured. 'It's real. Really really real.'

Head down, the beast charged through the lift doors as they closed. Jake shoved Sadie clear and threw himself left with Tom still hanging from his shoulders.

The beast barrelled down the corridor, lifting the

stunned nurse from her feet and tossing her into the air. She collided with the ceiling, smashing the light there, then fell to the ground whimpering. In two great bounds, the beast was upon her. Its vicious teeth tore at her throat. The nurse screamed, and then she stopped. Sadie couldn't look.

'Enough!'

Jake was on his feet again. His voice echoed down the hall. He held up Tom's bloodied T-shirt.

'I'm the one you came for.'

The beast stopped, raised its shoulders and turned to glare down the hall. Strands of viscera trailed from its bristled chin. Its nostrils flared in Jake's direction.

'Don't be stupid,' Sadie said. 'You can't fight that.'

'Get in the lift,' Jake replied.

'There's a dead man in the lift.'

'I don't think he'll mind. Take Tom, go back to Ocean Street. I'll meet you there.'

The beast was stamping the floor. Sadie helped Tom to his feet, but she hesitated by the lift door.

'Jake, seriously. That thing will tear you apart.'

'Quite possibly. But I'll still meet you there.' Jake braced himself, standing between the creature and the lift, putting up two fists as if boxing in some gentleman's match. The lift door was open behind Sadie. Tom stood there, with his finger on the button.

'Come on Sades,' he said.

She should get in, she knew that. She should run. But there was Jake, standing brave and magnificent in his old man's clothes. She had the strange urge to protect him. Where had that come from? She looked back at Tom, standing impatient and appalled. He was pale and sweaty, barely able to stand. Glancing between him and Jake, Sadie saw the fire extinguisher on the wall.

'I'll meet you downstairs,' she said to Tom. When he kept his finger on the button, she snapped at him. 'Hurry up and go!'

Tom held up both hands in surrender.

With a fierce, guttural roar, the beast charged again, closing the distance between them with terrifying speed. Its black lips peeled back and fire sparked in its eyes.

Tom swore. The doors began to close, taking their time.

Sadie grabbed the extinguisher from the wall and pointed its nozzle at the floor. A wide spray of foam coated the linoleum. The beast's feet slid away and it hit the ground hard, sprawling and snarling as it scudded into the closing lift doors.

Jake gazed at Sadie, astonished and impressed. He snatched the extinguisher and shoved it under his arm. The beast scrambled about on the floor, attempting to right itself, but Sadie and Jake were already running. They passed no one else. The alarm was still sounding, but the panic was happening elsewhere.

At the end of the corridor, glass doors opened on to a large balcony. It was empty.

Jake hurried through the doors, pointed at a bench seat to the far right. 'Sit there.'

Sadie frowned. 'Yeah right, great idea. It won't notice us if we're sitting down.'

Jake held up Tom's bloodied T-shirt. 'It won't notice you. It's only interested in me.'

'You can't still be thinking of fighting it?'

Before Jake could respond, the balcony doors exploded in a paroxysm of bent steel and shattered glass. Jake grabbed Sadie by the shoulders and shoved her backwards onto the bench. A dark mass flew through the air and collided with him, throwing him to the paving. The beast was taller than Jake and twice his width. Its thick arms easily pinned him to the ground. Having found its quarry, the beast threw back its head and bellowed at the night. Its triumph reverberated out across the city, echoing off the dark apartment blocks and around the empty market.

Jake struggled, unable to shift the beast's bulk. Sure of its victory, the creature took its time, sniffing at its prey. Its shoulders shook with what might have breathlessness or laughter. Its anthracite eyes gleamed, its spine arched and—

Jake lashed out with his knee, lifting the tattered loincloth and connecting with the organs behind. The beast howled and bent over in pain. Jake was instantly on his feet, brandishing the fire extinguisher. He clubbed the beast's skull with the steel canister. Once, twice, three times. Dark blood gushed from a wound above the creature's right eye, and the beast staggered backwards blindly. Again, Jake swung with the extinguisher, cracking it down on the back of the beast's head. There was a terrible crunch, like a boot on a gravel drive, but Jake kept on. His eyes were wild. As he raised the extinguisher again, the beast struck out with its left fist. The impact knocked Jake a metre up and two back, sending the extinguisher flying over the edge of the balcony into the car park below.

Jake hit his head against one of the large pots but managed to stagger back up. The beast roared, mouth wide, spraying blood and spittle. Its head went down and it stormed towards Jake, horns thrusting.

Jake stood his ground. When the beast was upon him, he fell backwards, rolling with his attacker. He gripped the beast by its shoulders and, using its weight and momentum, diverted it up and over his head. The Minotaur cleared the balcony wall and disappeared, sprawling, into the darkness below. There was the soft crunch of bone and metal, and a car alarm sounded.

Sadie peered over the balcony. Five floors down, the most incredible and deadly creature she had ever seen lay prone on the crumpled roof of a 4WD. She wasn't sure how she felt, seeing the beast so still, so dead. It had killed two people in front of her, it had gored her best friend and it had tried to kill Jake. And yet, now that it was dead, she felt sorry for it.

Jake was standing beside her. His nose was bloodied and a graze ran from his right elbow to his shoulder, staining the sleeve of his shirt.

'It frightens you,' he said quietly.

'That thing would have frightened anyone,' Sadie snapped.

'I don't mean the Minotaur. I mean death.'

'Yes. Of course. Totally.' Sadie turned to face him, drawing in her bottom lip between her teeth. 'Yesterday we found your friend murdered and you didn't bat an eyelid. Like his death meant nothing. Is that what happens when you don't ever die?' she asked, her chin tilted at his. 'You stop caring?'

Jake didn't look away. 'You didn't run. The Minotaur could have killed you. You could have escaped in the lift. You made sure Tom did.'

They were connected now, Sadie realised, she and Jake. Connected by this violence, more tangibly than they had been by secrets, by confessions. This was real.

Below, the dark figure of the Minotaur twitched and lifted its head. It dropped to the ground and limped away into the shadows, towards the harbour. Above, dirty pink daylight was rising behind the hospital.

~

Downstairs, there were police and fire-fighters and frantic paramedics. Plastic tape unfurled and lights flashed. Tom waited with the other hospital evacuees, wrapped in a blanket. In the confusion, it was easy enough for the three of them to slip out into the morning and find a taxi.

The taxi stopped three houses down from Sadie's. She got out and peered back in at Tom, who was shivering in his seat. His eyes were pale and wide. Jake craned his head around him from the far side of the back seat.

'If you're free tomorrow, perhaps you could take me shopping. For new shoes.'

He wasn't talking about shopping. The relic was out there, and Sadie knew, as she nodded, that she was agreeing to help Jake find it. 'Okay, sure.'

Tom's frown deepened. 'I thought we were hanging out tomorrow?'

'Oh yeah,' Sadie winced. Maybe she was surprised to realise which offer appealed more. Maybe she wasn't surprised at all. 'It's just, this is kind of important.'

'Shopping? For shoes?'

It all sounded awful. 'Yeah. The thing is—'

Tom shrugged. 'Nah, forget it, it's cool.' He looked towards her front gate. 'Stan'll be off fishing soon.'

Sadie nodded. She glanced at Jake, bloodied and battered. He smiled. The door closed, the taxi drove off, and Sadie walked along the silent street.

She wished Tom hadn't been sitting there between

them, and maybe she felt guilty about that. Without him there, Jake might have walked her up the side of the house. The idea seemed strangely irresistible. There was something new beneath her skin. Something halfway between anxiety and anticipation.

The house was quiet and she made it unseen from the back door to her bedroom. Through her window, the garden was a still and perfect scene of bright greens and warm light. Magpies were carolling. Sadie took off her boots and sat on the end of her bed, feeling suddenly exhausted.

Head on her pillow, she remembered the rose. It was still in her bag, which had been carelessly thrown onto taxi floor and along hospital corridor. She imagined the flower would be torn and bruised, but there it was, as perfect as the moment Jake had picked it. She used the mug on her bedside table as an impromptu vase. It was the last thing she saw as she fell asleep.

12
LOST TREASURES FOUND

Sadie slept four and a half hours, but only felt impatient on waking. She hurried through a piece of toast and a quick shower and pulled on the first dress she found in her cupboard. Wheeling her bike through the front gate, she called out an easy lie about meeting Tom at the beach.

Tom answered his phone on the second ring.

'Hey Sades.'

'Hey, look, I have a favour to ask. Okay, I lie. Two favours.'

'You sound out of breath.'

'I'm on my bike. If Nan or Grandpa ask, can you say I'm with you today?'

For a few seconds, all Sadie could hear was the echoed rush of the morning air. 'Yeah, sure. Cool.'

He agreed too easily. Now she felt even worse. 'You don't have to.'

'Nah, it's cool.'

'Are you sure?'

'It's cool, really.'

'Thanks Tom. You are awesome.'

'Right.' Tom didn't sound convinced. He hesitated, allowing the wind to again echo down the wire. 'What was the other favour?'

'Oh yeah. I've had a look at this website, but there's no street address. You reckon you could find out who it belongs to?'

'Maybe. What's the website?'

Sadie told him. In the background, she could hear typing. Trust a boy to be in front of his computer.

'Right, yeah, got it. Looks like lots of antiques stuff, is that it?'

'That's the one.'

'Lots of those Greek vase things—'

'Amphorae.'

'—some old maps, goblets, jewellery. International shipping is available. Yeah, you're right. There's no address, just an email.'

'I know. So?'

'So give me a sec. Shouldn't be too tricky.'

'You'll do it now?'

'Sure.'

'Thanks Tom. Two thumbs up.'

A beat. 'Sades.'

'Yeah?'

'Be careful.'

'It's just shopping.'

'Right. Look, I don't want to sound ungrateful or anything, but he beat that thing to a pulp.'

'Yeah, well. If he picks up a fire extinguisher, I'll jump straight back on my bike.'

'Sades, I'm serious.'

Only half-listening for traffic, Sadie cut across a corner and collided with a cyclist coming in the other direction. Her first warning was a young man's yelp, before her front wheel tangled with his, throwing her sideways to the dry grass of the kerb. Her phone bounced away from her.

She was already apologising when she saw the man's messenger bag. The buckles had popped open, unleashing a manilla folder. Five photographs slid out. Each was grainy and speckled with colour fuzz. There was Sadie, wheeling her bike through her front gate. There was Tom, hands in his pockets, crossing her drive. And Sadie and Jake leaving the house in the early hours.

Sadie looked up, outraged, and saw the God squad staring down at her.

'I knew it. You are stalking me!'

She tried to snatch the bag, but the blond one— Brother Jason, his name badge claimed—was too quick, swooping down and clutching it to his chest, as if rescuing a fallen bird.

'What's he like?' he asked.

'What's who like?'

'You've met him, we've seen it, you know we have. What's he like?' He was Australian, Sadie realised, unlike most of his two-wheeled brethren who sounded like they'd been shipped in from Ohio.

Her legs still tangled in her bike frame, Sadie scrambled to reach her phone. 'I'm calling the police, psycho.' It was an empty threat, and the man seemed to realise.

'What is he like? Where does he live? How can we get in touch with him?'

These questions burst from him at high pressure. It was all Sadie could do to back away, drag her bike upright and get her feet onto the pedals. Even as she hurried off towards the railway, queries and demands skittered along the bitumen behind her.

'Is he the one? Will he save us? Is he the one?'

Jake came to the front door in bare feet, carrying a Turkish coffee on a small china saucer. For a moment, Sadie wasn't sure it was him. The old man clothes were gone, and instead he wore a tight-fitting white T-shirt and dark blue jeans rolled up to his calves. A battered grey trilby was squashed down to his brow. He might have modelled himself on black and white snaps of some fifties film star. It really had been a while since he was young, Sadie thought. But the new look suited him.

Sadie had stopped halfway up the wooden steps. Her teeth clicked as she closed her mouth, far too late. She really hoped Jake hadn't noticed.

'I wasn't sure what time to expect you,' Jake said. Walking back into the house, he seemed more relaxed than she had yet seen him, almost smiling as he indicated the freshly cleaned lounge-room, the polished floorboards of the hall and the newly stocked shelves of the pantry. He stirred the coffee pot and poured Sadie a cup of the sweet, earthy brew. There was a plate of fresh pastries on the kitchen table and a bowl of fruit. Light fell through blinds that hadn't been opened in years. Sadie barely noticed.

She told Jake about the morning's altercation, trying to ignore the new heat rising in her cheeks. Jake sat across from her at the kitchen table and listened with an irritating calm.

'They must be after the relic.'

'Oh right. No biggie then. Thing is, they weren't asking about that, they were asking about you.'

'Sadie, I told you. Whoever killed Frobisher wanted to get to me. Because I had the relic.'

'Yeah, but it was weird. They wanted to know all about you. They were all like: *Is he the one? Will he save us?*'

'Save them? I haven't even met them.'

'Right, weird. But you think they killed Frobisher?'

'Evangelists on bicycles?'

'Okay, so not obvious suspects. But we should tell the police. I mean, they are stalking me. I have stalkers. There must be a hotline or something.'

'No.' He put down his coffee cup. 'Right now, the relic is the only thing that matters. The police would only get in the way. I want you to tell me about this website. Starting by telling me exactly what a website is.'

Sadie nodded, reaching into her handbag for her phone. With two swipes of her thumb, she opened the message Tom had sent as she pedalled down Ocean Street. A name and an address in East Perth. Jake peered at the screen with curious, quiet amusement, which quickly broke into astonishment.

'Vincent Pirandello. That's him. That was on the website?'

'Sort of. I had to be a bit clever. And you should thank Tom next time you see him.'

Leaning down under the table, Jake snatched up a pair of black canvas shoes. 'I'll call a taxi.'

'Everything's an emergency with you.' Sadie sighed, picking up a pastry. But she was already on her feet, following him to the door.

There was no escaping the heat in this city of concrete and glass, where no architect had ever thought of shade.

Sunlight glared from polished steel railings and scared shadows across wide, scalding pavements. It was all Sadie could do not to walk with a palm outstretched, like a lion tamer, hoping to quell the beast's fury.

The address was tucked down a laneway, nothing more than one of a dozen steel roller doors. A hatch in the roller door was ajar and cold air wafted through, luring them out of the sun. Jake leaned against the door. It went nowhere, so he gave it a shove with his shoulder. Somewhere inside, a bell tinkled.

'So much for the element of surprise,' Sadie whispered.

The warehouse was larger than it had seemed from the outside, but still not large enough for all the stuff inside. Crammed shelves created narrow aisles into which dusty books and ancient magazines spilled. Sadie looked down and wondered where to put her feet.

The man behind the counter looked older than he probably was. Deep lines cut down from cheekbone to stubbled jaw and there were the shadows of too many late nights beneath his eyes. Dark hair fell long and wild to his shoulders. He wore an embroidered waistcoat without any shirt and his bony wrists were encircled by leather bands and bracelets. He was reading an old issue of *Fortean Times*. One hand held the magazine, the other trawled in a bag of nuts.

'You're early,' he said, sighing heavily.

'Vincent, it's Jacob.'

The shopkeeper still didn't look up. 'What is?'

'He is,' Sadie told him.

The man's jaw slackened, taking in the tall boy in the crumpled hat. The magazine dropped to the floor. 'Jacob?'

'Vincent.'

'Wait, no. It can't be you. How do I know it's you?'

His voice was thin and parched, choked with the same dust that now gathered hot and thick at the back of Sadie's throat.

Jake lunged forward, grabbed both sides of Vincent's waistcoat and dragged him across the counter, scattering paperbacks and pistachio shells.

'I should break you in two, right here.'

Vincent's shoulders melted away, disappointed. 'Oh, it is you. I like the new face. Young always suits you.'

'Where is it?' Jake snarled.

'Where's what?'

'The relic. What have you done with it?'

Vincent seemed genuinely astonished. 'Me? Can you see a coward like me going near that thing? This body's never been up to much. Its heart would just give in, like an old balloon. You know how I feel about dying. I hate it, hate it. Every single time.'

Jake threw Vincent into the shelf behind him. 'Vincent, she's found us, after all this time. She's out there now, waiting in the water.'

Vincent licked at his lips, nervous. 'Are you certain? You can't be certain.'

'They killed me. I'm certain.'

'Then you'll be wanting us to leave, pronto.'

Jake frowned. 'We can't run. Frobisher's dead. We've no passports, nothing. It'll take too long to arrange anything.'

'They got Frobisher?'

'Somebody got him. I'm stuck here. We're all stuck here. And if I have to do something about it, then you, of all people, will damn well help me.'

Vincent seemed to struggle for air. 'You don't mean you're thinking of fighting? But, well, no. I mean, yeah, easy for you to say, your family were fighters. You can't expect me to fight. I'm a pacifist. I want to be a pacifist.' His right hand bunched the front of his T-shirt and his breath rattled. 'This is it, I can feel it. I'm going. My shoulder is tingling. I feel so far away.'

Jake slapped the old man, hard across his left cheek. 'Shut up. Dying won't get you out of this. We both know what they're coming for. What have you done with it?'

'Nothing, honestly.' Vincent had sunk to his knees, one hand at his chest, the other nursing his cheek. 'You're the guardian. You're the one who's supposed to keep it safe.'

'I have. For centuries. But I never realised I'd have to keep it safe from you.'

'I didn't steal it,' Vincent insisted, wheedling. 'Maybe you just misplaced it. I mean, you were old, you know what these brains get like.'

'Don't insult me.'

'Maybe it's for the best. Maybe you should just let it stay lost. Maybe that way we'll all be safe. Oxygen, I need oxygen. Call an ambulance. I'm serious, I've died like this before.'

Sadie prodded Jake's shoulder. 'Is he bluffing?'

'I don't care.' Jake put both palms down on the counter and leaned over to glare down at Vincent. 'Whoever stole the relic knew I had it. If it wasn't you, then who was it?'

Vincent shrugged. 'How would I know? It's not like any of you ever drop by for a chat.' He thrust a wizened finger at the countertop. 'I'm staying, even if she is out there. I'm gonna be invisible.' The same finger now turned towards the ceiling. 'They'll never miss me. What am I? They don't care about me, never have.'

The shop's bell tinkled. A young man in a well-cut suit stood there, clasping a black leather briefcase. He might have been a real-estate agent, except that his brief-case was handcuffed to his wrist. Seeing Vincent had company, the new arrival stopped his shiny shoes on the doormat.

'Sorry,' Vincent called. 'Think you want next door.'

The man nodded and backed out into the laneway.

'Anyway,' Vincent said brightly, returning his

attention to Jake. 'What was I saying? Oh yeah, I don't have any numbers, any addresses. No friends. Sorry.' He was grinning, for the first time since they had arrived.

Sadie lightly touched Jake's elbow. 'That man,' she said. 'He had a name badge on his pocket.'

'And?'

'I told you about the God squad, yeah?'

Jake turned back to Vincent. 'You've been watching the door the whole time we've been here. Like you were expecting someone, someone you didn't want us to see.'

'I don't know what you mean.' Vincent's grin had become a grimace.

'Stay here!' Jake barked, presumably at Sadie. He bolted for the door and threw it open.

Sadie didn't even consider staying put. She followed Jake into the startling heat of the alley, just in time to see the man sprinting away. A black 4WD waited at the alley's end, its engine throbbing impatiently, and the suited man ran towards it. He had fifty metres on Jake, but was slowed by the briefcase he clutched to his chest. Jake's legs sliced through the still air, making ground on his quarry. The 4WD's rear door was thrown open, the man dived for the back seat and the vehicle swerved off into traffic. Jake skidded to a stop on the kerb, then immediately turned on his heels.

Seeing Sadie watching in the alley, he swore breathlessly and pointed over her shoulder. 'Vincent!' he shouted.

Vincent was making quiet steps behind her, edging out through the door. Sadie grabbed him by the arm. He jerked back in her grasp, peering down at her fingers with some disappointment.

'You want to let me go,' he said.

'Fat chance.'

Vincent's dark eyes looked for hers. 'You want to let me go.'

Sadie was about to insist that she didn't, even if the idea of touching him wasn't exactly appealing, when she found her fingers lifting from his arm and her hand dropping to her hip. She couldn't remember why it had ever been a good idea to grab hold of him.

'Good girl,' Vincent told her. 'Now fall over.'

There was nothing Sadie wanted to do more. With both hands at her side, she toppled over on the cobbles like a felled tree. Her right shoulder took most of the impact, electric pain singing to her fingertips. The side of her head cracked on the hot stone.

Jake appeared beside her and lifted her upright. 'Sadie, are you all right?'

'Ask me how many fingers you're holding up.'

'I'm not holding up any fingers.'

'Then I'm fine.'

At the end of the alleyway, Vincent was getting into a taxi. Sadie somehow felt happy to see him go, even if she knew she shouldn't.

'I'm sorry,' Jake was saying. 'Vincent can be very persuasive, if you're not expecting it. I should have warned you.'

'It was like the Drowners, their song.'

'Same principle. I told you, each Old One has his own talent.'

Sadie leaned against the white brick wall, trying to gauge how firmly her head was attached. A new headache pressed at her temples. 'Guess you were right, my stalkers were after the relic. You think that was money in the briefcase?'

'It wouldn't have been hard for Vincent to find a buyer. There's no shortage of collectors out there.'

'I don't suppose you memorised their licence plates?'

Jake frowned. 'I suppose that would have been a good idea.'

'What would the God squad want with a demon anyway?'

'Sadie, I'm not sure even you could resist it.'

'You think?'

He met her defiant glare. 'You've known more death than anyone your age deserves to. If someone offered a chance to change that, wouldn't you say yes?'

Sadie's voice dried in her throat. Of course she thought of her parents. Of course she thought of that book under her mattress, full of scrawled questions she would never ask them.

'What, and that's possible?' She was angry at herself for asking.

'That demon makes anything possible.'

'But you must have managed to resist it. I mean, you've been looking after it for ages.'

Jake looked down. 'Every dream has its price, Sadie. I'm not sure that's one I could ever bring myself to pay.'

They took a taxi back to Ocean Street. As they turned right off the highway and rolled downhill towards the beach, sunset flared in the windscreen. Sadie sat at one end of the back seat, Jake at the other.

'So Vincent's always been seriously dodgy?' she asked.

'I'm afraid so. He and I have been bound together since the beginning. All Old Ones were assigned to a regiment of seven. Squadrons, we call them. When I came here fifty years ago, mine came with me. Moaning all the way.'

'So you're what, the squadron leader?'

'Yes.'

'And you didn't do anything helpful like stay in touch?'

'They know where to find me.'

It wasn't hard to picture Jake leading troops into battle, but it was a surprise to realise there were five more of his lot—his *squadron*—in Perth. Were they all leading small, ordinary lives? Were they all so alone?

Jake had lapsed into silence again, digging down into his own thoughts. There was more he had to say, more he was avoiding saying. Sadie nudged his thigh with her knee.

'And?'

He was scowling now. 'And what?'

'You promised you'd tell me the whole truth,' Sadie said, carefully. 'But when I ask about some things, it's like there's this anger just steaming off you.'

'I'm not angry at you.'

'Oh, that's a happy face?'

Jake looked out the window at the setting sun. He didn't shift on the seat, but Sadie felt him pull away from her. 'Your parents,' he said. 'You never talk about them, do you?'

Sadie flinched. 'What's that got to do with anything?'

He turned back to her. 'You don't, do you?'

For a moment, Sadie worried she couldn't explain herself. She had spent so long not thinking about it, buttressing herself against the sharp edges of grief and anger and loss. 'When it first happened, people wanted to talk about it all the time. Like they thought I had to talk it through, talk it out of me. But I didn't want to talk about it, not then.'

'It was your loss, not theirs.'

'Yeah, that's it exactly. It sounds stupid, but I didn't want to share it with anyone else. Nobody else was going to understand. It was like every time someone wanted to talk about it, they were stealing a bit of it from me.'

Jake nodded, waited for her to go on.

'After a while, a few months, people stopped wanting to talk about it. They stopped giving me these pathetic frowns and started smiling. All the time. Like if they smiled enough, I'd just have to join in.'

'What did happen to your parents?'

Sadie took a deep breath and told him. Told him everything. What she remembered. What she didn't. How she couldn't look at the eastern hills without thinking about that day. How Christmas still made her angry. How there were streets and suburbs and shops she couldn't go near without her stomach hollowing out. The geography of loss.

'I think, in the end, people just get impatient. They wait for you to get over it, to get back to normal.' Sadie met Jake's gaze and held it. 'But I'm never going to get over it.'

'No,' Jake said quietly. He leaned forwards, grappling his knees as if gathering reinforcements, and took a deep breath. 'During the last war, I fought in Egypt with the British army. The locals warned us of demons living in the desert. Powerful spirits who would lead men astray. Ifrit, they were called. Demons of fire and sand and dust. Forbidden creatures.' He frowned. 'I already knew these stories, just as I knew the worst demons lived at sea, waiting to be summoned to shore. They were creatures of immense power and immeasurable mischief. Praise them or threaten them, make them choose you as their master and they'll grant any wish.'

'That's what's inside the relic. A sea demon?'

'Vincent taught Lysandra how to become its master, and she asked it for immortality. I should have known what they were up to. Each squadron was given a city to care for. Lysandra's was mine.'

'You feel responsible.'

'What do you think?' he snapped, then held up his palms in apology. 'By the time I found out, it was too late. All I could do was trick the demon into a box, before it could grant any more wishes. Demons can be bound to objects, you see—a bottle, a lamp, a chest.'

'It was you,' Sadie realised. 'You put it in the box. You made the relic.'

'Yes. I closed the box and I'm the only one who can open it. That's why it's my responsibility. Why it always has been. I carved the box from the woods of Mount Olympus, from divine timber. To cut down a tree, I needed the blessing of the Gods. I had to tell them what Lysandra had done.' Jake watched Sadie carefully, searching for approval. 'I had to betray the people I was supposed to care for.'

Sadie waited for him to go on.

'I stood on the shore. I watched a volcano spew burning rock and ash and fire into a blue sky. I watched the sun disappear. The sea rose up and scattered the merchant ships. I watched it swallow my city. Swallow everything.'

He breathed in hard and straightened his shoulders.

'Even in servitude, a demon delights in being mischievous. Lysandra and her people still drowned. Only their souls had been made immortal, not their flesh. They were left halfway to divinity, halfway to hell.' He sniffed, shook his head and pretended to be impressed by the sunset, as if he was suddenly embarrassed by his honesty.

Sadie recognised something of herself in Jake. He was navigating the brittle edge of dark emotions. She knew how that was done. A quick joke, a smart remark, and her course remained steady.

'Okay, questions. If the demon tricked her, why would Lysandra want it back?'

'It's been imprisoned for thousands of years. If she sets it free, it will choose her as its master and give her its power. Finish the job.'

'Even if she starts a war?'

'I doubt there's anything she wouldn't risk for immortal life.'

'Right. So, second question. You said you were the only person who can open the box. If that's true, she can't get at the demon. So why all the fuss?'

Jake smiled, but only just. 'Sadie, it's not just the relic

I've been hiding. It's me. I know Lysandra. She'll find a way to make me open that box. Whatever it takes.'

The taxi had pulled up outside Ocean Street.

'Shouldn't we be looking for the God squad?'

'We need to get into Frobisher's office and get his address book. I need to find the rest of my people. Someone must know something.'

'And we're back here because—?'

Jake plucked at the front of his T-shirt. 'First rule of burglary. Never wear white.'

'Burglary, right.'

He frowned, looking for her eyes. 'You don't have to come with me.'

Sadie already had her door open. 'Shut up,' she said, smiling.

Sadie buzzed with a strange, nervous electricity. It wasn't just the hunt for the relic, it was Jake. Being with him, sharing this adventure. He was leaning on the dining table, looking serious, in a tight black T-shirt. The newspaper was unwrapped and spread out in front of him.

'What's wrong?' she asked.

Jake held up the paper to show her the front page. *Cold Blooded Murder*, it read, above a photo of a suburban shop surrounded by police tape and a fuzzy snapshot of a middle-aged man smiling at the camera.

If anything, Sadie felt relieved. It was someone else's tragedy. 'Oh, that's terrible,' she said, but her tone was elsewhere. 'Do they know what happened?'

'I know what happened.'

'You do?'

'Last night you asked me if we could ever die. Well we can. If you know how, you can pull out our souls. Or, you can do this.' He tapped at the front page. 'He was shot three times. Once in the gut, once in the heart and once in the head.' Jake's hands identified each wound. 'Anything metal will do the trick. A knife, a sword, a bullet.'

Sadie took the paper off him, skimming the details. A newsagent. 'That's the man you went to see about Vincent.'

'Patrick.' Jake threw the paper aside and thumped his fist on the kitchen table. 'The address book!'

'You think that's why Frobisher was killed?'

'Maybe it's not just the relic they're after. Maybe they're hunting us down, one by one.'

'Why would anyone do that?'

There was a knock at the door. Those three raps chilled Sadie more than any talk of murder.

Jake started for the door, but Sadie held him back.

'That's either a murderer or my grandparents. Do you really want to answer it?'

'I'm not scared, Sadie.'

'You haven't met my grandpa.' There was another

knock, more insistent this time. A murderer wouldn't knock, she decided. 'I'll go.'

It wasn't a murderer waiting on the tatty doormat and neither was it Stan. As the door opened, Sergeant Bradbury glared in. He had an announcement ready but, seeing Sadie, forgot all about it.

'What the bloody hell are you doing here?'

'This is my house.'

'Yeah, right.'

'It is.' Sadie was more nervous than she sounded. She remembered lying to him in Frobisher's office. *I'm watching you*, he'd said.

'Sarge.' Behind him, Sadie saw Constable Williams shake her head, sinking her hands further into her pockets. There was another woman there too. She was in her mid-forties, probably, and craning her head anxiously to peer around the policeman, at Sadie—no, beyond Sadie, to the hallway. Her eyes were glassy with tears.

'Yeah, anyway.' Bradbury cleared his throat. 'This isn't about you, Miss Miller. We're looking for Sam Mitchell.'

'Who's Sam Mitchell?'

'Kid's been missing for a week. Picture's been in the papers. Neighbours think they've seen him. You going to let us in?'

'There's no Sam Mitchell here. I've never heard of him.'

But, at that moment, the woman broke whatever

invisible tether had held her back and hurried up the wonky stairs. 'Sam! Sam!' She shoved both Sadie and Bradbury aside, running along the hall to where she had glimpsed Jake waiting in the shadows.

'Oh Sam!' she cried, grabbing Jake in a fierce hug. Her tears soaked his T-shirt.

Sadie didn't understand any of this, but she could see Jake did. There wasn't any confusion in the brief, guilty look he gave her. His head lowered and his shoulders slumped.

Bradbury stepped back from the doorstep, clearing a path for Sadie from hallway to police car. 'I think you'd both better come down to the station.'

PART TWO

THE
OLD
ONES

13
THE KILLER INSIDE

The woman had barely sat still in the hour since they had arrived at the station. At first, Sadie thought she had seemed relieved, if impatient. She had clutched Jake to her shoulder and promised him she would take him home. Then, when Jake hadn't recognised her, or hadn't said the right things, she had become angry, telling him to stop fooling around. When he still hadn't said the right things, she started looking scared.

She blamed Sadie, that much was certain. Sadie had done something to her son—lured him from his happy home. Now, waiting to be interviewed, it was all Sadie could do not to look guilty, shifting in her plastic seat.

Constable Williams assured Sadie she wasn't under arrest. 'Don't worry about the Sarge, it's all bark, no bite with him. Just a quick chat and you'll be off home.'

That was three hours ago. In the meantime, Sadie's grandparents had arrived. Stan paced the waiting room, making demands at the front desk, while Ida waved at her, a little forlornly. That simple gesture put heat in Sadie's cheeks and she needed to look away. She had lied to the two people she most cared about, and they knew it. But her grandmother still waved.

Finally, Constable Williams led her through to a small white room, where Bradbury waited with a manilla folder and a tape recorder. They were joined by her grandparents. Ida lightly touched her shoulder and Stan refused to sit down until Bradbury threatened to eject him if he didn't.

The policeman asked her where she had met Sam Mitchell and what he had told her. Had he been involved in Frobisher's murder? Was that why he was in hiding? She answered as truthfully as she could, leaving out the more outlandish details. With every answer, she felt Stan's folded arms tighten until his fingers dug bloodless into his shirtsleeves. With every answer, she felt more ashamed.

Finally, Bradbury lifted his biro and read back over his page of notes. 'So, in summary, you met Sam Mitchell when he was breaking into a house left to you by one Jacob Freeman. Mr Mitchell then claimed to *be* Mr Freeman and was present when you discovered Horace Frobisher's body. Mr Mitchell fled the scene before myself and Constable Williams arrived, although you insist he couldn't have committed the murder as he was with you at all times. Is that correct?'

Sadie shifted in her seat. 'Well, not at all times, now

you put it like that. I sort of, stormed off and left them there. But just for a few minutes.'

'So Mr Mitchell was alone with the lawyer, shortly before you found him dead.'

'Yes, but he wouldn't have killed him. They were friends. Frobisher had been Jake's—Mr Freeman's—lawyer for years.'

'Mr Freeman's. But not Mr Mitchell's?'

Sadie could feel a familiar red blush spread out across her collarbone and rise up into her cheeks. The policeman was over-complicating things. But Jake had been alone with Frobisher, just before the lawyer was killed. And Jake had been to see the newsagent. Could Jake be the killer? No, she wouldn't believe that. She needed to talk to him; she needed him to explain all of this away.

'I told you. Frobisher recognised him. He called him Mr Freeman. Look, don't think I don't know how it sounds, okay? But maybe that woman out there's got it wrong, maybe Jake isn't her missing son. Maybe he just looks a bit similar?'

Bradbury nodded, as if accepting the possibility, and opened the folder in front of him. From it, he produced three grainy black-and-white photographs, each of which showed three or four dark figures in a hospital hallway. Sadie's face was clearly visible in one.

'Don't suppose that face looks a bit similar to anyone you know?'

Caught off guard, Sadie could only nod.

'You want to tell me what the bloody hell went on there? From what we can make out, some kind of wild animal went crazy in the wards, killing two nurses and one doctor. S'pose it was just coincidence you and Mr Mitchell were there too?'

Sadie nodded again.

'And I s'pose young Mr Mitchell had nothing to do with it? It wasn't some stupid prank that went wrong?'

Stan took the prints from the policeman and studied each in turn, his face impassive. He handed them to Ida, who murmured, 'She never said anything about this.'

'It wasn't a prank,' Sadie insisted, trying not to look at either of her grandparents. 'Jake wouldn't have anything to do with stupid pranks. If you really want to know, he stopped that thing killing a whole lot more people.'

Bradbury tutted. 'You keep calling him Jake.'

'That's his name. I told you, that woman out there has made a mistake.'

With barely concealed pleasure, Bradbury returned to the folder, taking out two sets of near-identical inky fingerprints. 'I'm afraid Mr Mitchell is known to us from past misadventure, sweetheart. Shoplifting, vandalism. The usual dumb stuff. So, yeah, he's exactly the sort of guy who'd have a lot to do with stupid pranks.'

Sadie wanted to object, but found herself silent. The fingerprints were a precise match and, there beside them, was a colour snap of a younger, miserable-looking Jake in a flannel shirt, with his wrists in cuffs.

'His mother thinks he's lost it. Maybe he actually believes he is the late Mr Freeman. Certainly threw himself into the part, with the voice and the accent and everything. But that doesn't really excuse you, does it, sweetheart?'

'I'm sorry?'

There was a smirk behind that red moustache. 'Well, maybe the kid is crazy. But why would you believe the bullshit story he fed you? Most people would have spotted a mile off he had a screw loose. Not you though, huh?'

Sadie could hear her teeth click in a hollow mouth.

The strangest thing was, her grandfather wasn't angry. Leaving the interview room, he put his arm around Sadie's shoulders and pulled her into him, guiding her towards the door. There was strength in that grasp, and more comfort than she might have expected.

'Excuse me, it's Sadie, isn't it?'

Sadie had entered the station foyer with her head down, looking at her boots as they scuffed the carpet tiles. She had hoped the woman—Mrs Mitchell—would stay sitting on the hard plastic chairs. At worst, she had imagined the woman might hurl abuse as Stan and Ida bundled her out to their waiting car. No, this was even worse.

'I'm Dianne Mitchell,' she said. 'I just wanted to say,

I don't blame you at all.'

Sadie nodded, but she was no longer sure what she thought. Her skin felt raw, her tongue was loose and her muscles twanged like rubber bands.

'The girl's tired,' Stan said. 'It's late, and she needs to go home.'

'It's okay Grandpa,' Sadie said, releasing herself from his hug.

Ida patted her elbow. 'We'll be in the car.'

Dianne still held out her hand, so Sadie took it, a little weakly. 'Hi.'

'I think you've done an amazing job, dealing with all this. We thought we'd lost him, forever.' She put a hand on Sadie's shoulder. 'I just want you to know, we'll look after him now. He'll get the help he needs and, soon, he'll get better.'

Sadie trembled. She nodded and tried half a smile, as if she was pleased for this woman.

The truth was, the more she heard people say Jake was crazy, the less she believed it. She had seen things. Things that couldn't be explained away. Blood and viscera glistening on the Minotaur's jaw. The Drowners erupting from the harbour waters. A perfect, eternal rose.

No, believing Jake wasn't the problem. What troubled Sadie was that she also believed Dianne. The boy she knew as Jake was also Sam Mitchell, or had been, until recently. Behind Dianne, across the white brick wall, were a dozen posters of missing children, teenagers, parents and grandparents.

Sadie stared at the faces staring back at her from the noticeboard. She almost marvelled no one else had seen the full horror of what had happened. She was thinking back a week to that hot morning in the lawyer's stuffy office. Thinking about the Dalai Lama.

How can you be here, she had asked, *that age, this week?* And Jake had fobbed her off with some half-hearted mumbo jumbo. *A gift from the Gods.*

Now, the answer was clear to her. This wasn't re-incarnation. Jake hadn't been given a new body. He had stolen one. He had crawled into a young boy's head and booted him out. Sam Mitchell, the real Sam Mitchell, was gone, and he wasn't coming back.

Dianne took a sharp breath and stepped back. For a moment, Sadie worried the woman had read her mind.

No. It was Jake being led through to the interview room. Seeing Sadie in the foyer, he moved towards her, then stopped. He saw the pale horror about her cheeks and he flinched. He knew she knew. For a second he looked guilty and then nodded, as if offering the smallest of confessions. Yes, it must be true. He had killed Sam Mitchell and taken his body. Then his head went down and he let the policeman lead him away.

Sadie never wanted to see him again.

14
NOT THE GIRL YOU THINK YOU ARE

It was two days before Sadie agreed to see Tom. He went in shuffling his sneakers across the carpet like he was sure the floor was booby-trapped. Any minute, Sadie would hit the switch and consign him to the flames.

She was reading, with Nick Cave playing in the background. Tom sat on the edge of the sofa, trying and failing to make himself comfortable. His torso was still tightly bandaged and the stitches in his side made him lean so that he looked like he might topple sideways at any moment. He waited for Sadie to say something, but it was clear she wasn't in the mood.

'They're saying it probably fell off the back of a cattle truck,' he said.

Sadie didn't look up and didn't ask what he was talking about. 'Yeah?'

'Yeah. My dad's all over it. The way he sees it, there's always someone to sue.'

'Right.'

Another silence arrived. Tom was left holding the conversation.

'Probably gonna have to give up athletics, for a couple of months anyway…Dad reckons I could've got a scholarship to some university over east or something. You know, a sports scholarship.'

Sadie's book dipped, but only for a moment. 'You don't want a sports scholarship.'

'I know. It's all about the suing. He wants to say I missed out.'

Tom licked his lips, pressing on.

'The doctor says all that other stuff was endorphins. You know, the stuff about—' he trailed off, unable to think of a word that didn't sound ridiculous. 'Pain can make you see weird shit, he reckons.'

Sadie sighed, throwing the book aside. She got up and changed the CD.

'Kim was asking about you.'

'Yeah?' Sadie was thumbing through the booklet, skim-reading lyrics she already knew by heart. 'What was she asking? "Who was that weird chick we used to hang out with?"'

Tom laughed, but just once. 'He was a bit weird, wasn't he? Jake, I mean, or whatever his name really is.'

'He wasn't weird,' Sadie spat, with such force that it surprised them both. 'What is wrong with everyone? This isn't just some funny story about some crazy guy. We're not just going to laugh it off.'

Now, Tom was silent, but felt no less uncomfortable.

'I mean, listen to yourself, Tom. All that crap about endorphins. You can't really think it's that simple. You thought you'd seen the devil, remember? But it wasn't the devil, it was the Minotaur. An ancient, impossible monster. We saw it kill two people. It almost killed you. I mean, seriously, that's not a funny story, is it? People *died*.'

Sadie swung her legs around and over the foot of her bed, to face Tom. Her eyes were wide and red. 'Jake isn't strange; he isn't wacky. He's a killer, Tom. I've seen him, you've seen him. Maybe that cop's right, maybe he did kill the lawyer, maybe he's still killing people.'

'But I heard, I mean, he's not even really called Jake, is he? That was all made up. He's just some kid called Sam.'

'Sam's gone, Tom. That's what Jake and his people do. That's how he came back from the dead. They creep into your head and take you over. I saw it in the police station—all those posters, all those people who go missing.' She pointed at the flyscreen. 'There could be hundreds of them out there, thousands maybe. It's how they live forever—they steal other people's lives.'

Tom shifted on the sofa. He had never seen her so worked up. It worried him. 'Sades, you can't say stuff like that.'

'Why not?'

'Because you sound as crazy as him. Like you believed all the stuff he told you.'

'I don't have to believe him. I saw it. You saw it.'

'Yeah, well. I don't know what I saw. But I know what I'm saying. I saw nothing. If you don't want people thinking you've lost it, you should say the same.'

'You think I give a shit what anyone else thinks? This is serious, Tom. I'm not going to—'

'Shut up.' Tom was on his feet before he realised, standing over Sadie. She shrank back from him. 'I'm just saying, you know, I'm your friend. And I want to stay your friend. Maybe some weird stuff did happen, but maybe we should work that out before we go telling anyone. Serious now Sades, do you want to try telling Kim any of this?'

Sadie thought a moment before she said anything. 'Maybe not.'

'I don't want you making it easy for them to have a go at you. You're the smart one Sades. You're the sane one. That's the way it's gotta be.'

Sadie's chin quivered. 'I trusted him,' she said. 'I don't know why, but I wanted to trust him.'

Tom was already moving back and away from her. He was worried he had upset her. 'Well, yeah. Maybe that was a bit stupid, hey?'

Sadie put her face in her hands. 'I'm such an idiot.'

'Are you grounded?' he asked, when enough nothing had been said.

'No. I don't think so. I don't know. I don't care. Why?'

'Just, maybe you should get out of the house for a bit.'

'I think maybe I should never see anybody, ever again.'

'The thing is, Kim's asked you to come sailing tonight. Her dad's doing that twilight sail thing near the uni. Kim says it's really boring, so we're all invited.'

'How thoughtful.'

'Seriously Sades, you need to get out of the house. Do something normal.'

'Normal.' Sadie nodded. 'Suppose I could give that a go.'

Every shop was in darkness along the highway, even those open for business. An announcement had gone out that morning, banning the unnecessary use of electricity. The state's power supply was straining under the demands of a million air-conditioners as Perth wilted.

The Royal Perth Yacht Club was a twenty-minute drive from the coast, on a fork in the Swan River. From here, the brown waters went three ways: tracing the freeway south, winding east past the Perth city centre, and curling back west towards the harbour at Fremantle. There was no breeze, but the place was still busy with middle-aged men in striped polo shirts and white cotton caps, twanging ropes and spraying down the decks. Nobody was letting the still evening stop them. A few already had beer bottles in stubby holders, preparing to set off.

Kimberley met Sadie with air kisses. 'It's so cool of you to come,' she trilled, taking Sadie by the arm. 'I told Tom, these things are seriously boring. Although, there's this guy who works in the sheds here who has the most awesome six pack. It's not even a six pack, it's like a fifteen pack or something. I don't know what you'd call it.'

'A keg?'

Kimberley looked at Sadie as if for the first time. 'You're funny,' she said.

This unusual friendliness on the part of her cousin surprised Sadie, but she soon understood. Kimberley wanted gossip. She pulled Sadie up the jetty steps, leaving Tom on dry land.

'So,' she whispered, 'is he hot?'

'Is who hot?'

'I suppose he's kind of alternative, yeah? Wears op-shop clothes and listens to all that weird music you always have on? He must be a bit hot Sades. You wouldn't get in so much trouble otherwise.'

Kimberley had never called her Sades in her life. 'Who said I was in trouble?'

'Everybody knows. Have you even been on Face-book this week?'

Luckily, Sadie's uncle, Steven, spotted them then and gave her a wave.

'Kim, go tell your mother to get her backside off her barstool and onto the boat. We're leaving in exactly four minutes and I don't want her complaining that I forgot her again.'

'Why do I have to go? I was just over there.'

'Because she's not answering her phone and because I keep a roof over your head. Quick smart.'

Kimberley's shoulders sank and she began to slouch back to shore. Then a better idea occurred to her. 'Heather,' she shrieked at her black-clad twin sister, who was making a slow path up the steps. 'Dad says you have to go get Mum out of the bar. We're leaving in four minutes exactly.'

'Ugh.' Heather groaned and slunk back towards the clubhouse.

Within ten minutes, a small flotilla of yachts drifted out across the bay, their engines murmuring. A few hundred metres from shore, they turned off the motors and waited, as if hoping to lure in a breeze. Sunset warmed the glass towers of the city and polished the brown river until it shone. Headlights glowed on the far shores. A returning ferry sliced a path between flashing buoys, but Sadie had the impression that nothing was going anywhere. Still, she was glad she had come now. Above her head, sails hung loose as bed sheets forgotten on a clothesline. Here, the world had stopped.

Tom was at the stern with a beer, pulling whichever rope Steven suggested. He seemed to know his stuff, but there was little for him, or anyone else, to do.

Sadie sat at the bow with her legs dangling over the edge. She had once seen dolphins here, ten kilometres inland, and there were stories of lost sharks circling sailboarders.

Kimberley came to sit beside her with a Diet Coke. She glanced towards the stern. 'Come on then, did you?'

Sadie looked up, blinking. 'Did I what?'

Kimberley's eyes flared. 'Mum said they found the two of you in that old house. That's why you were there, wasn't it? Come on, you can tell me. Did you do it?'

'Bloody hell.' Sadie tugged her arm free. 'You really have no idea what you're talking about. It's nothing like that. I mean, it *wasn't* anything like that.'

'It's okay.' Kimberley was whispering now. 'We've all done it. Well, I mean, not all of us, sure. Heather's still waiting for her vampire. Look, I'm really happy for you, everyone thought you were a lezzo. Or, you know, frigid.'

Sadie opened her mouth to argue, but then closed it again. She didn't know where to start. Was it that simple, that cheap and tacky? Had she trusted Jake for no better reason than he set her hormones bubbling? And what about now that she knew what he was? Surely she couldn't still care for him, for a killer?

It was almost a relief when someone started screaming.

The woman screaming stood on the spacious stern of a particularly grand vessel, gripping an empty platter. Tiny pastries were scattered on the deck. A wan figure in chain mail clambered aboard the yacht.

Sadie's uncle cupped a hand against the low sun to get a better view. 'What the bloody hell's going on? Where did he come from?'

Then, from the yacht behind them, came the sounds of men shouting. Another intruder in rotting finery had climbed aboard. Two men were trying to wrestle him to the floor. Voices came clearly through the still evening air.

'Make a citizen's arrest! Make a citizen's arrest!'

'Just hit the bugger!'

'Get your phone out, someone should be filming this!'

Another boat had been boarded. Its attacker shot up from the river and landed heavily on the deck. He casually knocked a burly man overboard.

Then, another! And another! The skipper took a swing at his opponent with a wine bottle, but the intruder leapt aside and skittered up the mast. Then he pounced, sending the skipper and his wife sprawling over the railing. Similar scuffles were breaking out on all of the boats. Twenty furious bodies bobbed in the bay.

Sadie's uncle dropped his beer as his own yacht shook.

Sadie's knees collapsed and she fell to the deck. Pulling herself back up on to her feet, she could see the figure in his tarnished armour. His skin was blue and puckered and his long hair was matted with seaweed and salt. His mouth dropped open in a war cry—howling in rage and delight.

Sadie's uncle charged at the man, yelling in terror. The Drowner didn't shift, but his chest swelled and Sadie knew what was coming next. A fierce jet of water and bile hit Steven square in the chest, lifting him from his feet and thrusting him overboard. Tom stepped forward, but Sadie grabbed him and shoved him downstairs into the cabin.

'What on earth is going on out there?' Margot asked, sipping her white wine. 'It sounds like one of those terrible party boats.'

'There are men,' Tom gabbled, 'coming out of the water.'

'Oh, not more swimming? Give them a few beers and they're teenagers again.'

Sadie didn't have time to explain. She needed a weapon. 'Margot, the flares, where are they?'

'How should I know? Ask your uncle.'

'Uncle Steven's gone overboard,' Sadie said flatly.

Margot tutted. 'They never grow up.'

Tom was opening cupboards in the cabin kitchen.

'There are some cheeses in the fridge, if you're hungry,' Margot said, returning to the magazine open on her lap. 'And sushi.'

The boat rocked to starboard and Heather looked up, unplugging one of her earphones. 'Is that Kim messing about?'

Sadie and Tom looked at each other in panic. Kimberley was still out there on the deck, and she wasn't alone. Heavy boots thudded overhead.

'Hurry up!' Sadie yelled at Tom. He pulled another drawer from the kitchen cabinet.

Heather frowned, annoyed by all this fuss. 'What are you after?'

'The flares,' Sadie told her. 'Doesn't every boat have flares?'

'Oh, them,' Heather said blandly. 'They're in that thing.' She gestured to the orange box above the sink.

Sadie ran across and pulled the box from the wall. Inside she found a whistle, a compass, two lifejackets and, yes, four flares. Two of the tubes were yellow, and two red. She threw one of each to Tom, who began grappling with the strings.

'Am I signalling for help?' he asked.

'No,' Sadie said, picking up the remaining flares, 'we're fighting for our lives.'

Margot lowered her wine glass. 'Sadie, Tom, darlings, I really don't think you should be messing about with those.'

Another great howl came from the stern and there,

at the top of the stairs, was the Drowner who had washed Steven away.

Margot peered up at him. 'Heather, that's not one of your friends, is it?'

'Tom, do it!' Sadie screamed. 'Do it now!'

Tom thrust the flare away from him, towards the stairs, and yanked the cord. There was a deafening bang and the cabin filled with smoke. Heather and Margot coughed and spluttered. Sadie's eyes were streaming. Squinting through the acrid haze, she could make out the lettering on the side of the yellow flare in her hand: SMOKE. She threw it aside and fumbled with the red tube. The dark shape of the figure was halfway down the stairs. Her fingers found the pull cord and she thrust it in his direction, but she hesitated. In the thickening, choking smoke, it was impossible to be sure she had the flare facing away from herself. If she didn't, she was about to be blinded in a searing shower of sparks.

The Drowner was nearly at the foot of the stairs. Sadie's eyes were streaming and her chest burned.

She tore at the cord. Nothing happened. There was a little fizzle and spark, no more impressive than a birthday sparkler. Then the tube kicked in her hand and a cascade of crimson light erupted, turning the thick smoke a brilliant pink.

A horrified shriek came from the direction of the stairs.

Sadie charged forward, holding the flare out in front of her, and the shape retreated up the stairs, clawing at the light. Hearing the Drowner crash into the water, she hurried up onto the deck. Already the flare was beginning to gutter; its sparks were thinning and losing enthusiasm. But her efforts didn't go unnoticed. A cry went out and was quickly passed from vessel to vessel: *the flares, get the damn flares!* Within a minute, jets of crimson lit every deck, as the sailors repelled their howling attackers.

Still, Sadie wasn't done. There was another Drowner at the prow. He was a tall, lithe creature, with ragged armour loose around wiry limbs. He had one arm crooked around Kimberley's neck and a blue-skinned hand clasped across her mouth. As Sadie turned her sparking weapon towards him, he hissed through his rotting teeth.

'Let her go,' Sadie insisted, wishing her voice was firmer. She edged on along the railings.

Kimberley was paralysed by fear.

The Drowner's eyes narrowed and his mouth opened. With her free hand, Sadie braced herself against the rail, ready for a blast of seawater. Instead, the shouts from the other yachts faded away. All she could hear was the rustle of the water against the hull and the distant call of seagulls. Somewhere, a wave was unfolding across a shore, taking its time, luxuriating. The song was the most seductive she had ever heard. It reminded her of the beauty of the water, its irresistible depths and darknesses. Nothing else seemed important. She looked at the flare in her hand and couldn't remember what it was doing there. She tossed it overboard and it sizzled away to nothing.

As the Drowner's song continued, Sadie felt her legs move, carrying her towards him. Part of her was all terror, willing herself to stop. The rest of her wanted to be taken.

'Sadie! Get out of the way!'

It was Tom, she knew, but most of her didn't care. She was going with the Drowner, down into the dark waters. Then, a searing streak of crimson fire tore past her. Tom had lit his red flare, bringing the Drowner's song to an abrupt end.

Sadie clung dizzily to the rail as Tom edged forward, waving the flare about. Her head was heavy, tipping forward on her weak neck, and she sank to her knees.

A loud splash spattered her with river water. Tom was standing over her. He had thrown the flare overboard and was grabbing her by the shoulders with both hands.

'Sades, Sades, are you okay?'

Sadie managed a nod. She was aware of calm returning to the bay, as the Drowners retreated into the water. Had they been driven back by the sailors? No, maybe that wasn't it. Maybe they had taken what they had come for. Slowly, fearfully, Sadie twisted her head towards the yacht's prow.

All that was left on the deck were wet footprints.

'It took her, Sades. That thing took Kimberley.'

Nearby, Sadie could hear a yacht fire up its engine.

'We'll get her back,' she slurred, every word an effort. She flapped an arm in Tom's direction. 'We need to get Jake.'

15
JACOB'S WAY

The journey back to the jetty was intolerably slow. Sadie paced the deck as her uncle brought the boat around. He was soaked through, but otherwise unharmed. Burping up river water, his face glowed with fury and he didn't dare look at anyone.

Margot sobbed in the kitchen. So did Heather. Tom stood by, occasionally laying a hand on someone's shoulder and then removing it again.

There were few injuries among the other sailors, although the paramedics waiting on the pier treated almost everyone for shock. Nobody else had gone missing; those thrown overboard were all safely pulled back on deck. Everyone except Kimberley.

Sadie knew it wasn't her cousin the Drowners wanted. They had come for her.

The police wanted details, but no one seemed too sure what had happened.

'Kids,' someone said, 'just kids mucking about.'

A white-haired gent shook his head. 'Ask me, they looked Japanese.'

As soon as they were docked, Sadie hurried down into the kitchen and tugged at Tom's elbow. 'Come on,' she said. 'You're driving.'

Margot looked up. Her face was bloated. 'Driving? Driving where? You can't just leave. Kimberley's gone!' This last word was wrought across a dozen syllables. It only ended with Margot's head dropping to the table-top.

'She's right,' Tom said. 'I mean, you know, there's the police and stuff.'

'They can't do anything,' Sadie told him. 'We can. Get your car keys.'

There were faces and voices Tom had learned not to argue with. Sadie was using both. As they left, Heather stood up. Her cheeks were streaked with mascara. She tried to speak but said nothing.

Nobody stopped them as they walked along the jetty and back to shore. Just in case anyone tried, Sadie wore her best look of distress, keeping her shoulders stiff and her hands in front of her, as if she was about to collapse in tears at any moment. It wasn't that hard, she only needed to listen to the ugly thought tugging at her gut. *This is all your fault*, it said.

Turning his key in the ignition, Tom looked across at her. 'Where are we going?'

'I don't know, a pizza? No, idiot. We're going to get Jake.'

Tom was more patient than ever. 'Yeah, I worked that much out. But, I mean, he's back with his mum. Where's that?'

'He's not going to be there. You didn't see him at the police station, he seriously didn't recognise that woman. There's no way he's going to be staying with her. He'll be at Ocean Street.'

With his hand on the handbrake, Tom paused. 'You don't think she's dead, do you?'

'No, I don't. I think they wanted a hostage. I think they want to trade her for something. Something they think Jake has.'

'Okay. So how long have we got to get her back?'

Sadie was trying not to think about it. She put her hand on Tom's. 'Please Tom, just drive.'

There was a light on at the back of the Ocean Street house. As Sadie and Tom hurried up the path, a curtain twitched and the light went out. Still, the front door fell open as Sadie knocked on the glass.

She raised her chin, and called up the stairs.

'Jake, it's Sadie. You've got to help us.'

There was movement upstairs, but no one answered.

'The Drowners came back. They've taken Kimberley.

Jake, don't muck about, we need your help.'

As they edged inside, the front door slammed shut. A man appeared behind them, his features lost in street-light silhouette. He had the physique of a bouncer and he was holding a cricket bat, which he slapped meaningfully across his free palm.

'You made a mistake,' he said. 'Coming here.'

Sadie held her ground. 'I need to speak to Jake,' she insisted. 'Jake Freeman. I'm a friend of his.'

'Jacob Freeman is dead.'

'Yeah right. I think we both know that's not totally true.'

A young woman appeared from the kitchen, at the other end of the hall. She was holding a baby to her shoulder. 'She doesn't look like a murderer to me, Aaron,' she said.

'Excuse our Aaron,' another voice said from the top of the stairs. 'It seems our little group is being hunted down and killed, so we're all feeling a tad jumpy.'

A light went on overhead, giving Sadie a clear view of the tall woman descending the stairs. She wore a long-sleeved, black dress that contrasted neatly with her crisp bob of white hair.

'Who are you?' Sadie asked.

'My name is Agatha Penglis. You have already met Aaron, and this is Maud. You must be Sadie Miller.' Arriving at the bottom step, Agatha held out her hand, but Sadie ignored it.

'Where's Jake?'

Agatha reclaimed her hand. 'Jacob is in hiding while he finds the relic.'

'You're all like him, aren't you?'

'That's right.'

'You're all killers.'

'Erm, Sades,' Tom tapped her left elbow. 'Don't go into one, hey?'

Agatha's neat smile remained in place. She was probably in her early sixties, and she moved with the grace of a ballerina. She looked at Tom and reached for his bandaged side.

'You're hurt,' she said.

She pressed her hand against his side and Tom gasped. A moment later he blinked—surprised, but no longer in pain.

'And now,' Agatha said, 'you're not.' She turned back to Sadie. 'My little gift. Not quite the act of a killer.'

Tom had his T-shirt up and was gingerly peeling back his dressing. The stitches fell away like dead hair, leaving only the palest of scars. 'Holy shit,' he murmured.

'I don't care about your fancy tricks,' Sadie said, firmly. 'Where's Jake?'

'Ah.' Agatha nodded. She looked to the man with the cricket bat. 'Aaron, I wonder if you'd be a dear and put the kettle on. Jacob always has a rather sumptuous collection of teas.'

'There isn't time!' Sadie barked.

Agatha pushed gently past Sadie to the living room. Growling with frustration, Sadie followed Agatha and found her sitting comfortably in one of the leather armchairs.

The young woman—scarcely older than Sadie herself—came in from the kitchen, still carrying her baby, and took a seat on the floral three-seater. She was wearing thongs, jogging shorts, and an orange T-shirt emblazoned with a Balinese sunset. Oblivious of the horrified attention Sadie gave her, she rolled up her T-shirt and began breastfeeding the infant. Tom cleared his throat and went to stand by the window.

Agatha gestured to the armchair across from her. 'Sit down dear, please.'

Sadie was twitching with impatience. 'You must be joking. I don't want anything else to do with you people. The whole thing disgusts me. All I care about right now is getting my cousin back.'

'I think you may be labouring under something of a misapprehension, Sadie. Jacob isn't a killer. None of us is.'

'Tell that to Sam Mitchell.'

'I'm sorry?'

'Sam Mitchell was seventeen years old. Last week, he suddenly started calling himself Jacob Freeman.'

'Ah, now I understand you. I don't know the first thing about this Sam Mitchell, Sadie, but I can tell you one thing. Jacob didn't kill him. Sam was already dead.'

Sadie scoffed. 'What, he was some kind of willing sacrifice? That's even worse.'

'Oh jeez, will you just shut up?' The young mother, feeding her baby, had suddenly found her voice. 'Jacob isn't a killer. He's practically a vegetarian.'

Sadie put her palms out towards the woman. 'I can't even look at you. I mean, really, that is so wrong. You're breastfeeding the baby of the woman you killed. Seriously, it's sick.'

The harsh whistle of the kettle broke the mood.

'Come on,' Sadie said to Tom. 'They're not going to help. Let's get out of here.'

Tom caught her arm as she turned to leave and shook his head.

'Oh, you want to stay for tea?' Sadie snapped. 'She takes out your stitches and you're suddenly best friends?'

Tom let her rant at him, without so much as blinking. 'Kim.'

Agatha went to the window, peeling back one of the drapes to look out at the empty street. 'You've found yourself in a new world, Sadie. If you want our help, you need to know exactly what is at stake.'

'I don't want more fairy stories. I don't care. My cousin could be dying, if she isn't dead already.'

Agatha let the drape fall shut once more. She began to roll up the sleeves of her cotton dress from first her left wrist, and then her right. Sadie wondered if she was about to end her evening brawling with a retiree. 'When the Gods left, we stayed behind to watch over you. Jacob has told you about the demon. If Lysandra gets a second wish, she'll start a war. The Gods will expect us to fight alongside them. To fight against you, the same people we've lived among for thousands of years. You think we haven't come to care for you?'

The older woman spoke with compelling passion, but Sadie held her nerve. 'You kill people to save your own skins. How is that caring?'

'Sadie, please. Look.' Agatha held both her wrists out towards her. Even in the poor light of a low-watt globe, scars glistened in her arms like marble ridges. 'This body was thirty-eight when she overdosed in a St Kilda flat. When I found her, her heart had stopped. There was nothing of her left, not here.' Agatha tapped at her right temple. 'She died alone, a terrible accident, yes, but an accident. We Old Ones are stronger than most mortals. I had the strength she didn't, the strength to crawl to a phone. To heal myself.'

Aaron came in, carrying a tray with a teapot, five mugs and an open packet of ginger nuts. 'Mining accident,' he said, arranging coasters on a low coffee table. 'Poison gas. Twelve men died. Agatha fixed me.'

'It's true, once we took whoever we wished,' Agatha said. 'But Jacob found a better way. We only choose those who are already lost.'

Without thinking, Sadie found herself looking again to the young mother on the couch. The woman had finished breastfeeding, and now twirled a finger before the cooing infant. The finger was glowing brightly of its own accord, holding a narrow white flame. She glared at Sadie, reluctant to share anything. 'Hairdryer,' she said, finally. 'She'd been dead a minute, in a puddle on the bathroom floor. First thing I heard was the baby crying in the other room. She had no family. No parents, grand-parents, brothers or sisters, nothing. Grew up in care. I checked.' She scowled at Sadie. 'Suppose you think I should have just left her there, a dead single mother, miles out of town, with a crying baby. You think Tenielle here would have been happier with that? She's not my child, no. But I care for her, I even love her. Without me, she'd probably be dead too.'

'I'm sorry,' Sadie said, mostly automatically. The truth was, she was no longer sure what she thought. Right now, all that mattered was seeing Kimberley safe. She turned to Agatha. 'Okay, so maybe you do care. But are you actually going to help us find Jake?'

Agatha pulled down her sleeves, smoothing the cuffs. She walked across to one of the towering bookshelves and removed a copy of *The Great Gatsby*. From its pages she produced a small, folded square of paper and held it out to Sadie.

'His address. But be careful, Sadie. Jacob has a duty, one he's fulfilled for thousands of years. He's kept the relic safe. If he helps you save your cousin, if he gives Lysandra what she wants, all of you will be in danger. From the Gods, and from us.'

The paper wavered in Agatha's outstretched hand. 'Are you ready to take that risk?'

16
ELECTRICAL STORM

It was almost ten o'clock when Tom parked his 4WD outside the brown brick bungalow with its open, dry grass front yard and painted concrete drive. A light was on in the kitchen window and another over the doorstep. The scene was so ordinary it was hard to imagine they had the right house.

'You want me to come in?' Tom said, turning off the engine.

'Yeah,' Sadie nodded. 'Actually no. Actually yeah, probably a good idea.' She opened her door and then shut it again. 'Actually no, I'll be fine.'

She smiled. So did Tom.

Dianne answered the doorbell and watched Sadie through the locked screen door.

'It's very late Sadie, and it's not a good idea for you to just call around like this,' she said, allowing Sadie to step inside. 'Sam's still, well,' she pursed her lips. 'To be honest, he hasn't really come back to us yet.'

Sadie nodded, hoping to avoid a pointless conversation. 'Is he in?'

Jake was lying on a bed, his feet bare and his hands tucked behind his head. He stared at the ceiling like a prisoner resigned to a long stretch.

'Not another psychiatrist?'

But then he saw Sadie and he jumped up. For a second, he might have run to her, but there was a new distance between them. This wasn't a happy reunion.

'I'll be just outside,' Dianne promised, reassuring no one in particular, as the door clicked shut.

This wasn't the sort of place Sadie would have expected to find Jake. It was so typically a boy's room, with band posters on the wall, dirty clothes across the floor and an overall sense of barely constrained chaos. But, of course, this wasn't the place to find Jake. These weren't his things, just as it wasn't his mother outside the door.

Sadie straightened her shoulders and held her gaze firm. None of that could matter now. Later, maybe.

'We need your help,' she said.

Jake nodded. If he was disappointed, it didn't show. 'I assumed you wanted something.'

'The Drowners have taken Kimberley,' she said. 'Taken her underwater.' She couldn't bring herself to say *drowned her*.

'I see.'

Sadie swallowed hard. 'Is she dead?'

Jake's calm face betrayed nothing. 'Possibly.'

'Possibly? What does *possibly* mean?'

'Probably not.'

Encouraged, Sadie took another step towards him. 'That's what I thought. The thing is, they didn't attack any old boat, did they? They wanted me.'

Jake sighed. 'Yes. They used you to send me a message. Really, it's good news.'

'How is any of this good news?'

'It means Lysandra doesn't have the relic. Either Vincent still has it or he's sold it.'

'Right. So Lysandra wants to trade. You said she'd find a way to make you open it. If we find it, hand it over, she'll give Kimberley back, won't she?'

'No,' Jake said firmly. 'Sadie, it isn't that simple. You know what will happen if Lysandra gets her hands on that box.'

'We're talking about Kimberley, my cousin. I can't just let her die.'

Jake's jaw set. 'One girl's life, or everyone's lives? No contest.'

'She's my *cousin*.'

'That can't mean more to me. I can't care.'

'But you do! I know you do. You saved Tom. You fought the Minotaur to save his life. And you fought the Drowners to save mine.'

'Mistakes. I should have stayed hidden.'

'I don't believe you,' Sadie insisted. 'The Drowners don't believe it either. They took Kimberley because they know you care. They know you won't let her die.' Her hand went out for his, but fell short.

'You know I trusted you,' she said, her voice shrunken with hurt. 'I thought I knew you. All that stuff about telling me the truth and you still didn't tell me the first thing about you. The most important thing.'

'Sadie, I'm sorry.'

She met his eye. 'Prove it.'

Jake sat down on the edge of his bed. Sadie wondered if he was anchoring himself to the spot, but he began feeling about under the bed.

'I'll need a length of rope,' he said, retrieving his shoes.

'Why?'

'Do you want me to save your cousin, or not?'

Sadie almost smiled. 'There's rope in Tom's car. And a roof rack.'

'I won't need a roof rack.' Jake stood bolt upright, snatching his satchel from the carpet. 'Mrs Mitchell!'

Dianne appeared in the open door. 'Sam? Is everything okay?'

'We're going out.'

'It's nearly eleven,' Dianne began, 'I don't think…'

But Jake had already pushed past her and was striding off down the hall.

The last ute pulled out of the Cottesloe beach car park and there was nothing left but broken beer bottles and seagulls. Jake leaned on the handrail at the top of the grass terraces, and faced the invisible horizon with its cargo ship tea-lights and lighthouse flares. Further out, an electrical storm was sparking. Soon it would be leaping from cloud to cloud, like the announcement of some distant war. Sadie wondered if that was exactly what it was.

They hurried down towards the groyne. Sadie slung the rope over her shoulder and took off her boots, while Tom hopped about to avoid the surges of surf. Jake merely strode on, some metres ahead of them, ignoring the waves that soaked his jeans.

Most nights, there were fishermen on the far side of the groyne. Tonight, the sea was still and black, and there was nothing on the concrete promenade but salt stains and fish scales.

'Here,' Jake said, taking the rope from Sadie. 'Go stand against the lamppost, both of you.'

Tom and Sadie looked at each other, uncertain. Jake tutted.

'Sadie, just trust me.'

'Yeah, I've seen where that gets me.' Sadie scowled at him, but nodded. 'Come on,' she told Tom. 'He knows what he's doing.'

Jake made quick work of tying the two of them to the steel lamppost. He stood back and his gaze met Sadie's. His lips parted. There was more he wanted to say. Maybe now he saw his chance.

'Kimberley's down there,' Sadie snapped. 'That's all that matters.'

Nodding, Jake turned and strode the short distance to the end of the groyne.

Sadie didn't know what she was expecting to see. Maybe she thought they would wait here by the water until the Drowners noticed. As it was, there was no waiting. She glanced down at her sandy feet, and when she looked up, a dozen of the Drowners were there. Each one stood on a rock with a gnarled hand to the barnacled hilt of a sword or axe-handle. Six on either side of the path, they formed a loose aisle, as if presenting themselves for inspection.

Jake stood at one end, and lightning flashed at the other.

A wave crashed heavily against the groyne. Spray seasoned the still air. A sodden bundle of rags had been dumped on the concrete. As Sadie watched, the rags unfolded into a tall, slender figure.

She wore the flowing robes of a priestess, but the linen was stained and mildewed. Around her wasted neck hung an iron key on a length of tarred string. Her long dark hair was knotted with seaweed and it twitched about her shoulders as if it were alive. As she stepped forward, her bare feet left tidy puddles on the pier.

'My love,' her voice rustled like dry leaves on a warm wind. 'Can it be you?'

At first, Sadie thought the woman was confused. Then she understood.

For a moment, Jake said nothing. His shoulders were turned away from the priestess, as if he could hardly bear to be near her.

'Lysandra,' he said.

'Always so beautiful. So vain. You were born beautiful, born young. Perhaps it never occurs to you to be anything else.' She touched his cheek with her weathered fingers. There was a smile on her lips, but it quickly fell away to nothing. 'This is how you greet me, after so many lifetimes. With such coldness.'

Jake stepped back from her. 'I'll discuss nothing until the girl is returned.'

'Discuss? Elders discuss. Politicians discuss. When do lovers discuss?'

Sadie shifted against the lamppost—the rope bit at her wrists. Something about this woman set her fingers clenching.

Lysandra paced a slow orbit around Jake. Her right hand went, tenderly, flirtatiously, to the key around her neck. 'Lovers sing, lovers swoon. Lovers sacrifice everything to tie their destinies together.'

'We were never lovers,' Jake said. His teeth locked, marking the edge of his patience. 'Lysandra, give me the girl.'

The priestess tilted her head with curiosity. 'What can she possibly be to you?'

'I've never met her. But, if you want to talk to me, bring her here.'

Lysandra hesitated, but Jake's glare held fast. 'She is nothing to us,' she said.

Another Drowner shot up from the dark waters and landed beside Lysandra on the concrete path. He was carrying a bedraggled Kimberley, soaked through but otherwise unharmed. He set her down on her bare feet. Her eyes were open, but she swayed blankly.

'Kim!' Tom shouted.

'She can't say anything,' Sadie told him. 'She's in a sort of trance thing. She'll be okay.'

As relieved as Sadie was, she couldn't help worrying. Lysandra had given Kimberley back far too easily. If Jake was right, if the priestess did intend to bargain for the relic, then she must have something else to trade, something bigger.

'For millennia, I have waited for you to return with my prize,' Lysandra said. 'It calls to me, its power crackles in my veins. I'm tired of waiting. Give it to me and let us walk together on dry land.'

'Lysandra, you know I can't.'

'What did I do to deserve such cruelty?'

'You betrayed your people, all of humanity. You betrayed me.'

'I adored you. I did everything to be with you.'

Jake turned on her, all spittle and fury. 'Don't you dare. Don't you dare suggest this had anything to do with me. You didn't adore me. You were jealous of me.'

'I frightened you. I tore at the barriers between us and you, you went running scared to your masters.'

'You think I wanted to? You think that was easy? You left me no choice.'

He almost looked scared, Sadie thought. She had never seen him so emotional.

'There is always a choice, lover. You chose to destroy us. The city you had pledged to protect.'

'You angered the Gods. You brought down their vengeance.'

The priestess held out her hands. Her fingers were worn back to polished bone. 'I suppose you call this justice?'

'Lysandra, I'm begging you.' Jake took a step forward, so that toes of his sneakers touched Lysandra's robes. His fury had left him. His eyes were wide, pleading. 'Forget about the demon. It's too late for you and your people, but you could still save everyone else. There's a whole world you could spare now by letting go.'

'After everything, you ask me for compassion? Me?'

'Yes.'

Lysandra laughed. It was a high, cold sound. 'So this is what the centuries have done to you, lover. You've lived so long like a man, you've mistaken yourself for one of them.' Her lips bent in a cruel smile. 'But I know the truth. I know what makes a man. It is the sure knowledge that one day he will die. You can't live forever and still be a man. What would a man think of you, if he knew the truth? He would call you a monster.' She moved close to Jake, and her voice became a whisper. 'You and I, we are both monsters.'

She raised her right arm in a twitching gesture. Two Drowners were suddenly beside the lamppost, one pressing a blade to Sadie's throat and another to Tom's.

'Sades,' Tom muttered.

'Be quiet!' Sadie hissed.

Lysandra's smile was a glassy, gruesome thing. 'You were wise to tether your acolytes. We might have sung them to their deaths. But they can still bleed.'

'Touch them and I will destroy you,' Jake said, so quietly that his words were almost lost beneath the wash against the rocks. It was less a threat, Sadie thought, than an admission of defeat. 'There will be no more hiding, for either of us.'

'This is your justice? You refuse me my prize, yet you would sacrifice everything for the sake of two lives?'

'I would.'

Lysandra floated down the concrete path to sneer at Sadie. 'Such cruelty, for this...driftwood.'

Sadie met the woman's glare. She wasn't sure she had ever hated anyone or anything as much as she hated the priestess.

'For her,' Jake said.

Tom mumbled something that Sadie tried not to hear.

'Then let me give you a new ultimatum.' The priestess's arm swept out along the coast, from Fremantle to Scarborough. 'Her city for mine.'

'Don't be ridiculous.'

'You will bring me my prize by sunrise, or I will sink this city, her city, to the ocean floor. Just as you once sank mine.'

'I can't give it to you.'

'Then she drowns, my love. Her city drowns.'

A breeze moved across the groyne and the Drowners were gone. Jake stayed where he was, alone in a trembling puddle. His hands seemed to pull his shoulders down towards the concrete. Sadie cleared her throat and he looked up, remembering himself. He untied the ropes.

'Was she serious?' Sadie asked. 'Can she really do that?'

Jake spoke quickly, impatient with his own explanations. 'The demon has already given her a good dose of its power, enough to keep her and her people going for thousands of years. She's not a God, not yet, but there's no saying what her limits are.'

'So, short answer?'

Now Jake looked at her, his eyes bright with fear. 'Yes, she could do it.'

Even while that was sinking in, Sadie couldn't help changing the subject. 'She called you her lover.'

'I was curious when I met Lysandra. I wanted to know what it was like to be human. To truly face death.' He shook his head, briskly.

There was a shriek, a whoop and another shriek. Kimberley was awake, struggling with both her balance and her bearings.

'I've been spiked!'

Sadie went to her cousin and hugged her. 'You're fine Kim, everything's okay.'

'I was seeing things. There were these fish people. And this city, but underwater. Sonia always says I'll be the one to get spiked. She says I should stop letting guys bring me drinks.' Kimberley began to cry. Sadie cradled her cousin's head, but she was looking at Jake. He was still staring at the rope in his hands, while Tom checked the damage to his wrists.

Behind him, beyond the horizon, the storm was drawing in.

17
LIVE FOREVER

Tom wasn't sure he should leave Sadie with Jake at the Ocean Street house. Kimberley was shivering in the passenger seat, sobbing and rambling. He had agreed to drive her home, but had hoped Sadie would come with him.

Sadie was angry at Jake, that much was clear, but she was still having trouble looking away. Tom couldn't understand it. Two hours ago she had never wanted to see Jake again, had called him a killer. Now he threw open his front gate, striding up the path in silent fury, and she was just following him.

Tom wound down his window. He should call her back and tell her to be sensible.

'Sades!'

With one foot up on the veranda, Sadie turned. She looked irritated. 'What?'

'You want me to come back?'

'Whatever. I don't care.' Seeming to hear herself, she frowned. 'Yes. Please.'

'Cool.'

There was nothing else to say. Tom nodded, once accidentally and once with conviction, then pulled away from the kerb.

Kingsley followed Sadie through to the lounge and into an argument.

'Where's everyone else?'

Agatha was resolute. 'Patrick is dead. Isaac decided to take his own chances.'

'But no sign of Vincent?'

'Did you really think there would be?'

Maud sat sideways on the couch, both feet up on the armrest. She looked exhausted and made no effort to join the discussion. Aaron was swigging lager from a dark brown bottle. Each time he picked up the bottle, it was less empty than it had been when he put it down.

Agatha stepped forward, touching Jake's arm. 'You've made contact, haven't you? After so long. It must have hurt.'

Jake snatched his arm clear. 'It doesn't matter. We're getting out.'

'Without the relic? Without Frobisher?'

Ignoring her, Jake strode through to the kitchen, slapping at Maud's soles. 'Get your damn feet off my furniture.'

~

Sadie found Jake and Kingsley sitting on the back step, watching the lightning draw in. Jake didn't turn as the screen door banged and Sadie felt anger tense her shoulders. Why was she doing the following? Arms tightly folded, she passed him on the steps, scattered dirt with the toe of her boot and came back around to him.

'You can't really be thinking of just running away?' she said.

Jake's eyes flashed up at her, grey and angry. 'Sadie, I made the relic. I'm the only one who can open it. If I leave now, there might still be a chance.'

'Not for me and not for Perth. Are you really going to let us all drown? Let me drown?'

A pause.

'You could come with me.'

'You can't be serious.'

He was on his feet now, his shoulders bunched like a boxer's. 'You think I want to run?'

Kingsley shuffled off into the garden, as if excusing himself from an awkward conversation.

Jake turned to Sadie, ready to argue. Instead, he merely nodded. 'There's nothing I can do, Sadie. I've done everything I can these last days to find the relic, to find Vincent. Now there isn't time. I can't give Lysandra what she wants. I can't stop her. And I can't watch. Not again.'

'So that's your plan, is it? To make sure you're looking the other way while everyone I know, my whole city, drowns.'

'I'm sorry.'

'Don't say sorry. There has to be something we can do.'

'Vincent sold the relic to the God squad. And there's no way of finding it, them or him. He's probably halfway around the world by now.'

'But say he isn't. Say we do find the relic.'

'In five hours?'

Jake had surrendered. He looked at her with pity, like she was deluding herself. Like he knew she would give in. But Sadie wasn't giving in. 'Say we do. Would you give it to Lysandra?'

He didn't have to think about his answer, but he still took his time. 'No.'

'Even if it would save me, and everyone in the city?'

'But it wouldn't. It would only put you and everyone else on the planet at risk.'

'You're honestly saying you'd let two million people die?'

'Two million or seven billion? No contest.'

Even though she was expecting it, that still shook her. She couldn't believe he was that cold.

'But it's not down to you to make that choice. You can't just do the numbers, decide who lives, who dies.

You know what we call people who think they can? We call them monsters. Maybe Lysandra was right about you.'

She was thinking of her grandfather. Of the black-and-white photographs of Hiroshima pinned to the study wall. Thinking of the mushroom clouds that ended the war he had thought just. Clouds that saw him spend the next sixty years marching for peace. Other clippings came and went, but those stayed, even as the paper curled and yellowed.

Jake said nothing. He walked away from her, into the long grass. Sadie could feel the storm closing in, the air damp against her bare arms.

'You told Lysandra you'd destroy her, if she hurt me,' she said. 'Did you mean that?'

'You know I did.'

'So there is another way.'

Jake winced, but didn't turn.

Sadie glared at the back of his head, trying to remember everything he had told her. Trying to find a solution. She thought of him standing on the Fremantle pier, catching his breath and talking of Gods and demons for the first time. 'You said the demon was a weapon.'

Jake kept his back to her. 'No, Sadie.'

'A weapon powerful enough to scare the Gods.'

'Please.'

He was begging now, quietly desperate. And there it was, simple as anything. Another way. 'That's what we do. We find the demon. You use it to stop Lysandra, once and for all. Save my city.'

Jake rounded on her, more astonished than angry. 'Doing that would mean betraying the Gods. They'd hunt me down.'

'You said if anyone human asks the demon for anything, then the Gods will destroy all of us. But what if it's someone who isn't human, isn't a Drowner? What if it's one of their own?'

'They'd still be furious.'

Sadie held his gaze. 'But would they still destroy the rest of us?'

Jake rubbed at the back of his neck. He turned a small circle in the dirt, and came around to face her. His cheeks were bloodless, his eyes pale. 'It's a terrible risk, Sadie. There's no knowing that the demon can be trusted, no saying what would happen. To you, to humanity. To me.'

'But if we don't try, we know exactly what will happen.'

'You realise what you're asking?'

Sadie held her ground. 'Yeah, I do. I'm asking you to decide where you belong. With Gods, monsters, or the rest of us. Who do you care about, really?' She bit her lip. 'Agatha told me, about what you do. What you are.'

Jake flinched as if she'd raised a hand to slap him.

'Sadie, I'm sorry I didn't tell you, but you wouldn't have understood.'

'Too right. Where's Sam? What happened to him?'

'Sam's dead. He's gone and he can't come back.'

'What was he like? I mean, what sort of boy was he?'

'I don't know. I found him at the bottom of the river, near Blackwell Reach. You know those cliffs, kids are always daring each other to jump off.' Jake touched his right temple. 'There was a wound, here. I think he hit his head, was probably dead before he hit the water.'

'But maybe he could have been resuscitated. Maybe someone could have saved him.'

'Nobody did. Believe me, I know how death feels. He had been dead three minutes, at least.' A small smile pinched his lips. 'We must have died around the same time.'

'Only you came back, and stole his body.'

'Sadie, it's how the Gods made me. It's taken me centuries just to control how I come back, and even now it's not an exact science. I've learned how to wake up in darkness, in cold skin and airless muscle. I can't help living, but I can try to live without hurting anyone.'

'What about Sam's mum? His brother? You don't think this hurts them?'

'Usually, I'd be halfway around the world by now. When I can, I find a way to let them know their loved one is dead.' He took a step forward, looking for her eyes.

'Because Sam is dead Sadie. I'm all that's left of him.' He frowned. 'Is that okay?'

'Of course it isn't.'

'Say you needed a new liver, a new kidney, a new heart. Say you needed a donor's help to stay alive. Would that be wrong too?'

Sadie's teeth clicked. 'It's not the same.'

'Isn't it? This is the best way I know to live, Sadie.'

Sadie shook her head, slowly. 'It's still cruel,' she said. 'If the Gods made you that way then they were wrong. They were cruel.' She reached for his hand, but fell short. 'I don't think you're cruel, Jake. I don't think you're a monster. I think you've found the best way you can of doing the wrong thing. But it's still wrong. You shouldn't have the right to steal a body and trample on someone like Dianne.'

'Then tell me, Sadie. Tell me what's right.'

'I think you already know. That's why I knew you'd help me save Kimberley tonight.'

He stepped back, then towards her. Back again. His hand held his forehead as if he was suddenly dizzy. 'Stop Lysandra? Stop serving the Gods? Stop coming back?'

'If that's what it takes, yes.'

Jake stared at his hands, hanging low and empty by his thighs. 'I've thought about it, over the years. But I'm not sure I have it in me.'

'To betray the Gods?'

'To destroy Lysandra What happened to her people, all those years ago. It was my fault.'

'No it wasn't. It was her fault. Just like tonight is her fault.'

He was silent. It might have been a minute before he moved.

'I can't,' he said. 'The relic's gone. We've lost, Sadie. I'm sorry.'

Somewhere behind them, Kingsley started barking. It began as a low growl, but quickly roused into throaty snarls and snaps. His fleshy muzzle was pressed into the dirt under the garage doors. Twice he raised himself on his hind legs to rattle the hinges.

'That door's been unlocked,' Jake noted, indicating a padlock hanging loose. He seemed glad of the distraction, puffing out his chest and squaring his shoulders. He moved to open the doors, but Sadie stopped him.

'There's a killer looking for you, remember?'

Jake nodded, then tore the doors open. A stack of tin cans fell at his feet. Spaghetti, beans, stews. Kingsley hurdled them all and bolted to the back of the shed. His barking became savage. It almost drowned out the man's squeals and pleas for help.

There was an old sports car inside the garage, a green MG. It was infested with rust and its tyres had crumbled on the sandy floor. Jake squeezed alongside it, towards the back of the shed. Sadie followed.

They found a man by the rear bumper, writhing and flapping on a makeshift bed constructed from flattened cardboard boxes. A small pile of paperbacks made an impromptu bedside table, lit by a tiny gaslight. Three bottles of wine stood next to it.

'Get it off me! Get it off me!' the man wailed.

Jake called Kingsley and the dog reluctantly returned to his master.

The man sat up, tidying his hair and straightening the denim jacket knotted around his waist.

It was Vincent. Seeing Jake, he clambered up the back of the car.

'I had to come. There's a killer out there, someone's killing us all.'

Jake snatched Vincent by the front of his singlet and slid him up the garage wall, until the smaller man's head bumped two tins of paint from a precarious shelf.

'I haven't got it,' Vincent bleated. 'It's gone, I sold it.'

Jake said nothing. Vincent's head thumped another a tin from the shelf.

'But it's safe, I know where it is.'

Still, Jake said nothing. A glass of nails toppled, scattering in the shadows below.

'I mean, I'll get it back for you. Right now. Ow.'

18
FIND THE RIVER

Jake dragged Vincent across to the back veranda by the front of his filthy singlet, and threw him down on the top step.

'How long have you been stealing from me?'

'You know, it's easy for you,' Vincent spluttered. 'You had a sweet deal set up with Frobisher, you were always moving money about. Some of us had to struggle to make a living, had to set ourselves up from scratch each time.'

'We've got five hours Vincent, maybe less,' Jake spat. 'Talk quickly.'

'Look, I had a few contacts in the antique trade. I mean, back in Blighty, there's a market, sure, but here people go crazy for anything old.' He looked at Sadie, smiling, as if hoping for an ally. 'It's all this newness, you see. All you have to do is give them a whiff of something dusty, and they pay.'

Jake stood back, crossing his arms. 'And I'd got old, careless. So you took what you thought I wouldn't miss.

But then, you became greedy.'

'I guess I got a name for myself. I mean, you do, in a place like this. You don't have to be a big fish to make a splash. People started to ask about my sources. Last thing I wanted was them snooping around here.' He glanced in the direction of the screen door. 'It's been days since I had a cuppa.'

Jake slapped him with the back of his right hand. 'The relic. Where is it?'

'A man came to the shop. He looked like a bloody door-knocker, I thought. Nearly turfed him straight out. But then he said he'd heard my name about the place. He said I was the man to get him something special. And then he asked for it, just like that. The box of fire, he called it. I mean, I'm careful. He could have been anyone. I said I was just a bookseller. But he wrote me a cheque, then and there on the counter. Ten thousand dollars. That's small change, he says. Just a taste of things to come. His client would pay ten times that if I delivered.' Vincent stopped nursing his slapped cheek and turned out both his palms. 'I mean, I've got debts. Now here's this bloke offering me a retirement fund.'

'You broke into my house. You stole the most precious thing in it. The most dangerous thing. And, for what? A few debts?'

'Oh, come on, man. I did my research. I'm not going to sell it off to just anyone, am I? His client was some religious group. Live out of town in an old—what do you call it?—seminary. Just mortals though, nothing sinister. All they wanted was to lock it up behind glass and admire it. You know what mortals are like.' Vincent straightened up in his chair. 'You were dead, I figured it would be safer with them. There's no way Lysandra would go looking for them, is there?'

Jake fumed. 'Don't you dare suggest you were acting in anyone's interest but your own. If we don't get that box back, this city, and your shop, and your fortune, will be lost. And I will make you suffer.'

Vincent swallowed hard. 'Look, I didn't know she was out there, honest. I didn't know she would go crazy trying to get it. You think I want this city sunk?' He sat forward in his seat, clasping his hands together in a desperate prayer. 'I know where they are. I went out there, didn't I? Just to make sure, to be careful. I knew you'd make everything all right, in the end. I mean, hell, that's why I'm here. There's a killer out there, but I knew I'd be safe with you. You're our leader, you'll protect us.' He threw himself from the steps and dropped to his knees in the dirt.

Jake recoiled from him. He turned away and kicked at the dry grass. Sadie followed him.

'We can do it,' she said quietly, so that Vincent, sobbing by the back steps, wouldn't hear. 'We can get the relic.'

'We can.'

'You can stop Lysandra.'

'I could.'

Sadie waited for him to say more. She wanted him to look at her. 'Will you?' she asked.

Jake stared at his hands. He stared at Sadie, his chin trembling. His fingers entwined themselves in the brass chain around his neck.

'You said I should choose. Choose where I belonged. Who I cared about.'

Sadie nodded.

'Do you care about me, Sadie Miller?'

She took a deep breath. 'I want to.'

Jake tore the chain away from his throat and stared at the talisman in his palm. He looked as if he might cry, or be sick. Slowly, he tilted his palm and let the disc fall to the dirt by his shoes. 'We'll find the relic,' he said, with sudden determination. 'I'll use the demon's power to stop Lysandra. I'll save your city. And I'll face the consequences as a mortal.'

A fat droplet of rain landed squarely on his forehead, like an anointment. Within seconds, they were caught in a downpour. The water was clean and blissfully cold. From here to the Darling Ranges, sweaty figures in their underwear ran from airless rooms to dance on wet lawns. Another rumble of thunder rolled up and over the dunes towards them. In the rain, Sadie couldn't tell if Jake was upset, or relieved.

At his feet, new mud swallowed the tarnished talisman and its broken chain.

There was no respite from the rain. Furious torrents roared down Ocean Street, along footpaths and gutters, as if determined to wash away any trace of the heat.

Tom pulled up at the kerb at around one. The tyres of the 4WD parted the rising water. He hit the horn, twice, each time only lightly, worried about the neighbours.

Sadie had eighteen missed calls on her mobile, but she couldn't bring herself to check them. She sent Kimberley a text, asking her to tell Margot that she was fine and that she would be home soon. That way, her grandparents could stop worrying and she could postpone any trouble until morning.

But, as she opened the passenger door, her cousin looked out at her, confused. 'You just sent me a text saying you're okay. I know you're okay, I can see you're okay. Why wouldn't you be okay?'

Sadie had been bent over to shelter from the rain, but now she straightened up. 'Oh, bloody hell. Tom was supposed to drop you home.'

'He did, I got changed. I mean, come on Sadie, a midnight road trip? You are never this exciting.'

'Get out.'

'No way! It's pissing down.'

'Get out or none of us are going anywhere. I'm shotgun.'

Kimberley reluctantly unbuckled her belt and squeezed between the seats to join Heather in the back. Sliding into the passenger seat, Sadie could see them both in the rear-view mirror.

'Oh, seriously? What is she doing here?'

'Mum said she had to come. Like it makes things safer. Like she could protect anyone from anything. I mean, from a good time, maybe.'

'There isn't room,' Sadie growled. 'Jake and Vincent are coming too.'

Kimberley sniffed. 'Heather, get in the boot.'

Heather climbed over the back seat and dropped down into the boot.

Soon Tom was turning right onto Marine Parade. To the west, the storm was low and close over the dark sea. There was little gap now between the electric flash and shattering thunder.

Kimberley had insisted on sitting in the middle, pressed tightly between Vincent and Jake. She now seemed to regret this, recoiling from the odorous man on her left. Every time she looked west, her nose bunched. When she looked east, she batted her eyelids.

Sadie watched her cousin in the rear-view. 'I can't believe your mum and dad let you out of the house.'

Kimberley shrugged. 'Come on, you know what mum's like. She thinks worry gives you wrinkles. Dad's a lawyer. He knows when it's not worth arguing.'

'Kim, you nearly died.'

'I know. It's all over Facebook that I drowned. Seriously, people are so upset. Celia Black's going to be totally pissed off. Her dog got run over last week but, come on, that was a dog. This pisses all over her dead dog.'

On her right, Jake winced. 'What a delightful turn of phrase.'

Kimberley turned to him, feinting a shiver. 'I am seriously in love with your accent.'

Sadie rolled her eyes.

As they drove east, through white rain, Sadie plugged her iPod into the stereo.

'This is worse than Heather's stuff,' Kimberley complained. 'At least some of those singers are cute. You know, in an emo kind of way. These people sound *old*.'

'If you don't like it, you can taxi home,' Sadie said. 'This is my road trip.'

Still, Sadie was touched by a strange sense of camaraderie. She was no longer an unwanted stray. This was her adventure, and the others wanted to share it.

Through the windscreen, the hills rose up against the low sky like a damp memorial. Memories littered the roadside. The past's geography surrounded her but it no longer seemed to be a map of her loss. There were wonderful things that had once happened here, just as there were terrible things. Which wasn't to say that she didn't think of that wet afternoon, bobbing and weaving along steep roads. Her mum had been lightly scolding her dad, who always pushed the speed limit. On empty country roads, he would hunch over the wheel and cackle like a cartoon racer.

That was how Sadie remembered them, playfully arguing. She didn't think they ever shouted, and she knew they loved each other. She had always felt lucky, when she saw other kids' parents. Tonight, somehow, she still felt lucky.

The handbrake crunched on and Tom leaned across to turn down the music. They had left the main road and were on a soggy dirt track that traced the first twists and turns of the Swan River. The city was half an hour's drive behind them, but felt much further away. Even in high summer, the greenery here was dense around the brown water. Tom had parked by a steel gate. A hand-painted sign warned trespassers to keep out. Beyond it, a gravel path was quickly swallowed up by greying trees.

'I don't know why I had to come with you,' Vincent complained, pressing himself flat in his seat. 'I could have drawn you a map. I mean, what am I going to do? I'm not a talker. I shake. My palms sweat. I drop things. And you can forget violence, I'm no fighter. I wasn't made that way.'

Jake and Tom shouldered the gate open and soon the 4WD was edging along the muddy track. The headlights seemed to find faces in pale tree trunks.

Finally the path opened onto a broad, wet clearing and a large sandstone mansion. Two utes, a station wagon and a shiny black Merc were parked beside a rainwater tank, but there were no lights in any of the windows.

Jake leaned forwards between the seats. 'Turn off the engine,' he muttered.

They waited in silence. A wet possum poked through the undergrowth then, spotting its audience, scurried away.

'Maybe there's nobody home?' Sadie suggested.

At the sound of her voice, the back window on the driver's side imploded. Heather shrieked, scrabbling about in the glass rubble.

Bright lights flared above the front veranda. A bearded man in singlet, shorts and thongs was striding purposefully towards them, a shotgun thrust out in front of him. With a free hand, he gestured for Tom to roll down his window.

'Do it,' Jake muttered.

Despite the gun pointing in her direction, Sadie saw little sign of aggression, merely a wry twist to the man's top lip.

'G'day,' he called, spitting rainwater, as Tom wound his window down. 'Been expecting you for a coupla days now.'

Tom's mouth opened and shut again with little more said than, 'Well' and 'Cool', strung together by a few 'ums'.

'Jeez Louise, I hope you're not the one we've been waitin' for. Don't just sit there, mate. Get your arse out of the car.' He ducked his head to peer in at Sadie. 'Same goes for you darlin', and your pals in the back.'

'He's got a gu-un,' Kimberley noted in a high whisper.

'Well spotted Hawkeye,' Sadie muttered.

'This is what we came for,' Jake said. 'Just do what he asks.'

'But it's raining!' Kimberley trilled.

'Open the door,' Jake said.

Kimberley jolted into action. Her long legs unfolded and she quickly flattened herself against the side of the car.

'Hands up now darlin',' the man said. 'All of you keep everything where I can see it.'

Dropping down from the passenger seat, Sadie moved around the bonnet to join the others. Tom was squinting into the light, Kimberley was squeaking and Jake was somehow managing to look casual while holding his hands in the air. The heavy rain soaked their clothes and gave each of them an excuse to tremble. Vincent got out last. He took long, arched steps that kept him low to the ground. The house's front door flew open and another three men appeared, each of them holding a weapon.

'All good Alan?' the youngest of them shouted. Even from this distance, Sadie recognised him as one of the God squad men.

'Get the women and kids to stay inside,' the first man yelled back. 'Jason, take this lot around the back.'

At that, Kimberley whimpered and Sadie found it hard to keep holding her defiant sneer. *Around the back* sounded bad. Clearly Vincent thought so too, as his hands dropped and he spun on the balls of his feet, making a run for the trees.

Jason, panicking, let loose both barrels from the veranda stairs. Sadie threw herself left as the windscreen shattered. Behind her, Kimberley was screaming and Jake was shouting at everyone to stay calm.

Too late, Sadie thought. She crouched in the black mud, watching Jason fumbling shells into his shotgun. She saw Kimberley make a break for it. There wasn't time to think. She ran after her.

Alan fired again, shattering the driver-side window. Tom and Jake dropped to their knees, keeping their hands behind their heads. Another shot went off and Sadie weaved right. Her cousin was already crashing through the scrub.

It was strange, but Sadie felt responsible. She couldn't let Kimberley get herself killed. Tom and Heather would be all right, she knew that. Jake was there.

Bloody hell, she thought, as a bullet thudded into a nearby tree, *do I trust him?*

There were men chasing her. She could hear their shouts. Despite the downpour, it was a bright night—crisp shards of moonlight made her an easy target. Her hair was plastered to her face. The sharp leaves of the undergrowth scratched her legs. Her dress snagged on a branch and tore to her waist.

She ran downhill, skidding and sliding towards the river. She had some idea of swimming to safety. Across the river, there might be a farm or a winery. Maybe she could find help. Would she call the police? Could they help? Her own phone was back in the glove box.

Halfway down the hill, she tripped and ploughed headfirst into the mud. She somersaulted twice, then rolled sideways into bushes, spitting black earth. Her right cheek and bare arms were bleeding, her left ankle was twisted. Her lungs felt raw and breathless and her ears were ringing. She lay in her sparse shelter and waited to be found.

Heavy footsteps approached. Branches were snapped and tossed aside. Peering out from her bush, Sadie could see it was Jason, the trigger-happy cyclist.

'I saw you come down here. You and your friend. You better come out, unless you want the snakes to get you.'

It was an empty threat, probably intended to scare a

city girl who didn't know better. It was an insult to Sadie's intelligence, but told her a bit about his.

Her fingers felt the edges of something warm, hard and uneven in the mud. It was a rock, still holding the day's heat. Without shifting her shoulders or the bush around her, she prised the rock free. It was heavier than she expected. She was barely able to lift it.

'Last chance,' Jason taunted. 'I've got two shells here. At least one of them's got your name on it.'

He crashed through a thick bush, cursing. He was close enough to make Sadie jump.

She rolled the rock towards her hips with her fingertips. Twice it slipped from her touch and almost rolled downhill.

Jason slid in the mud and landed on his backside. He was even closer now. It was all Sadie could do not to flinch and betray herself.

She rolled the rock closer. Finally, she could feel its crags against her hip. She drew it to her chest.

'Out you come now.'

He was nearly on top of her. She gritted her teeth and thrust the rock out and away from her.

It crashed through the bushes and thundered away downhill. As she'd hoped, Jason was stupid enough to mistake it for her in the heavy rain. She waited for him to move away, then raised her head above the shrub-line. There was no sign of anyone else.

Five minutes later, Jason retraced his steps, but still didn't find her. As he continued uphill, she could hear him on his walkie-talkie.

'Guess they all coulda doubled back, yeah.'

They. Were both Vincent and Kimberley out there?

The river was a murky brown, run through with moonlight and shadows. About its edges, small dark yabbies twitched. Sadie followed the bank downstream until she reached a rusty iron fence, topped with barbed wire. The fence was high and ran out a metre or so into the river, making it impossible to climb over or around it. Anyway, she was no longer sure that was such a good plan. She was already thinking of an impossible rescue. What other choice was there?

A nearby bush shivered, announcing an interloper. Sadie dropped into a squat, hoping for invisibility.

A pair of tanned legs appeared. Like hers, they were scratched and bloody.

'Kim!' Sadie hissed.

Kimberley dropped to her knees. Her cheeks were streaked with tears and mud.

'Oh wow, you're alive! We're both alive! There was this tree trunk thing and I'm like no way am I going in there, but I can hear someone coming, and he's like, stay still you little bitch, so I'm like I'm going to have to crawl in there, even though there's probably snakes or spiders or shit. Oh wow Sadie, I thought, no way has anyone else got away.' She held up her phone. 'I tried to phone everyone, but there's seriously no signal here.' Kimberley sat down and drew her blackened knees up to her chest. 'I mean, how do people even live out here?'

Sadie took her cousin's phone. There was still no signal. 'You didn't try calling the police, I suppose.'

'Yeah right. Like they could do anything. Besides, aren't they after Jake, or something? He's like a fugitive, isn't he?'

'No Kim, he's not a fugitive.'

'Oh.' Kimberley seemed disappointed. 'So, are you and he—?'

'Because this is totally the best time to be having that conversation.'

'Wow, touchy or what?' Kimberley stuck out her bottom lip. 'Why are you always so prickly?'

'I'm not prickly.'

'We've all made an effort, you know. But you really don't make it easy.'

Sadie squirmed. She really wasn't prepared for such acute analysis from her dippiest cousin. 'Shut up.'

'You shut up. You saved my life tonight. You know that was the first time I'd ever thought that maybe you actually like me.'

'Seriously Kim, shut up.' Sadie sat forward and pressed a finger to her lips. Nearby, a man was shouting.

'Maybe one of us should, like, make a run for it or

something,' Kim said. 'You know, to cause a distraction.'

'I've sprained my ankle,' Sadie whispered. 'It'll have to be you.'

'Okay, bad idea.' She smiled. At Sadie, at herself.

Sadie felt a new tenderness for her cousin. Maybe any distance between them was, partly, her fault. Maybe she had been too busy looking at the horizon. 'I do like you,' she said, her eyes to the mud.

The shouting was getting closer. Someone was crashing through the undergrowth towards them. Sadie could hear a high, panicked tenor in his voice.

'Someone please! Please, help!'

Sadie hauled herself up into a crouch, pressing her hands down into the mud. She ignored the stinging in her palm and the burning in her ankle. Was it Tom? Her first instinct was to go and help, but if they did capture Tom, wouldn't it be better if she were still free?

Kim saw her waver and tugged at Sadie's shoulder, holding her back. 'I don't wanna get shot Sades, please.'

Then the screaming started. It was a noise neither of the girls had ever heard, or even imagined to exist. It was the sound of someone who no longer feared anything, because the worst was already happening to them.

Before she even thought about it, Sadie was running, ignoring her bad ankle. Kim was behind her. The screaming continued. Sadie's feet sank in the soft riverbank. Brambles scratched at her shins. The rain made her dress tight and heavy.

Then, up ahead, she saw it. A dark shape behind the spiny branches of the tea tree. The shape shook, flexed and took off uphill, uprooting small trees and shrubs as it ran. Sadie stopped, transfixed, until it disappeared behind the broad trunk of a Karri. Nobody was screaming anymore.

She pressed forward along the bank, edging around the tea tree. That was where they found Vincent. Most of him, anyway. He had been torn open and his insides were strewn upstream. His throat was ragged and bloody and his pale eyes rolled back in his head.

'What is that?' Kimberley asked, catching her breath. Realising, she vomited into the river.

The thing had ripped through the hillside. Sadie knew what this meant. The Minotaur was alive. It had followed them here, perhaps swimming upriver from the coast. It was still on the hunt, still tracking that taste of blood from a Cottesloe laneway.

'It's coming for Tom,' she told her retching cousin. 'Maybe Jake too.' Her jaw set and her chin rose. 'We have to warn them.'

19
THE HUMAN DEFENCE LEAGUE

There were three of them, each shouldering a shotgun. The men—boys really—circled the house, looking serious and enjoying it.

Sadie and Kimberley crouched behind the generator shed. The corrugated walls shivered and hummed in tune with the engine; hot, oily air lurked in a dizzying haze.

'I am totally going to die in this rain,' Kimberley said. 'Can't we just tell them we give in and go home? You know, game over.'

Sadie ignored her. She was wondering how she could cause a distraction and get into the house to stage that impossible rescue. Could she ask Kimberley to run screaming into the bush and hope the guards followed? What about the generator? Could she blow it up somehow?

Yeah, right. *Sadie Miller: explosives expert.*

Shaking her head at herself, Sadie glanced towards Tom's abandoned 4WD. Something moved behind the backseat. A dark head appeared in the tinted glass, then disappeared again. Heather. She was lying down when they were forced out of the car and, it seemed, she had stayed put.

'No way,' Kimberley whispered. 'That is so typical. We've been getting killed and chased and drowned and she's just been lying around listening to music.'

'Wait here,' Sadie said.

It was only a few metres from the edge of the bush to the car, and Sadie was willing to chance it. She already had a plan. Well, half a plan, but it was a start. She waited for one of the men to pass the fender and then darted to the left rear wheel. She figured she had about thirty seconds before she was in clear view. Reaching up, she popped open the rear door and jumped in to lie across the back seat. The door clicked shut behind her.

'Heather,' she whispered, 'it's Sadie. Don't move.'

'Sadie?'

'I did just say it was me.'

'I had to pee in a Coke bottle.'

'Okay…'

'And my iPod's out of batteries.'

'Heather, shush. You've had driving lessons, yeah?'

'Dad banned me. I reversed into a phone box.'

It took a minute for Sadie to explain her plan. Actually, it took about ten seconds, but convincing Heather took a lot longer. Closing the door behind her, Sadie dropped down to the mud. She watched one of the men disappear around the side of the house, checked she was alone in the clearing, and ran back to Kim.

'Okay,' Sadie said, squatting down beside her cousin. 'I think I've got it sussed.'

Kim said nothing. Her eyes were wide and she was trembling.

Sadie felt something hard bite into her shoulder. She heard the shotgun click.

'On your feet,' Jason hissed, then he whistled sharply and shouted towards the house: 'I've got two of them here!'

They had all been pretty nice about it, Tom thought. There was friendly banter as they were led into the cool mansion, and a dumpy woman in a paisley dress had offered him and Jake tea. Tom had looked at Jake, unsure if taking tea was the sort of thing you did when someone had a gun pointed at you. Jake nodded.

Alan sat in the corner of the large kitchen, with the shotgun on his lap. Whenever Tom glanced at him, he smiled, so Tom stopped glancing. Jake didn't look at anyone.

There were at least twenty people in the place. It was two in the morning but new smiling faces kept appearing in the kitchen doorway. Everyone seemed excited to see them. Small clusters of pyjama-clad children gathered and waved and were shooed away by the woman with the teapot.

According to the clock above the stove, it was about two fifteen when a grey-haired bloke in a short-sleeved white shirt came in and sat at the kitchen table. No, that wasn't quite what he did. First he got down on both knees and bowed to Jake.

'We are truly blessed,' he said, as the woman poured everyone another mug of tea. Jake didn't say anything.

There was something familiar about this new bloke, Tom thought. He was probably in his seventies, but he had kept himself fit. He moved with the confidence of a wealthy man and spoke like Tom's dad, sure everyone was interested and not caring if they weren't.

'My name is Steve Cooper. I'm the founder of our little society here. We've been waiting for you.'

Steve Cooper. The name was familiar too.

Jake sat back in his chair, folding his arms. 'You have something of mine,' he said.

'That's right. We hoped it would bring you to us.'

'Me?'

'You or someone like you. You see, Lord—'

Jake twitched. 'Don't call me that.'

'Sir, then.'

'Call me Jake.'

'Jake.' Steve seemed disappointed, but only for a second. 'You see, Jake, in 1964, I wrote a book called *Gods*

& *Monsters*. Perhaps you've read it? At the time, I considered it a work of fiction. Science fiction, to be exact. The premise was that Gods had once walked the Earth, but humanity had done something to anger them. I won't spoil the ending for you.' He smiled, revealing good teeth. 'Now, when the Gods left us to our own devices, they left behind a few guardians. Ambassadors, if you like. Does this sound familiar?'

Jake shook his head. 'I don't read modern fiction.'

'You're Stephen Cooper,' Tom said. 'I read those horror books of yours when I was a kid. *Skinpricklers*.'

Steve nodded graciously. 'Always good to meet a fan.'

Tom didn't say what else he now remembered. The stories from school, that Stephen Cooper had gone crazy and started his own cult. Stories that now appeared to be true. The author's smile was friendly enough, but his eyes were steady and intense. He didn't seem to blink.

'Strange as it might seem, I always thought of the book as mere fantasy. I didn't realise until years later that it was a gift. The Gods speak through me.'

Yeah, Tom thought, *stone cold crazy.*

'At first there were just a few letters. People from all over the world, saying they'd had the same dreams. Of course, I dismissed them as delusional. But then people started to come to me. A man travelled all the way from Miami to tell me he'd met a demi-god, living in a motel. To my shame, I called the police. Then six months later, a woman appeared on my doorstep. She was an archaeologist from a Greek university. She told me about the Minoans, an ancient civilisation swallowed by the sea. That was when I stopped doubting. I'd never been religious, but this wasn't faith, this was proof. Proof that Gods had once moved among us, that they would come back, and that we were all in danger.'

Tom looked at Jake, wondering how seriously he should be taking this. Jake sipped his tea.

'More and more people came to me,' Steve continued. 'By the 1990s, we had the funds to buy this place, to establish a refuge from the end days. We even thought of a name for ourselves—the Human Defence League. Then, just months ago, a man called Vincent approached me. He'd read my book. He said that the final battle was coming. But there was more. An ambassador from the Gods, one of the Old Ones, was still alive. More than that, he was actually living in Perth. Can you imagine our excitement? This was our chance.'

Steve paused, expectant. Jake gave nothing away. Tom felt obliged to say something.

'Uh, your chance?'

Steve turned back to Jake. 'Is he one of your acolytes?'

'I don't have acolytes,' Jake said.

'We are all your acolytes,' Steve assured him. 'That's why we knew we had to make contact. I knew that, if we went to you, you would turn us away. But Vincent said he had something in his possession—the box of fire—that would bring you to us. It looks like he was right.'

'Vincent's never been right,' Jake muttered. 'So, I'm here. What do you want me to do for you?'

The question seemed to surprise everyone in the room. The children at the door giggled and the woman with the teapot smiled down into her apron.

'I think you have things the wrong way round,' Steve said. 'It's more about what we want to do for you. We will worship you. Worship you and your masters.'

'Why would you want to do that?'

'To prove our loyalty. To show the Gods we haven't forgotten them. To beg for mercy.'

Jake nodded and jumped to his feet. 'Understood. Give me the box and I'll put in a good word.'

Steve stayed sitting. Alan clutched his shotgun.

'We can't let you go, not just like that. You see, Jake, we've done our research. We know the rituals of devotion, the ceremonies.'

'Good for you. But I'm afraid I'm on a tight schedule.'

'Unfortunately, I insist,' Steve said. 'You can have the box, but first we will prove our devotion to you. With worship. And with blood.'

Everyone in the room was suddenly looking at Tom.

'Don't be an idiot,' Jake said. His cheeks were pale.

Steve pushed back his chair. 'The Gods demand a sacrifice.'

They were taken through to a large hall in the centre of the mansion. Tom was put on a chair. A long rope was tied in a noose around his neck, and work began to tie it to an overhead rafter. Women and children, young men and old, gawped down from first-floor walkways. Part of Tom thought they should be wearing something religious, instead of T-shirts and jeans. Most of him just thought *help*.

Jake had been bound to a stone pillar with another length of rope. It had taken six of the larger men to hold him down. He now glared silently at Steve, as the old man came down a set of stairs, carrying a battered wooden casket before him. It was little bigger than a jewellery box. Any sharp edges it once had were worn to soft curves. The lid was fastened shut but there was no sign of a latch or keyhole. Tom guessed this was the relic. Jake never once took his eyes from it.

Steve laid the box in the centre of some circular chalk patterns on the slate floor. Then he stepped back from it, with care.

'Some of us say the box speaks to them,' Steve said to Jake. 'In their heads, a quiet voice. Trying to make deals, trying to persuade them to open it.'

'You won't be able to,' Jake snapped. 'I'm the only one who can open it.'

'I imagine it plays some part in the final battle?'

'It started it.'

'Fascinating. Honestly, the way you said that just then made my spine tingle. To think I was holding something so old, something part of the very fabric of history, past, present and future.'

'For the last time, this ceremony is pointless,' Jake told him. 'The Gods don't care. They've gone and, if you're very lucky, they'll never come back.'

'No Jake. They're already coming back to us. You can feel them, can't you? Moving through the night sky, towards us. Ready for battle.'

The rope around Tom's neck tightened. Panic rose in his gut. This couldn't be happening. He looked at Jake, waiting for him to do something. Right now, he trusted no one else to do it.

'When the sacrifice is kicking, we will slit his throat and collect his blood. It shall stand in tribute to our returning masters, proof of our loyalty. You will represent them, bear witness.'

The doors to the hall burst open then and two sunburned men dragged in Sadie and Kimberley. Seeing Tom, Sadie's eyes widened in horror, but she made the effort to joke.

'Why are you standing up there?'

'I'm being sacrificed. To the Gods.'

Sadie's smile wavered, but only just. 'Is this what

boys do, when you're left on your own?' She nodded at Jake. 'Hey, you remember the you-know-what from the hospital?'

'Of course.'

'Cool, because it's here. It killed Vincent. Well, sort of ate him, really.'

'It was totally gross,' Kimberley added. 'I spewed. Seriously. Big chunks.'

Steve ignored this intrusion. He laid a curved steel blade on a small wooden altar, beside a silver goblet. Then he glanced at the new arrivals. 'Get those kids out of the way.'

As Sadie and Kimberley were dragged off, Steve kneeled down before the altar and kissed the blade. He murmured some words that nobody else heard. Then he stood and strode across to Tom.

'Thank you,' he said. 'Humanity will survive, because of your sacrifice.'

'Uh, Jake did say the Gods weren't watching,' Tom said quickly. He could barely speak. His throat was tight and his tongue was dry. Sweat stung his eyes. This was really happening. He looked across, with new desperation, at the bound boy across from him. 'And, uh, Jake does kind of know what he's talking about.'

'Wait!' Sadie ripped her arm free and made a break for Steve. Jason snatched at her hair and yanked her back into him. She bellowed with pain and frustration.

'Thank you,' Steve said again and bowed his head. Then he kicked Tom's chair out from beneath him.

20
EVERYONE DIES

Tom writhed and choked at the end of the rope. His fingers clawed at the noose. Steve knelt down before his altar, stretched his arms out and began chanting. The words were low and round, as if especially crafted for echoing about the hall.

Jake was straining at his bonds. His veins pulsed in his temple.

'Cut him down!' he barked.

The chanting continued. Murmured echoes descended from the overhead walkways. Children poked their excited faces through the banisters. Women put out their palms as if checking for rain, and raised their eyes to the ceiling.

Sadie howled. It was a noise she'd never heard before. A noise she'd never imagined she could make. Tom's head was full of blood, his eyes were aflame. Her best friend was choking to death. Tom. Dying.

She looked to Jake. He was doing everything he

could to free himself. She had to do something.

Sadie kicked out backwards at Jason's shins. He didn't buckle; his fingers dug into her upper arms. Sadie pulled forward and he simply snatched her back.

'Soon as this is done, I'm gonna make you regret that,' he snarled in her ear.

'Let me go!' Sadie shouted.

And then Jason gurgled, as if washing his mouth out. He rose in the air and flew over Sadie's head, into the centre of the gathering. He landed hard on the slate by Tom's overturned chair and put a hand to his shirtfront. He seemed astonished when it came away covered in blood.

The chanting stopped.

Kimberley screamed.

Sadie turned. Behind her, the Minotaur roared, lifting its scarred muzzle to the ceiling. It was even taller than she'd remembered, and it stank of sweat and seaweed and rotting meat. Its right horn glistened to the hilt with bright red blood.

'A demon!'

Steve had been lost to a moment's terror. Now, he was returning to the altar.

'It comes from the underworld, to test our loyalty to the true Gods.' He snapped his fingers at Alan, whose startled hands fumbled his shotgun. 'Kill it!'

Sadie ignored the beast, snatching up Jason's fallen

gun. Shoving it in her armpit, she saw Kimberley shivering on the tiles, transfixed by the Minotaur.

'Kim?'

'It's a monster,' Kim said, her jaw slack. 'A cow monster.'

'Get out of here, Kim. Run. We'll meet you in the car.'

Kimberley nodded, slowly, never taking her eyes off the creature. Sadie hurried over to Jake and untied his knots.

'You were a soldier,' she said. 'You can fire a gun, can't you?'

The rope came loose from Jake's wrist. He grabbed the shotgun from Sadie, pointed it towards the rafter above Tom and pulled the trigger. The report was deafening. Sadie squeaked. The rope snapped at the rafter and Tom fell to the floor. He lay still on the slate, his blue lips pursed.

It's too late, Sadie thought *He's dead*.

The gunshot spurred the hall into action. Those armed opened fire at the Minotaur. The creature ducked and darted. Bullets sparked against stone. As one young man attempted to reload, the Minotaur tore out his throat. Another man crashed a chair across its head, only to have his own skull crushed by a casual flick of the beast's wrist. In the corridor outside, men pulled more guns from a cupboard.

Everything was panic, but Jake was calmly on his feet.

'Get behind me,' he told Sadie, tightening the strap of his satchel across his chest.

'No chance.' Sadie hurried over to Tom, getting her fingers under the rope around his neck. 'Tom? Can you hear me?'

There was no response.

'Don't let him go anywhere!' Steve shouted, pointing madly at Jake. 'Our salvation depends on it!'

A thick-set man with red hair nodded and charged at Jake, who casually knocked him unconscious. A second man lunged and, without even looking at him, Jake broke his nose. Reaching Sadie's side, Jake knelt down and lifted Tom by his armpits. The bloodied corpse of a young woman was thrown against his shoulder, but he only brushed it aside.

'Is he okay?' Sadie asked.

Jake didn't look at her. 'He's not breathing.'

'We need to get him to the car,' Sadie said.

Jake nodded, heading for the door. Sadie didn't watch him go. She was looking at the relic, forgotten on the slate. She slid across the tiles and grabbed it to her chest. Her fingertips tingled.

Ignoring the screams and the blood and the bullets streaking in every direction, she jumped to her feet and hurried after Jake. If the Minotaur had come for him, or for Tom, it seemed to have forgotten. Instead, its dark eyes sparked with bloodlust at finding itself thrust into an arena of artless gladiators. It slashed and stabbed with its horns, and ripped and gutted with its talons.

It was only as Sadie reached the doors to the main corridor and opened them for Jake, that its nose twitched and shifted in their direction. Its latest, whimpering victim was discarded, and the creature charged towards them.

Kimberley had crawled to the door on her knees. Safe in the hall, she climbed up the wall. 'I really want this to be a dream,' she mewed.

Sadie put a hand on her shoulder. 'Run,' she said. 'We'll catch you up.'

Kimberley ran for the front door, but Sadie didn't move. Maybe she felt safer beside Jake. Maybe she couldn't bring herself to leave Tom. The Minotaur was almost upon them. Jake lifted the shotgun and fired once. At such short range, the blast was enough to throw the beast backwards. Its bare chest was stippled with blood and pellets. Jake pulled the heavy doors shut and jammed the gun across the handles.

'Here,' Sadie thrust the relic towards him. Jake shoved it into his satchel and she turned her attention to Tom.

Tom was flat out on the corridor boards. Sadie tilted his head and lowered his jaw. She murmured the mnemonic the school nurse had taught her. *A* for *airway*,

B for *breathing*. And *C*, what was that for? *Chest?* Was there a *D*?

Jake lifted Tom's right wrist, and pressed two fingers to the base of his palm. 'There's no pulse.'

'Just watch the door!' Sadie snapped.

She pinched Tom's nose with her finger and thumb and breathed in until her lungs hurt. Then she pressed her mouth over his and cleared them out, watching Tom's chest rise.

The barred doors shook. The Minotaur was trying to break through. Jake dug his heels into the floorboards and pressed his shoulders against the barricade.

In. Out. In. Out. Each time Sadie watched Tom's ribs, praying they would take up her rhythm.

There was another crash and the doors bulged. The wood held, but the hinges flinched at the wall.

In. Out. In. Out.

Another thump at the doors knocked Jake to his knees. The shotgun barrels bent. From inside, more shots rang out. The Minotaur roared and men began screaming. Someone had bought them more time.

Tom spluttered. His body convulsed. For a wonderful moment, Sadie thought he might sit up and ask what was going on. That was what happened in films, wasn't it? At the last minute, the kiss of life had the hero back on his feet? But then Sadie saw the vivid welts around his neck and the rope burns and grazes. This was real.

Tom didn't sit up. The front of his T-shirt lifted, but only just. Jake darted forward and checked his pulse again.

'Barely there,' he frowned. 'He needs to get to hospital, now.'

'We're in a gunfight, in the middle of nowhere. Right, yeah, I'll just pop outside and flag down a taxi.'

Jake looked up at her, his bottom lip tucked behind his teeth. Sadie knew what that look meant.

'We can't.' There were tears on her cheeks. 'We have to do something. We can't let him die.'

'Everyone dies, Sadie.'

'You didn't. Look,' she sat up, leaning over her fallen friend. 'That rose you gave me. You said it would never wither, never die. That was your gift. You can do that here, can't you? You can save Tom.'

Jake flinched. 'You can't ask me to do that.'

'I'm asking. Save him.'

'If the damage is more than superficial, he'll always be like this, always a moment from death.'

'Agatha healed him before. She can do it again.'

'It's not that simple, Sadie.'

'Do it.'

Jake gritted his teeth and grunted through them. His shoulders tensed and he pressed both palms to Tom's chest. Tom convulsed again, as if electrified, then fell limp. His breathing remained shallow and sporadic.

There was another crash as the Minotaur threw itself against the doors. Jake snatched Tom from the floor and followed Sadie down the corridor.

They found Kimberley standing motionless on the threshold of the front door. Steve emerged from a room on the left. There was a shotgun in his hands and blood on his shirt. He looked at Jake, his eyes red but steady.

'I can't let you go,' he said. 'We need to show the Gods they haven't been forgotten.'

'Nothing you do here will make any difference,' Jake said.

Steve lifted the barrel to Kimberley's forehead. 'I've already made the offering. All I have to do now is complete the sacrifice. It doesn't have to be the boy.'

'My dad's a lawyer,' Kimberley squealed. 'You kill me and he'll totally sue your balls off.'

'Kill her and I'll kill you,' Jake said. 'Be sure of that.'

Standing behind Jake, Sadie checked her watch and stepped forward. 'Kim, walk over here.'

'Um, the gun, genius? He could totally shoot me.'

'Take the risk.'

Kimberley's mouth formed an appalled vowel. 'You are so mean!'

'Kim, please.'

Swallowing hard, Kimberley edged along the skirting board, until she was beside Jake. Steve traced her path with the gun barrel, coming around to stand on the doormat, blocking their exit.

'What about this one?' he said, jabbing the weapon towards Sadie.

Sadie lifted her chin, defiant. 'You've got ten seconds to put the gun down,' she said.

Steve laughed. 'Or what? You're just a child. You've got no weapon, nothing.'

'No. But I've got friends.'

Steve's finger slid up the trigger. He paused, hearing something behind him. An over-revved engine roared. Red tail-lights burned through frosted glass as Tom's 4WD reversed up—and partially demolished—the veranda. Steve attempted to throw himself clear, but his head collided with the door as the car's rear shoved it from its hinges.

The 4WD was showing no sign of slowing. Its sides scraped paint and sparks from the stone walls.

'Brake!' Sadie shrieked. 'Heather, brake!'

With barely a metre to spare, the car came to a shuddering halt. Heather's meek voice could be heard from the driver's seat. 'Whoops!'

Kimberley tutted. 'It's the phone booth all over again. The girl's a menace.'

Sadie quickly opened the back and helped Jake load Tom into the boot. Kimberley jumped in beside him.

'Oh my god. Is he dead? He looks dead.'

It was just Jake and Sadie then, standing by the rear bumper. Rain soaked the floorboards at their feet. Jake swung the satchel free of his shoulders. Sadie thought he was about to give it to her, but instead he rested the bag against his forehead. His eyes closed and his lips twitched with some silent prayer.

'What are you doing?' Sadie said. 'We need to get out of here.'

Opening his eyes, Jake looped the satchel's strap around Sadie's neck. 'Get to the ocean,' he said. 'Use the relic. Save your home.'

'You're coming, aren't you?'

A snarl of triumph echoed along the corridor. The Minotaur was through.

'Go!' Jake shouted, shoving Sadie into the boot. Immediately the 4WD lurched forwards.

'Wait for Jake!' Sadie shouted.

'I said, drive!' Jake yelled over her.

Steve had fallen against the nearest wall. He had a deep gash on his forehead. He was reaching for his shotgun as the Minotaur came around the corner and casually snapped his neck.

Kimberley shrieked. Heather panicked: her foot flattened the accelerator, and the 4WD tore itself free of the veranda. Swerving dangerously in the mud, the vehicle hurtled towards the road.

'Wait!' Sadie screamed, clinging onto Tom and the

back seat to stop herself falling out the open rear door. Heather wasn't listening. She was too busy making sure that she stayed on the gravel track and missed the rain-water tank.

Jake vaulted the smashed veranda and sprinted after them.

'He's coming,' Sadie called to Heather. 'Slow down, slow down.'

But then, there was the Minotaur. Its head was down and its horns were thrust forward. Snot and fury were streaming from its snout.

'It's chasing us!' Kimberley shrieked.

Sadie could see what was going to happen next so clearly that it seemed to have already happened. All the haste and panic boiled away, leaving nothing but a slow, terrible moment.

Jake stopped running and turned to face the beast.

He put up his fists.

Sadie screamed at Heather to stop, but Kimberley was screaming at her to go. The monster had Jake's leg in its teeth. It pulled him backwards and away, down into the mud. The car turned behind scorched trees and then there was nothing to see.

Soon they were winding a dangerous path back to the main road, heading back to their sinking city, but Sadie already knew it didn't matter.

Jake was dead.

PART THREE

THE DROWNED CITY

21
BRUISES

They stopped halfway down the hill and parked on the gravel beside the road. It was nobody's idea, but nobody argued. Heather simply pulled off onto the soft shoulder and switched off the engine.

Jake was dead. Jake was dead and it was Sadie's fault. It wasn't the Minotaur that had killed him, it was her. She had made him tear off that talisman, made him promise to betray the Gods. Was he out there somewhere now, being judged disloyal? Being denied a return ticket?

She pushed the door open and threw herself out of the car. The water streaming off the bitumen was ankle deep and the earth gave beneath her boots. She tripped twice, grazing her already-grazed knee. But she kept going, towards the glow over the next hill. Towards nothing, towards anything. The cold rain pulled her skin tight across every scratch and every bruise.

Kimberley's voice followed her. 'Where are you going?'

Sadie didn't answer. It didn't matter where she was going. Tom was in no state to drive and neither was the car. Both brake-lights were smashed, the windscreen was gone and there were worrying gouges in the bodywork. A torn tyre flapped around a buckled wheel. They were lucky to have made it this far.

She had always kept going. Moving on distracted her from the meaninglessness of her parents' death. She had walked away from that crash, and things were okay. Death hadn't won. But now, she didn't feel there was anywhere to go.

'You can't just leave us here,' Kimberley shouted. 'This is your bloody road trip. You can't just walk off!'

Tom slid down from the passenger seat. He was still unsteady on his feet and the welt around his neck was an ugly violet. But he snatched up Jake's satchel and stumbled after Sadie.

She heard him coming, sloshing through the water at the road's edge. Her own pace quickened, uselessly. She was too tired and too bruised to get any distance on him.

'Where are you going?' she sneered.

A hand flapped at his injured throat. He couldn't speak. He held the satchel out to her.

'Don't be stupid.'

Sadie kept going. Tom grabbed at her arm but she tore it back.

'Let go of me, okay?'

He ignored her. Again he thrust the satchel towards her.

'Oh right, yeah. We'll just jump on our white horse and ride back into town. It's too late. Don't you get that?'

Tom kept holding the satchel out to her, jabbing his finger west. When she didn't understand, he repeated the gesture.

'They've won, okay?' Sadie cried. 'Jake was the only one who knew how to open it, and he's dead. I got him killed and now we're all screwed.'

That was it. Tom snatched the bag back to his armpit, shook his head and started walking away from her, towards the glow, towards home.

'Oh right, yeah. Great idea. Walk back to the city. Yeah, that'll get you there in time.'

Tom kept walking.

'I'm the one who was storming off. You're supposed to run after me.'

He was still walking, with as much determination as his battered body could manage. Frustration percolated in Sadie's shoulders and her fingers curled.

'Seriously, Tom, stop. Come back.'

She took off, jogging across the gravel to catch him up.

'Come back. Tom, don't be stupid.'

She skipped alongside him, snatching at his elbow. She grabbed him near his right armpit, harder than she'd ever grabbed anyone, and spun him around.

'Stop being such an idiot,' she howled, trying to tear the satchel from him.

He wouldn't let go. Sadie pulled, and he pulled back. When she realised she couldn't win, she began slapping his arms. Before she knew it, she was thumping his chest with her fists and crying. She didn't know why. She was just crying at the whole, rotten world. She sobbed for a whole minute before she had enough breath to say it wasn't fair. None of it was fair. Nothing.

Somehow, Tom's arms were around her. He held her. He said nothing. Her tears steamed in his T-shirt. Whatever it was—anger, frustration, sorrow—soon boiled out of her.

Sadie stepped back and he let her go. She wiped her cheeks with her wrists and took the satchel. She could feel the relic through the canvas. Electricity sparked in her fingertips. It was the same tingling she'd felt back at Ocean Street, when she'd lifted it from the mantelpiece. The demon inside was reaching out for her.

Take me to the water, it said, or did she imagine it? *Release me*.

Sadie remembered Jake holding the satchel to his forehead. *Get to the ocean*, he had said. *Use the relic*.

Release me, the voice said again.

Maybe Jake had unlocked the box. Maybe he had trusted her that much.

Sadie held out her hand. 'Give me your phone.'

Tom pulled his mobile from his back pocket. There was enough of a signal to check the weather—sunrise and sunset. Lysandra had given them until dawn. That gave them about two and a half hours to get the relic out to sea.

'We'll need a boat.'

Tom nodded. They both knew where they could get one.

Sadie didn't know what she had done to deserve such friendship. But she hardly had time to wonder before she was blinded by a pair of high-beams coming over the next rise. Seconds later, a large vehicle—an old jeep, Sadie thought—rattled past. The brake-lights flared and it spun around to hurry back.

'Is that the police?' Sadie asked. By now, they might have found the dead bodies. It would look like a massacre, she realised, one of those horrific cult tragedies you heard about from the States. All those people.

She hadn't thought about them. Not once. She had only thought about her friends, and about getting away with the relic. Had she even flinched on the riverbank, when they found what was left of Vincent?

Even now, she was really only thinking of Jake. Jake, being pulled down into mud and blood by the Minotaur.

The jeep drove past Tom's abandoned 4WD and

pulled up a few metres from where he and Sadie were standing. Its headlights snatched at the rain. The driver's door opened.

'Sadie, is that you?'

Agatha emerged from the jeep. She had a silk scarf tied around her head.

'I hoped we'd find you,' she said. 'Are you all okay?'

Sadie wanted to run and hug this woman she barely knew. She felt that Agatha would understand.

'We got what we came for,' she said, holding up the satchel.

Agatha was marvellously blasé. 'Oh, that's it, is it? What all this hoo-ha is about? Do you know, I've never seen it. Oh dear,' she frowned, noticing the wound on Tom's throat. 'Oh Tom, my poor love. That looks absolutely horrid. You must let me do something about it.'

Tom lowered his eyes and Sadie suspected he was blushing.

'Now, I think the lot of you should join us in the jeep,' Agatha said, linking elbows with both of them. 'It'll be a bit of a squeeze, but we should all fit.'

Sadie's spine straightened. 'Us?'

'Oh yes, there's someone in the car you might be surprised to see again so soon.'

Sadie pulled herself free from Agatha and ran into the light. A little spark of hope remembered itself. It couldn't be. Maybe the Gods hadn't blamed him for trying to use the demon. Maybe they understood. Or maybe they hadn't noticed.

Agatha's jeep was a few decades old, but as well-polished as a soldier's boot. Sadie could see a young man sitting in the passenger seat. He was tall and thin, with a powerful nose and thick dark hair above a high forehead.

'Jake?' It didn't look like him but, of course, it wouldn't. He was someone else, again.

'Sadie?' The boy leaned out through the open door. 'Oh, man, it's true then. He's gone,' he said.

Sadie's heart stuttered in her chest. 'Jake? Tell me it's you.'

'It's Vincent,' the boy said. 'I went straight to Agatha and told her what happened. Said she had to come and rescue you.'

Words formed on Sadie's lips, then dissolved in silence. It wasn't fair. Vincent, coward and cheat, had come back and Jake was gone.

'For once, Vincent is actually speaking the truth,' Agatha said, coming to stand by Sadie's shoulder. 'When I realised that, I knew things had to be serious. Sadie, this must be hard for you. You should know Jacob never has had much luck with his,' she considered the word carefully, '*bodies*.' She put a hand to Sadie's forearm. 'I felt him go.'

'You did?'

'I always do. We were very close once.'

This wasn't what Sadie wanted to hear. She had but the briefest of claims on Jake. Agatha had known him for longer than she had lived or would live.

'You felt him go,' she said, trying to hold back a note of hope. 'Did you feel him come back?'

Agatha considered the question. It seemed to unnerve her. 'No. Not yet.'

Sadie's knees sagged and Agatha had to dart forwards to catch her. 'Oh you poor dear. Let's go. I fear this night isn't over yet.'

22
RAIN

Agatha did her best to heal Tom's throat. His voice returned, as if breaking through a bad cold, but a raw welt remained, like a cruel smile beneath his chin. Sadie tried to smile encouragingly.

'It'll heal,' he assured her. Each word still scraped in his throat.

'Yeah,' she said, eyes down, and he started to worry.

He had nearly died, he knew that. The strange thing was, when it came to it, he had almost felt calm. He wasn't going to go easily, but part of him had just nodded and thought *yeah, fair enough*. But then he'd seen Sadie, seen her distress, and he'd fought back.

As they approached the city, the road shook beneath them, rattling the jeep. Car alarms honked and rubbish bins tipped over on drenched pavements. Agatha pulled up on the kerb until the quake subsided.

'Our friends are getting a mite impatient,' she said.

The relic had fallen from the dashboard to Sadie's

lap. Tom saw her reach to pick it up, then hesitate, as if fearing it.

'I hate that box,' Heather said. 'It makes me feel sick just looking at it. Like it doesn't want me looking at it. It doesn't like me.'

Kimberley snorted. 'You are such a freak. Who else feels picked on by furniture?'

'No,' Sadie said. 'It's alive. Seriously. I can hear it talking to me. It says it'll help us, if we do what it wants.'

Tom saw Sadie's hand tremble again over the lid. When he had held the box, he'd felt nothing but cool wood.

'What does it want?' Kimberley asked.

In the space behind the back seat, Vincent stirred. 'It wants to be free. But it won't be freed. Not without Jake.'

'No,' Sadie said. 'Jake did something to it. I think it'll open for me. We have to try.'

Heather looked to Sadie. 'You're not going to let it out?'

Sadie shook her head. 'Not yet. It isn't ready. It wants the water.' She put the box back on the dashboard. Goosebumps prickled the back of her arm. 'It's all we can do. If it doesn't help us, the city drowns.'

Another tremor, stronger than the last, knocked them about in their seats. Tom leaned forward and put his hand on Sadie's shoulder to steady her. She looked out, beyond the dark glass towers of the city.

'We've got two hours,' she said. 'If the sun comes up, we've had it.'

'And if it doesn't open?' Tom whispered.

'It'll open. It has to.'

Agatha had been listening to this conversation, not remotely fussed. But Tom had the feeling that, if asked, she would have turned and fled for the hills. She put her foot down, the jeep moved forwards and rain pelted at the windscreen.

There were roads that couldn't be taken. They were choked with traffic or flooded by dark, murky water. Yellow tape or orange barricades bisected intersections. Defunct traffic lights flashed silent warnings.

A short distance from the yacht club, flashing blue lights appeared through the downpour, and a plastic-coated policeman stepped out to flag them down.

'You'll have to turn back,' he said, peering in as Agatha wound down the window.

'It's an emergency,' Sadie said, leaning across. 'We need to get to the yacht club ASAP.'

'Yeah, every smart arse wants a boat.' The policeman flashed his torch in her face, making her blink. 'The club's closed off. It's flooded.'

'It's a yacht club,' Sadie said. 'It's supposed to be flooded.'

It was meant as a friendly joke, but Agatha waved a palm, hushing her. 'We won't be any trouble constable, and it is very important.'

The policeman gave a bored sigh. He turned his torch around to the back seat. 'Leaving town?'

Agatha remained a picture of innocence. 'Should we be?'

'Lotsa people are. Packing light, aren't you?' The torchlight glanced across Vincent's new, squinting face. 'Kid in the back there's not wearing a seatbelt. He's gonna have to get out.'

Sadie's frustration was boiling over. Dawn was barely an hour and a half away. 'Look, he just needed a lift. We're trying to get somewhere safe. You can understand that, can't you?'

The policeman ignored Sadie. His torchlight was on Vincent. 'Seen you before, haven't I, mate?'

Vincent shook his head.

'Stay there,' the cop commanded. He walked back towards the police car and reached through the driver's window for his radio.

Sadie turned in her seat. 'Okay then, so does he know you?'

Vincent shrugged. 'How would I know?'

'Who did you steal that body from, idiot? Who were you?'

'Don't have a clue. First thing I knew about this one,

he'd been pushed under a train. If I hadn't ducked in, got the body out of the way, it'd be nothing but cold cuts.'

'You came back here,' Sadie realised. 'You could have gone anywhere, but you came back here, knowing we'd probably be underwater by morning. Why?'

'I wanted to help!'

'Yeah, right.'

The policeman was watching them. Sadie tried to judge how serious his expression was.

'You could be a murderer sitting there,' she said, watching Vincent in the rear-view. 'You could get us all arrested. Why didn't you use your magic on him?'

'I couldn't see his eyes. I need to see the eyes.'

The policeman's conversation was over. He put the radio back, keeping his eyes on the jeep, and felt for the gun at his side. The holster stayed buckled, but his hand hovered over it, just in case. On the other side of the car, a policewoman got out into the rain.

In the back seat, Kimberley was already putting her hands up. 'Why does everyone want to shoot me all of a sudden?'

'What's with the *all of a sudden*?' Heather muttered.

It didn't occur to Sadie to feel scared. The relic sat on the dashboard in front of her.

'We need to get to that boat, now,' she said.

Agatha squared her jaw, feeling about for the gear-stick. 'Eight thousand years, Vincent, and you're still a pain in the arse.'

As the engine roared, both cops tensed, their hands snapping magnetically to their guns. Agatha pulled hard right. The car jerked as it mounted the broad traffic island. The rear wheels spun frantically, spitting yellow mud, before biting down on the wrong side of the highway.

The police ran back to their car and gave chase, siren blaring. Another police car, further up the road, did the same. Its headlights glared ahead of the jeep's. To avoid a collision, Agatha pulled right again, tipping the jeep up onto the kerb.

The university was between them and the yacht club and they were heading into it. A flooded lawn spread out in front of a limestone chapel. They lurched down a grassy bank, leaving a frothy path across the green. Through the spray on the rear windscreen, Sadie could see the police, already too close behind them. Agatha wrenched the wheel left, bumping up a smaller slope onto a pavement. The back of the jeep fishtailed on the concrete and the passenger door slammed against the edge of a stone archway. Agatha managed to straighten up, remarkably relaxed. She seemed to be enjoying herself.

As soon as the jeep had ducked through the arch, its headlights picked out a row of steel bollards, blocking the way to a brick path. Agatha dragged the car around, off the paving. The wheels juddered over the roots of a Moreton Bay fig tree.

Back on the path, the rush and wash of deeper waters sloshed through the jeep's steel floor. A high tide crept in around Sadie's boots.

'Oh blow.'

Ahead there was another set of bollards, with no path around them. Agatha checked the rear-view.

'Sadie, how far is it to the yacht club?' she asked, still pressing the accelerator to the floor. 'If you had to walk?'

'Ten minutes?' Tom guessed.

'Splendid,' Agatha said. 'Vincent, I want you running in the opposite direction. Make it look good, but let them catch you.'

'No way. I haven't done anything.'

'You don't know that, and it should keep them happy.'

'They have guns.'

'And if they use them, that should keep me happy.' Agatha looked across at Sadie. 'Be quick,' she said. 'And good luck.' She pulled on the handbrake and swung the car around.

Sadie was already clutching the relic, trying to ignore its tingling electricity. She shoved it back into Jake's satchel, put the strap over her head and wrenched at the door handle. It wouldn't budge. The collision with the archway had bent the frame. The door was jammed fast. She twisted around in her seat and kicked out with her boots. Nothing. Police lights scattered blue shadows about the jeep's cabin.

Knee deep in filthy water, Tom tore the door open. Kimberley, Heather and Vincent all stood behind him.

Sadie rounded on Vincent. 'What are you waiting for? You heard Agatha—you're our distraction. So get distracting.'

'But I don't know where the yacht club is.'

'It isn't that way,' Sadie said, pointing west. 'Go. Run!'

Vincent splashed off and away from them. In the floodwaters, he couldn't see the narrow duck pond that ran along the front of the library. He hadn't gone two metres before he tripped on its edge and plunged into the khaki murk.

So much for the distraction, Sadie thought.

She was already wading as quickly as she could, towards the car park, which was now more like an Olympic-sized pool. Behind her, car doors slammed and angry voices skimmed like vicious stones across the water. It was more difficult to run than she'd imagined. With each step the flood sucked at her boots and she had to fight to get them back. The satchel didn't help, thumping against her back as if chiding her. Her cousins were whimpering behind her, but Tom had surged ahead. He glanced back over his shoulder to make sure they hadn't drifted off.

Vincent was quickly caught and bundled with Agatha into the back of the police car. Even being shoved about, Agatha kept her grace.

Two cops—a man and a woman—had broken away and were plunging after Sadie, Tom and the twins in great strides. The man called out, but his words were lost in the rain.

Finally, reaching a set of pale brick buildings, Sadie was on solid ground. Her toes squelched in her sodden socks.

'Sades, look.'

Tom was looking back. Heather was lagging miserably, struggling to lift her knees. By contrast, the policeman was charging forward. Within seconds he had snatched the back of her T-shirt and held her mewling against his chest. The policewoman dived for Kimberley and tackled her down into the water.

Sadie faltered. Could she leave her cousins behind?

Forget them, a voice said. *Get me to the ocean.*

Sadie glanced towards the city's glass towers. There was little night left in those windows. She had to keep going.

Chasing Tom's heels, she could hear the stuttered fragments of an argument. 'My dad…lawyer…sue… your arse…'

They turned left, splashing across a concrete plaza. From here it was another five minutes, if they could keep running.

On the other side of the plaza, headlights flared on a

car parked in shadow, startling both Tom and Sadie. 'Stay right there,' a loudspeaker voice demanded. Two more policemen opened their doors and stepped out into the rain.

Tom looked at Sadie, his bottom lip bunched.

'One hour, twenty-three minutes,' he said, tapping his wrist. 'Then we all drown, right?'

'We're not going to drown.'

'You know what you're doing. Just get to the boat.'

'Don't be stupid. I can't sail a yacht.'

'Shut up. It's easy, okay? You won't need to sail, there's a motor. The rest is steering. You can do it.'

'Seriously, don't be an idiot.'

'Shut up.' Tom clapped a palm to each of her shoulders, staring into her. 'Look Sades, I know you like to boss me around.'

'I don't like to. I can't help it.'

'But now I'm telling you—you can do this. You have to.'

Tom's hands dropped and he ran towards the approaching policemen, veering off at the last second to lure them towards the student pub.

Sadie didn't wait to see him caught. She ran back across the plaza, up the brick path, hoping to avoid a dead end. She kept running, not worrying about the breath burning behind her ribs, until she reached the campus edge, where the yacht club waited across the street.

The yacht club car park was a clay-coloured swamp, its waters reflecting the last of the moonlight. Sadie splashed her way towards the darkened clubhouse. Nearly there, she saw another pair of torchlights dart about the white walls. The no-neck policeman was heading back from the jetty with his partner following. Within seconds, they would be upon her.

Sadie crouched by the clubhouse wall. The cold water was up to her ribs. There was nowhere to hide. Rain coursed in currents down her spine and she could hear the demon taunting her.

Is this the best you can do? Stupid, arrogant girl. I am history. You are dust.

She drove the satchel down into the muddy waters.

From around the corner of the building, she could hear the policeman, close now. 'Bloody kids, like we don't have enough to do. Buggered if I know what they think they're doing.'

'Sure you recognised that kid in the back?'

'I could have sworn I'd seen his face back at the station. Don't know now.'

Holding her nose, Sadie lay down into the flood. The back of her head bumped against stony ground. She closed her eyes and waited. Submarine hums echoed around her, but they didn't drown out the relic.

Always you hide. Perhaps you should just lie down here and drown. Maybe it will take someone better than you to set me free. Someone worthy.

Her empty chest burned and pressure built behind her eyes. Her fingers clenched. Finally, she felt the police wade past. Sparks rose before her and her lips pursed, but still she waited for silence, for stillness. Finally, she let herself sit up, gasping and dizzy.

'Hey!'

Torchlight threw her shadow across the clubhouse wall. The policeman was only a few metres away. He had turned back for a final look towards the jetty.

Sadie clambered to her feet. The jetty was all but invisible beneath the swollen river. Boats rattled against each other; some had grounded themselves on its walkway. She waded quickly across the submerged lawns and plunged into the river. The water lapped at her armpits. Seconds later, the policeman jumped in after her.

Are you ready to surrender yet, Sadie? As if a girl like you could hope to set me free. The Old One was a fool to have entrusted me to your care.

The demon was right, but she tried not to believe it. Jake had died to get her this far. Her cousins and Tom and Agatha had all been arrested. Even if she made it onto the jetty, even if she made it to the boat, there wouldn't be time to get the engine started.

Her left foot snagged on something and she stumbled,

getting a lungful of salty river water. It was a step. She had reached the jetty stairs. Pulling her foot free, she climbed. With each step, the weight of the water fell away from her. Soon she was as light as she could remember ever being, splashing along the pier. Boats poked at her like frightened cattle. One wrong step and she would tumble into the narrow gap between vessels. She could see her uncle's boat towards the end of the jetty, bucking in its mooring. Just another thirty seconds—

'That's far enough!'

Sadie stopped and turned back towards the stairs. The policeman was on the walkway. He had his gun pointed in her direction.

'Turn yourself around and walk back towards me, young lady. Nice and slow.'

Sadie nodded, but took a step backwards. When the policeman didn't shoot, she took another. It was the only thing she could do. She couldn't imagine that she wouldn't make it to the boat and sail off with the relic.

'I'm not going to tell you again. I will shoot.'

He will, the demon told her. *What are you going to do? How are you going to get the boat started?*

Sadie took another step backwards. The policeman held his gun out to his right, towards the river, and pulled the trigger.

'Walk back towards me,' he instructed.

Pathetic, the relic chided.

Shut up, Sadie thought. She understood now what it was doing; it wasn't mocking her, it was goading her on. It knew her better than she had thought.

'This is a bomb.' She lifted the satchel from her hip and held it out in front of her. 'This is a bomb,' she said again, with more conviction this time. 'Get any closer and I'll blow us both into little pink pieces.'

The policeman wavered. He probably didn't believe her, but he wasn't going to take the risk. She took another step backwards, testing him. The gun lowered, then snapped back up at her.

'Put the bag down,' the cop ordered. 'If that is a bomb, I really will have to shoot you.'

Sadie winced. 'Okay, fair call, so it's not a bomb.'

Then, from behind her, came the splutter and throb of an engine. Both Sadie and the policeman turned to see her uncle's boat pull free from the crowded jetty, nudging its neighbours aside. That nudge ran like a shiver along the walkway. At its end, a boat lurched forward, knocking the policeman off his feet.

Sadie turned and ran. The boat was already some distance from its dock, heading out into dark waters.

'Stop!'

The policeman was feeling about in the shallows for his gun. Abandoning the search, he ran, limping, towards her.

Sadie dived, clutching the satchel to her chest. She

surfaced quickly and began swimming sidestroke after the departing boat. The policeman reached the empty dock and paused, glancing at the neighbouring yachts, which seemed to tremble in anticipation. Biting down on his resolve, he threw himself in after her, but his plastic raincoat hampered his breaststroke and he floundered in the dark waters.

Sadie swam frantically, kicking with desperation. Finally, she drew up alongside the boat and two hands reached down to help her up. Tom.

'I ran for the river,' he said, breathless. 'Swam out.'

'How long do we have?' she asked.

'An hour fifteen. We'll make it.'

He pulled her up onto the deck. Sadie lay, flat on her back, laughing with relief. Her breathing calmed, but she stayed where she was: in a moment's stillness, watching the sky begin to change colour.

They raced the sun west around the curves of the Swan River, heading for the ocean. Under Tom's control, the boat zigzagged across bends and cut every corner. Sadie sat on the deck, hugging her knees to stop herself rocking.

Finally, they reached the harbour at Fremantle, where the river surrendered them to the sea. Pale light was spreading across the green water. The sheep ships and cargo vessels sat high in their docks, threatening to topple over. The harbour was utterly still.

They passed one of the abandoned lighthouses on its rocky spit, where a faded sign welcomed sailors. And then the harbour was gone and they were in open sea. The swell lifted the boat up into the rain, then changed its mind. Suddenly, the rain stopped. A white haze fell over the city and its suburbs, stretching east towards the hills. Outside the city limits, clear, purple skies revealed the first moments of a warm morning. Waves were golden tipped. It was dawn.

Tom switched off the engine and they coasted on, sliding over the swell. Leaning on the pilot rail, he looked across at Sadie. 'Five twenty-nine,' he said. 'Did we make it?'

Sadie knelt down and picked up the satchel. As she tried to stand, the boat lurched, knocking her back onto the deck. The ocean was moving beneath them, not in its usual soporific rhythm, but in a panicked rush. Sadie could see the waters pulling back from the shore, like a clumsy magician might tug at a tablecloth. The yacht was being dragged with them, spinning and lurching as it hurtled out to sea.

Tom's jaw went slack. 'Sades?'

Sadie saw it then, rising up before them. The ocean creased in a towering ridge of blue water that blotted out the horizon. The wave was soon ten, twenty metres tall.

Sadie swallowed hard. They were too late. The

Drowners were really going to do it. With one hand clinging hard to the guide-rail, she pulled the relic from the satchel. Her fingers prised at the lid, but it remained stuck fast.

'Okay, we're here,' she said. 'I release you, you're free. Come on, save us. Please.'

She couldn't be sure if the wave was rushing towards them, or they were rushing towards it. It didn't matter. Within seconds they would be shattered like a pair of crash-test dummies.

Her nails dug at the edges of the lid. It wouldn't budge. The relic was cold in her hands.

'It won't open!' she told Tom. 'I can't even hear it anymore. It's not saying anything.'

Time didn't slow down, as Sadie imagined it might at the end. There weren't a few final, slow moments for her to consider her fate. The wave was upon them, tilting the stern back into the water. She clung to the railing and closed her eyes.

Nothing happened.

Sadie opened her eyes. Her reflection blinked at her, trembling on a wall of water. The boat's prow sent ripples across its surface.

She turned back to see Tom standing wide-eyed at the helm.

Sadie turned the relic over in her hands. 'Maybe that's it. Maybe it saved us. Maybe we're okay.'

'Um, Sades?' Tom's right hand flapped in the direction of the stalled tsunami. A cluster of dark shapes could be seen behind its surface. There were a dozen of them, maybe more. Within moments, the first had burst free, landing on the deck with a roar of triumph. Another touched down on the bow, and two more in the stern. One dropped beside Tom, its blue hand drawing a ragged blade from his rotting belt. Grey lips peeled back on blackened teeth.

Now Sadie could hear the demon again. And it was laughing.

Good girl, it said. *You brought me home.*

Before she could say anything, a cold, soggy palm was pressed over her mouth and she was pulled backwards over the railing. And into the water.

23
THE SMOKELESS FLAME

Sadie expected to drown. Her shoulders shook as she gasped for air. But opening her eyes, she found herself alone in a bubble of air. All around her was dark water. Above her, the morning sun flickered, retreating. There was no sign of Tom.

Her ears popped. She was being pulled rapidly downwards. A Drowner's narrow fingers tugged at her tight bubble of safety.

Occasionally a curious fish swam in her direction, then peeled away. A stingray glided above her—it was the most graceful bird she'd ever seen. Her attackers were no less graceful. They moved through the depths like they themselves were the currents, their mouths in silent song.

Then she saw it: the drowned city with its weathered coral towers and turrets, and limestone houses painted with algae and roofed with seaweed. Even in the murky light, it was the most beautiful thing she had ever seen— still, silent, and utterly serene. Brownish reeds drifted like long grass in a summer breeze. Sadie forgot her panic and felt a pang of sadness—not for the city's cursed citizens, but for herself, that she would never live somewhere so tranquil.

As she drifted on, a small figure bobbed up beside her, peering in. It was a child, but its once full cheeks were pallid and puckered. Wide, pale eyes regarded her, and a small hand—three of its fingers worn back to clean bone—pressed against the bubble's thin membrane. A tall woman swam up, snatched back the hand and tugged the child away. As they disappeared, they turned back for a final look at their visitor. It was a look of hope, Sadie realised, feeling the weight of the satchel.

Her bubble was tugged by a sudden current, down towards the black volcanic reef that was the city's foundation. Sadie plummeted down, then was swept up and carried towards a large, grey stone cathedral. At the last moment, barnacled doors opened and she was sucked into a cavernous space. It was lit only by marbled light through vast, arched windows. The bubble grazed the floor and Sadie found herself stumbling across slimy slate, struggling to hold herself upright. She slipped and a flat palm of water slapped her on the backside, knocking her back onto her feet. Then, finally, she was still. On each side of her, an escort stood to attention.

The bubble, which had contracted into a tight cocoon around her, continued shrinking. Soon the water kissed her knees and elbows and finally her cheeks. Seawater surged up her nose and down her throat. The satchel dropped from her hands and the relic tumbled out, cracking against the stone floor.

After everything, this was how she would die, alone on the ocean floor.

Then the water was gone. It dropped back and rushed away from her, scattering itself to the corners of the room. It scurried into narrow tunnels in the base of the wall, and glistened like dark, watchful eyes.

Lysandra swept into the chamber, flanked by a dozen guards. She wore a long, flowing gown that seemed to be woven from fine copper wire. The shoulders and breast-plate were tarnished by verdigris. Her knotted dark hair had been braided into heavy locks. Craning her neck, she gazed at her visitor in profound fascination. 'Brave, remarkable girl. I had nearly given up hope.'

'What happened to Tom?' Sadie asked, wishing she felt as brave as she sounded. When the priestess showed no sign of understanding, she added: 'My friend. We came here together.'

'The boy? He is unharmed.'

'Okay, that's something.' Sadie picked up the box and held it out to Lysandra. 'I brought you the relic. So you can leave us all alone now. That was the deal, yeah?'

'You deceive no one, child. You didn't bring my prize, it brought you.'

'The only thing that brought me here was a boat.'

The priestess nodded, staring hard at Sadie. Her once-dark eyes were clad in a milky film. 'Maybe you don't understand yourself well enough to know the truth. It was hunger that brought you here. A desire to change the world. You want the power in that box as badly as I do.'

She stretched out a long finger and tapped a taloned nail on Sadie's chin. 'I was like you once, Sadie. Ready to reach outside my world to find more.'

Sadie felt she had come prepared for anything but this conversation. She could feel something sour shifting in her gut. 'I don't want anything.' She threw the relic at Lysandra in fury, catching her square on her breastplate. 'Just take your stupid box and go, okay?'

Lysandra's pale eyes flickered at Sadie, but moved quickly to the relic. 'Oh Sadie. The power inside this box. The possibilities. I will make my people Gods. We will claim this world for our own, claim the stars and the sun and the land and the sea. Claim the sky.'

'I don't suppose it matters that you'll start a war?'

'We will win the war.'

'Against the Gods? Yeah, that totally sounds sane.' Sadie heard her voice tremble, and wished it hadn't.

A crowd had gathered in the chamber. Men, women and children took silent places along the walls.

Lysandra smiled. 'I feel your fear, Sadie. You have

held the box, you know the power it will grant me.'

Sadie felt her eyes sting and she tightened her jaw. 'Jake's dead, remember? If you wanted it open, maybe you shouldn't have let your stupid pet kill him.'

But was the box still locked? Sadie couldn't help staring at it, worrying the lid might lift beneath Lysandra's fingers.

The priestess raised her right hand in a grand gesture. The door behind her opened, revealing a shivering wall of water. Two figures crashed through, tumbling onto the slate in a wash of salt and spit and fury. They rolled about, until the larger found his feet and jerked the smaller upright. There was no mistaking the Minotaur, its dark hair matted with blood and seawater, but the second figure made Sadie's breath snag in her chest.

It couldn't be. His jeans were torn and bloody—a horrific gash ran from right knee to hip—and his T-shirt was stained and ragged. His long hair was plastered across his face and his shoulders shook as he fought for breath.

It was Jake.

'What the hell is she doing here?' Jake snapped at Lysandra. 'I told you to leave her on the surface.'

The priestess smiled palely. 'She is important to both of us.' She beckoned for Jake to be brought forward, and he was thrown to his knees beside Sadie.

Sadie bent down to help him up, but he shrugged

her off. She wondered what she had done to make him so angry.

'We saw you,' Sadie whispered. 'Agatha said she felt you go.'

'I wouldn't let him die,' the priestess said, her hand touching the key strung around her throat. 'Asterion is a useful servant. Useful but, as you say, stupid. He was told to bring us both the box and its maker. One is useless without the other.'

Sadie glanced at the Minotaur, towering behind them. Steam curled from its dark nostrils. Asterion. It had a name. It wasn't just a thing.

With a jolt, she felt the beast's dark eyes meet her own.

Lysandra thrust the box at Jake. 'Do it. Release our saviour.'

A murmur passed through the crowd.

'Do it, or we sink her city. Sink your home, as you sank ours.'

Jake looked at Sadie. His mouth was open, and his eyes were red and desperate. Sadie realised this was why Lysandra had brought her here—as leverage, to ensure Jake set the demon free.

'We had a plan, remember?' she said. 'It isn't too late.'

A heavy hand snatched at Sadie's shoulder, pulling her back against the beast's chest. Her hair was tugged, forcing her head down against her left shoulder and exposing her neck. Her temple cracked against the heavy lock chained around the beast's shoulders. She could feel its hot breath on her throat.

Lysandra tutted at Jake. 'Any trickery and Asterion will tear out the girl's throat. It will take but a second.'

'Sadie, you should have stayed on the surface,' Jack said.

She swallowed hard. 'Do what you have to do. Don't worry about me.'

He looked up at her and offered a sad smile. 'It's too late for that.' He stepped forward, grabbed the relic from Lysandra and tore it open.

Nothing happened. A gasp escaped the gathered crowd, echoing across the cathedral's curved ceiling. The box was empty. For a wonderful moment, Sadie thought Jake had fooled them. There was nothing in the box but an old myth.

But then she saw it, the flicker of a tiny fire, a pilot light for an impending blaze. The flame leapt from the box, skipping across the slate in joyful arcs. Before the stone altar, it erupted into a pillar of fire that scorched the overhead beams. Even the Minotaur recoiled, releasing its grip on Sadie and staggering backwards.

Lysandra knelt. Every Drowner in the cathedral followed her example. 'Creature of flame, we have released you from your prison. In return, we ask you to redeem us. Make me your master. Give us back our lives.

Give us justice. Give us vengeance on those who sent us to the depths.'

A wind shifted around the cathedral. To Sadie, it was the demon's voice, rustling and crackling. 'Centuries ago, you summoned me. You praised me. You begged me for immortality. Are you unhappy with my generous gift?'

Lysandra was still kneeling. 'My people have suffered for millennia.'

Sadie felt the demon's voice against her bare arms. 'I served you, priestess,' it said. 'And my reward was to be imprisoned in a box.'

Lysandra's jaw slackened. 'We have searched for an eternity to set you free.'

'And I have languished in darkness while this world has grown old. Soon the Gods will return to snuff it out. What will happen to me then?'

'Together, we will bring the Gods to their knees. With your power, we will have my revenge on those who wronged us both.'

'To be your servant, I would become a soldier?'

'No,' Lysandra said. 'You would become a weapon. A destroyer of Gods.'

The wind dropped for a moment, as if considering. Then it rushed at Sadie, so forcefully that she flinched. When the demon spoke, she felt the air tremble around her.

'You rescued me. You risked your life to bring me to

the water. What would you ask of me?'

Lysandra's mouth fell open in horror.

'Enough,' Jake snapped. 'She doesn't want anything, leave her alone.'

A limb of fire branched away from the column and a small flame darted from it to disappear down Jake's throat. He gasped, hand to his neck, and found his voice burned out.

'I have no interest in the words of Gods, or their envoys,' the demon said. 'You will not speak to me.'

Jake lifted his chin as a small gesture of defiance.

'The girl is nothing,' Lysandra said. 'She is merely a bystander. I freed you. I have earned the right—'

'Silence!' The demon's voice tore around the stone walls, then returned to Sadie as a whisper. 'Tell me what you would ask of me, girl, should I choose you as my master.'

Sadie blinked. Silenced, Jake couldn't ask anything of the demon. Either Sadie or Lysandra would become its master. Sadie could ask it to stop the priestess, but what then?

Sadie looked to Jake, needing him to tell her what to say, but he only smiled. The smile was a poor fit over the troubles beneath.

'Think what powers I might grant you,' the demon said. 'I have touched your mind. I have seen the darkness there. All that death. Would you have me erase it?'

Sadie's voice caught in her throat. 'Erase what, exactly?'

'Please, saviour.' Lysandra raised herself on a single knee, keeping her head lowered. She was trying to remain patient. 'She is nothing but a greedy child. She could never truly be your master.'

'You have had your say, priestess. Now the girl will speak.'

'I don't have anything to say,' Sadie insisted.

'Sadie?'

That voice froze her.

'Sadie, love. You haven't forgotten about us?'

There was her dad, as she always remembered him: corduroy jacket and elbow patches, two weeks late for a haircut, his glasses askew and smudged. And there was her mum, her hair pinned up, one handing resting on her hip. They stood where the flame had burned, in a corona of firelight.

It wasn't them, not really. Sadie knew that. But that didn't stop it hurting. The same air boiled in her chest. She cried the same tears. But she understood what the demon wanted. It didn't want to repay any debt, it wanted her in its debt, forever. She'd seen what it had done to Lysandra. The demon wasn't choosing a new master, not really. It was choosing a slave.

Her parents were gone now, and the flame flickered before her again.

'They are waiting for you, if you ask for them. If I choose you.'

'You want me to make a wish,' Sadie said.

'Perhaps the priestess is right. Perhaps I am a weapon. And a weapon is nothing if it is never used.'

Lysandra was on her feet now. 'A weapon needs a strong hand. It needs ambition. All she offers is grief and heartbreak.'

Sadie ignored her, addressing the flame. 'You could really bring them back?'

'Should I choose you, yes.'

'I could save my family.'

Again, Sadie looked at Jake. He didn't shake his head, or offer a gesture as a warning. It took her a moment to realise why. He knew she would make the right choice. She didn't need his help.

But it did help, thinking of Jake. Because she knew then that you couldn't cheat death, not really. She looked at Lysandra, with her cheekbones of coral. That was what immortality looked like. A dream that came at a terrible cost.

'There's so much I'd change,' Sadie said, quietly. 'I always thought I'd give anything.'

'Then ask. Make me your servant.'

'No.' Sadie's voice surprised her. Any doubts had gone. 'I wouldn't give anything.' Her eyes burned with tears. 'I love my mum, but she's gone. I love my dad, but he's gone. They'll always be gone.' She thought of her grandparents in their Mosman Park cottage. And Tom, on his father's boat. Her cousins, in a police cell. Everything she had done these last days wasn't for excitement. It wasn't to change the world. It was to protect the place she thought she hated, the place she had always dreamed of escaping. 'I wouldn't risk what I have left, not for anything.'

The flame spat impatient sparks. 'Then what is your wish?'

Sadie chose her words carefully. She could feel the Gods listening, waiting on her answer. She could feel their impatience, their anger. 'I ask for nothing. Keep your power to yourself.'

The voice swirled around her, scattering her damp hair. 'To be your servant, I would be free?'

'Yes. Forget all about us. Go back to the sea. Go home.'

Sadie felt the voice move away from her, rushing towards Lysandra.

'Two wishes,' it said. 'Two new masters. One who wants the world, one who wants nothing at all. One who wants war, one who would do anything to stop it.'

'You are a weapon,' the priestess said. 'Choose the master that will put you to the purpose you deserve. Together, we will wage war on the Gods.'

The air in the cathedral was still. Electric. Sadie felt

hairs lift from her arms.

The flame laughed. Quietly, then loud enough to scare dust from the stone walls. Cruel, mocking laughter.

'I am a weapon,' it said.

The column of flame erupted into blinding light. For a moment, Sadie could see a white, helmeted creature, its outstretched arms becoming a pair of powerful wings. Feathers of flame unfurled across the hall. Sadie staggered backwards from its glare, colliding with the stinking beast behind her.

Jake's arm wrapped around her and pulled her sideways.

'I've got you,' he said, his throat parched.

'I thought it would want to be free.'

'I'm sorry.'

'She's really going to do it, she's going to start a war.'

24
HIS LAST BREATH

The glare died down, but a new light poked into the cathedral's forgotten crevices. The stone walls sparkled, and the slate floor shone. The crowd appeared washed in warm sunlight, for the first time in millennia. They were human again, their skin flushed and pink, their eyes clear. Lysandra raised herself to her full height. Her eyes were dark and rich, and her skin was immaculate. Long, glossy hair fell across her elegant shoulders.

Sadie stumbled back, appalled. Lysandra's wish had been granted. Everything was lost. The Gods were coming.

Gliding forward, the priestess pointed at Jake. 'For thousands of years, you denied us our inheritance. You kept our salvation locked away in a box, dooming us to the depths. But those above never forgot us. They invented a name to remember us by, a legend. Atlantis. Today, they will meet that legend and tremble at our might. Today, Atlantis rises!'

'No,' Jake said, and that was all.

Lysandra's dark eyes narrowed. She paused, as if waiting for a punch line. 'Defiance, even now. I am on the threshold of divinity, about to do battle with the Gods themselves. You cannot deny me.'

'You never asked me why. Why I kept the demon from you.'

'You fear war.'

'Yes, but that wasn't all. Look at yourself Lysandra.'

'I am redeemed! We are all redeemed!'

'The demon is a creature of mischief. It has merely been toying with you, just as it toyed with you thousands of years ago. There was no choice for it to make. It already has a master.'

Lysandra flattened a palm across her breastplate. 'I am its master!'

'I hid from you for too long. I was scared, I was ashamed. I could have put an end to this long ago. It took Sadie to show me that.'

Sadie thought she understood. 'It's you,' she said. 'Back at the God squad place. You spoke to it. It chose you.'

Jake nodded. 'I told it you would bring it here. I said it would be free. On one condition. That it undid its last wish. That it put things right.'

Lysandra hissed. 'But I have my immortality!'

'You have your life,' Jake said. 'What little of it remains.'

Lysandra glanced at the glowing creature to her left: this strange, incandescent bird of flame hovering above the tiles. She turned her hands over. They were no longer beautiful. The skin was loose and liver-spotted, sagging about her long fingers. She lifted them to snatch at her slackening face. Heavy bags were pulling cheeks down and away from foggy eyes.

'No. No, this cannot be.' The protest turned to powder on Lysandra's dry tongue.

A terrified chorus rose from those gathered. Children split their clothes, growing up and then creasing over as they withered like old trees. The stones in the walls no longer sparkled. Cracks appeared, spitting grey dust. Water hissed and pressed at the windows. The roof began to crumble. The years, all those stolen centuries, were consuming the Drowners. Fathers and mothers and children were clattering to the uneven floor as rags and bones.

Sadie stared in horror, snatching at Jake's elbow. 'They're dying. All of them.'

'They should have died a long time ago.'

'But—I told you to stop her.'

Jake turned sharply towards her, gripping her jaw between finger and thumb, holding her gaze. 'And I did. But you were right, Sadie. It's not my fault, and it's certainly not yours. She did this. Lysandra, alone.'

The demon was laughing, delighting in the chaos

it had wrought. And then it was gone. A bird of light, a hawk, then a dove, then a sparrow, then a moth flickered against the dark windows. Then it was through the glass, fading away in the deep water. After thousands of years, it was home. The fire in the sea. Sadie watched it go, transfixed. Jake grabbed her hand and spun her towards the door. 'We're leaving!'

A great wooden beam came crashing down, bringing most of the ceiling with it. Jumping clear, Sadie saw Lysandra launch herself at Jake, shrieking. There was little of her left but sinew and skeleton. Only her rage kept her alive. She knocked him to the ground, and her spindly arms pinned his wrists to the slate. The box skidded away across the tiles.

'I will see you broken for this. I will tear out your soul.' Her right hand plunged down, forcing itself into Jake's open mouth.

Sadie had been knocked onto her backside and, with the city crumbling around her, took a few seconds to realise what was happening. The priestess was attempting to tear Jake from his body, just as the attackers had tried that first night at the beach. Sadie rushed at Lysandra, and tried to pull her off by her armpits, but the priestess was as stiff and sturdy as a sunbaked tree trunk. Sadie looked about for a weapon and grabbed the abandoned box. With a yell of desperation, she brought it crashing down on Lysandra's balding scalp.

The priestess flinched, weakening for only a moment. Still, it was time enough. Jake's shoulders buckled and he threw Lysandra off him and wrestled her back to the floor. The last of the fury seemed to go out of her. And she turned to dust in his hands.

Jake leapt to his feet, ready to run, as another girder fell. The roof was all but destroyed now, and there was no way to reach the door. Before Sadie could say anything, the windows shattered. The water rushed in with cruel relish, smashing the two of them against what remained of the walls. They were thrown and tumbled—currents passed them about like playground bullies tossing a stolen ball.

Sadie thought she might be lost forever in the fizz and spin. There was the sun, squinting down at her through the murk and the maelstrom. It was too far away, she could see that. She wasn't going to make it to the surface. As she watched, the light seemed to recede. She forced herself to concentrate, and forced her tired legs to kick. She looked for the light, pushed herself towards it. The city fell away beneath her. She could do this.

The water warmed around her. She swam towards the distant sun. But she could feel herself starting to slow. Her legs floundered, exhausted and useless. Too late, she thought. Her empty chest burned and it was all she could do to stop herself gulping down seawater.

Then Jake was in front of her, a smudge of colour in

the pale light. He took her face in both hands and pressed his lips to hers. Her cheeks filled and her lungs relaxed. He was giving her his last breath.

All the time, he kept kicking with his battered legs, lifting her towards the surface. As tiny bubbles escaped from the edges of his mouth, his kicks became sloppy. Finally, his body convulsed and he let go of her. His mouth opened and the sea filled it. He hung there, a broken thing, suspended in cold sunlight.

Sadie lifted her chin. The sun was looking for her, glancing through the choppy surface, feeling into the depths. She guessed she had another five metres. She could do that. She swam over to Jake, hooked her arms under his and kicked with the last of her energy. Her movements were clumsy and desperate, every muscle surrendering, but the sun swelled with each new kick. Slowly, slowly.

Her head was buzzing and there was panic in her stomach. The closer she got to the surface, the harder it was to hold her breath—Jake's breath. She kicked with new fury, with outrage. She was so close. She wouldn't be beaten by a few feet of water. And then, then—

25
SHORE LEAVE

The sun smacked Sadie in the face. She spat water and swallowed air. Each breath was a sweet salve for the burning in her chest.

Jake's head was heavy on her right shoulder. Numbness spread out to her fingertips, which clawed at his T-shirt. Below, Sadie's legs danced awkwardly. She couldn't keep both of them afloat for long.

The mid-morning sun spread out across the towering wave which still blocked the horizon. If the wave was still there, Sadie thought, then Perth was still there. For now. There wasn't time to be happy about that. They had to be at least five kilometres offshore, maybe more. There was no way she could make it that far and, besides, Jake wasn't breathing.

In the distance, something glinted. Something steel, something white. Sadie squinted, trying to make it out. It was getting closer. Could it be the yacht? She was sure she could hear the murmur of an engine.

'Sades!'

It was the yacht, tracing the wall of water. Tom thrashed his arms about in greeting.

Sadie almost sank with relief. She tried to wave, tried to shout, but only ended up gargling.

Within a minute, Tom was alongside. He reached over the side of the boat to her.

'Don't worry about me,' Sadie gasped. 'Get Jake on board.'

'He's alive?'

'He was. Come on, quick!'

Tom dragged Jake up onto the deck. 'Those guys, those things. They sort of became normal. They were cheering, like it was New Year's. You know, swords in the air. Then, I don't know, they just dropped their swords and wasted away. The boat started rocking. I thought we were gonna capsize.'

Sadie didn't say anything. The scene in the cathedral seemed a long way away now, and she wanted to leave it there. Clambering aboard, she fell forwards on her hands and knees. For a second, she thought she might be sick. In the stillness, on the boat deck, the panic and despair of the last hours threatened to overwhelm her.

'Did you do it?' Tom asked. 'Did you stop them?'

'Jake did it. Just like he promised.'

'So we're safe?'

Sadie glanced upwards at an angry sun. She didn't

know what she was expecting. Lightning bolts? A falling sky? 'I don't know. Not yet.'

She rolled Jake over on his side and found a weak pulse in his wrist. He was alive. He had survived the Minotaur and survived Lysandra. Surely he could survive this. Water flowed from his slack mouth. She pinched his nose and pressed her lips to his. She breathed out sharply, four times, and watched Jake's chest. Nothing. She gave Jake another four breaths. Still nothing.

The boat rocked, lurching forwards as the prow dipped. A heavy, dark figure had torn itself free of the water wall and landed on the deck. It threw back its bovine head and roared. Not the sound of triumph, but anguish.

Tom dropped to a crouch and scurried away, as far as he could get from the creature. He could barely look at it. His flushed cheeks seemed suddenly wan.

Keeping her eyes on the beast, Sadie slowly reached across the deck and dragged over one of the Drowners' fallen swords. She stood, even as the boat lurched again. The Minotaur moved towards her.

'You'll need to look after Jake,' she told Tom. 'Like I was doing, four breaths at a time.'

'Sades, that thing's deadly.'

'I know.'

Sadie edged forwards along the guide-rail. She held a palm out before her, as if hoping to calm an excited pup. The beast bellowed at her, all spittle and fury, squinting in the dazzling light off the water.

The sword was heavy. Every muscle in Sadie's arm strained to hold it steady. The point of the blade wavered in the direction of the beast's heart. If the Minotaur were to throw itself towards her, would she be strong enough to kill it? What was the alternative?

'Asterion? That's your name, yeah?'

Again the beast roared, swiping at her with its gruesome nails. Foul stenches leached from its matted fur. Rancid meat clung to its jaws. She took another step forward.

'It's just you and me now,' she said.

The creature roared again, spraying her with things she didn't want to think about. She resisted the urge to wipe her face, and moved closer still. The beast's foul breath made her gag, but she kept the sword's tip pointing towards its heart. She could kill it now, with one thrust of the blade.

Every moment she delayed, every second she postponed, she put her life at risk. And the lives of everyone onboard.

'Please,' Sadie said.

The Minotaur shifted, and a high, thin note chimed along the blade. The jagged edge had struck the lock strung around the creature's neck. Sadie had never thought about the chain. But now she remembered Lysandra's pendant—a key—on a length of foul string.

The sword trembled in her aching hand. Her gaze met the creature's dark glare. The eyes twitched and, behind them, she saw intelligence.

Sadie wasn't a killer. She thought of Lysandra's people, dying in darkness for thousands of years, their faces falling apart on the ocean floor. She thought of Frobisher, his blood setting in the carpet. And she thought of her parents. She had seen enough death.

Gritting her teeth, Sadie swiped forwards and upwards. The blade snagged on the chain around the creature's neck. She thrust her weight underneath it. A link buckled and finally, finally, the chain gave way, falling heavily to the deck.

There was a moment of absolute stillness. Even the waves seemed to pause as the Minotaur stared at its liberator. Then, it roared once more and threw itself at her. Sadie was knocked backwards. Heavy paws pinned her shoulders to the deck. A terrible jaw loomed above her, ready to snap shut around her throat.

Sadie closed her eyes and pulled her head back, just as the Minotaur lunged forwards and—

Licked her cheek. Its rough tongue sandpapered the line of her jaw.

Before Sadie could complain, there was a terrific crash overboard and she was alone on the front deck, with nothing but a length of rusted chain.

From the stern, she could hear spluttering. She

thought it might have been Jake, coming around, but the coughing belonged to Tom. Jake sat astride him, holding him down by his throat. Seeing Sadie, he released his grip.

'A bit disorientated,' he said, getting to his feet and helping Tom up. 'I thought he was attacking me.' He vigorously shook Tom's hand. 'My apologies. And thanks. You're a good man.'

Sadie threw both arms around Jake, causing him to stagger back under the impact. His skin was cold, but he was alive. They were both alive.

Tom cleared his throat.

'Sorry,' Sadie muttered, tightening her lips in an embarrassed smile.

Tom shrugged. 'Whatever.'

Jake was standing back from both of them. He wasn't celebrating. His hands were in pale fists by his jeans pockets, his face grim. He was watching the skies, waiting.

Sadie went to stand beside him. 'You think we're still in trouble. Are the Gods coming?'

He nodded. 'I can feel them,' he said.

At that, the sky seemed to shake. It was as if some great hands had lifted it by invisible corners to scatter the clouds like crumbs. The warm morning blue was gone, replaced by a darkness pricked by cold stars. The air hummed, then buzzed, then rumbled. The sea flexed and buckled. Sadie, Jake and Tom were thrown to the deck.

This was it. The Gods were here.

For some reason, Sadie's first instinct was to apologise. To nobody, to everybody. She had tried. She had played by their rules. She had asked the demon for nothing. It wasn't fair.

'No,' she said. Once with disbelief, then again with anger. 'No!'

Her hands gripped the edge of the yacht, pulling herself upright. She stood on the pitching deck and thrust her chin at the heavens. 'No!'

There was a rush of water and the boat lurched several metres in the air. Sadie felt she was being thrust into the sky to meet the descending army. Then the prow dipped and the boat dropped—a few seconds ahead of its crew's stomachs.

Then nothing.

Quiet. A clear sky was pulled tight above them. The sun made Sadie squint. The wave had flattened out. Once more the horizon was marked with cargo ships waiting to dock and the flat beaches of Rottnest Island.

'Is that it?' Sadie asked, looking at Jake, who was finding his feet. 'They're gone?'

He looked about, cautiously. Waited. 'It seems so.'

'I really thought they were going to do it. I thought we were all going to die.'

'Not today.'

Jake still didn't seem all that relieved. Maybe it was hard to let go of that much fear, that much anxiety, after so long.

'What changed their minds?' Sadie asked.

'You did.'

'The shouting?'

'No.' Jake gave her the smallest of smiles. 'You changed their minds because you changed my mind. Nobody born on this planet used that demon's power. Only I did. If they still have a problem, they'll take it up with me. In the end, they had no reason to be angry with you. Nothing to prove, no threat to vanquish.'

'But they peeled back the sky. The sun disappeared.'

'A bit of sabre-rattling, that's all. A final warning. You did it Sadie, you did the impossible. You saved your city, and the world too.'

'So they've forgiven us, for ever challenging them? For Lysandra?'

Jake's teeth tugged at his bottom lip. He nodded.

They were safe. There would be no war.

Sadie smiled. Laughed. Relief fizzed up into her shoulders. She pulled Tom to his feet and hugged the air out of him. He hugged her back.

Along the coast, low dark clouds boiled away into nothing. Sparkling sunlight began to clear away the mess. That wasn't all. Tom switched off the engine and unfurled the boat's white sail. The sea breeze had finally arrived, ready to take them back to shore.

~

Tom dropped Jake and Sadie at the harbour, pulling in at the quay behind a Norwegian container ship. He was planning to sail the boat upriver, back to the yacht club, but all Sadie could think about was her grandparents. She needed to be home.

Sadie kissed Tom's cheek and Jake shook his hand. The two of them clambered up the tall, rusted ladder to stand on the quay. They waited for Tom to pull away, his boat dwarfed by the freighter in the neighbouring dock.

No trains were running, so Sadie and Jake walked. For an hour and a half, they held each other's hand and said absolutely nothing.

On the corner of Swan Street, Jake stopped. He wasn't coming with her.

Sadie couldn't bring himself to let get of his hand. To let go of everything that had happened. Her legs trembled but her hand was steady.

Gently, Jake unpicked her fingers from his. 'You know where to find me,' he said.

The front door was open, letting in the long-awaited breeze. As soon as Sadie closed the front gate, Ida rushed out onto the veranda and threw her arms around her granddaughter.

As her cheek brushed her nan's, Sadie burst into tears. It was relief, but more than that, it was the warm love she felt for and from her grandmother. She knew then that she was already forgiven, that there would be time later to explain the last few days.

'Oh Sadie, my poor love, look at you. Are you hurt?'

'I'm fine, Nan. Just a few scratches.'

'Come inside, and I'll run you a bath.'

Stan was waiting by the door. He looked over Sadie's injuries as she was led inside, and his top lip tightened. He was angry at her for putting herself in danger. It was love, Sadie realised. He was angry because he cared. She wanted to explain, then and there, to tell him everything, but knew she couldn't. Not now. Maybe not ever.

She was home. But it wasn't quite the same place she had left.

26
A NEW GRAVITY

Sadie slept. A new gravity pulled her into the depths of slumber, where no sunlight could reach her. Her body was heavy and useless, sinking her to the ocean floor and making a mattress of the seabed. Her parents were there. She tried to call out to them, but the heavy water muffled her cries. She tried to swim towards them, but her limbs were tired and useless. As she watched, the current took them away from her.

When Sadie finally woke, there was stark afternoon sunlight behind the curtains and voices in the hall.

'Let him in, Nan,' she called, recognising Tom's voice.

Tom came in, a newspaper under one arm, a denim jacket under the other, and a mug of tea in each hand. He put Sadie's down on her bedside table and sat down on the end of the bed. There was a new recklessness to his movements, a new ease, that Sadie quite liked.

'I can't stay,' he said. 'Dad's down the road, getting a quote on the 4WD. You wouldn't believe how much it cost to tow it home. The back axle is completely busted. I am in some serious shit.'

'What did you tell him?'

'What do you reckon? I told him it was all your fault.'

Grinning, he threw the newspaper across the doona cover. A special wrap-around was plastered with images of destruction: crushed cars, flooded homes, broken buildings. Overleaf, there were a few blurry photographs of the tsunami waiting off the coast, evidently snapped on someone's mobile phone.

'You should check out page fifteen,' Tom said.

Sadie thumbed through, finding the breathless story of a car chase through the university grounds. Agatha was mentioned by name, as was someone Sadie didn't know. For a moment she was puzzled, then she twigged— Vincent. Both had been released on bail, the story noted with disappointment. There was no mention of the twins. It helped to have a lawyer for a father.

'There was something on the radio too, driving here,' Tom said, frowning. 'About Stephen Cooper. They're saying it was some kind of wild animal. Escaped from a private zoo, got freaked by the storm.'

'Just like at the hospital?'

'Old stories are the best, I guess.'

Sadie looked up, hearing an off note. 'Are you worried?'

'Yeah, a bit. I don't want to have to explain, if someone comes asking.'

'We didn't do anything wrong.'

'Maybe. Still, you know.'

'I know.' He just wanted to forget. She couldn't blame him.

Outside, a horn honked.

'What's he going to do, your dad?' she asked.

'I don't know. Send me off to boot camp.'

'I'll write every day.'

'Yeah, right.' Tom got to his feet and remembered the denim jacket he'd brought with him. 'Don't know whose this is, do you? I found it on the back seat.' He threw it at Sadie. It landed on the floor.

'It's Vincent's.' Sadie crinkled her nose. 'Probably won't fit him now.'

The horn honked again. Puffing his chest with exaggerated courage, Tom waved and left her alone with the paper.

After four pages of disaster reports, there was a second front page, where the paper proper commenced. The lead story startled her. There had been another shooting, this time a taxi driver, Isaac Thompson, gunned down in his driveway as he finished a night shift.

Sadie had forgotten about the murderer. She read through the report, allowing her tea to go cold. Someone was killing Jake's people.

She swung her legs off the mattress and planted both feet down on Vincent's jacket. Something hard and flat pressed against her right heel. Scooping the jacket up, she tugged the object free from its pocket. It was a small, hard-cover book—a diary, she thought. No, it wasn't a diary. It was an address book. Frobisher's address book.

Sadie flipped through the pages and found her own address near the middle. Why would Vincent have Frobisher's book? And when would he have taken it?

The truth landed on her like a slap—brutal, surprising, frightening. She opened the book and found Patrick's name and address. She snatched the paper from the bed and checked the lead story. Isaac Thompson. She found his name, and Maud and Agatha.

Sadie remembered what Jake had said, the night Mrs Mitchell turned up. He had been convinced the killer was using the address book to hunt his squadron down. But they had found Vincent hiding like the others, tucked away in the garage.

Hiding, Sadie wondered, or waiting? If he'd really been that scared, he could have run, with or without Frobisher's help. But he hadn't run. Even when the Minotaur had killed him, he came back. Like he still had a job to do. He had helped Lysandra, all those years ago, hadn't he? It was no stretch to imagine him helping her again.

But why kill his own squadron? His own friends?

Sadie glanced at the page her finger had bookmarked:

Agatha. Agatha had told her what would happen, if Lysandra started a war. Jake's squadron would fight alongside the Gods. Is that why Vincent killed them? Was he bumping off the opposition? That made a terrible sort of sense.

She needed to tell Jake. Vincent might still be a threat. He would know now that Lysandra had lost. He had lost. She couldn't really see him crawling back to beg forgiveness. He might be angry, might even—

The book fell from Sadie's hand. She dropped to her knees and grabbed her boots from underneath the bed.

That bike of hers had never moved so fast. Sadie wasn't even sure she breathed more than twice before she got to the top of the hill at Broome Street and hurried down to the sea. At the old house, she threw the bike on the kerb and sprinted up the cracked brick path. The front door was ajar.

There were no lights on in the hall. As she edged the door open, cold air surged out against the morning heat. She listened to the old house's whispers and complaints. From the front room, she could hear whimpering.

Maud was hidden behind an armchair, clutching Tenielle to her breast. The young woman's cheeks were flushed with tears, but the baby was sleeping. Seeing Sadie, Maud squeaked, then sighed with relief.

'It's Vincent,' she whispered. 'He had a gun.'

Sadie nodded. 'Where is he?'

'Upstairs. He wanted to speak to Jacob.'

A shot rang out from the first floor. Something heavy crashed down, shaking dust and plaster from the ceiling.

'Jake!'

Sadie forgot her caution and ran for the stairs. She took three steps at a time, arriving breathless on the landing.

From the end of the hall, another shot. Again, Sadie ran, ricocheting off the walls in her haste. She burst into Jake's bedroom. He was on the floor, a wound in his side and another in his thigh. Blood was pooling around his knees. 'Sadie,' he said, his eyes watering, 'get out of here.'

Vincent turned to her and the gun followed. He held it loosely in his hands, almost as if he couldn't bear to touch it, as if it were leading him on. His eyes were red and his cheeks were swollen. 'You,' he said. 'This is all your fault.'

'I found Frobisher's address book.'

'You got me killed by that thing. That animal. You have no idea how much that hurt.'

'Vincent, please.' Jake's forehead shone in the light through the window. 'She doesn't matter. Not to you.'

Vincent rounded on him, jabbing the gun towards Jake's chest. 'You ruined everything!' he shrieked. 'We could have torn down the heavens!'

'You were working for Lysandra,' Sadie said.

'She came to me three months ago. She promised to share her power, if I helped her get her revenge. On him.' He jabbed again at Jake. 'On the squadron that betrayed her.'

'Your friends.'

'They were never my friends. They'd have happily done the same to me.'

'And you weren't worried about what the Gods would do?'

Vincent sneered at her. 'Don't you get it? We would have been Gods. An army of new Gods, rising up against those who wronged us.'

Jake shook his head. 'Laying waste to this world… your battleground.'

'It wasn't just Lysandra who was wronged,' Vincent spat. 'I too deserved vengeance.'

'But why sell the relic to the God squad?' Sadie asked. Her hands were up now, just. She was moving into the room slowly, calmly. 'Why not just hold onto it?'

'Jacob would have taken it and run,' Vincent said. 'So I made sure it was somewhere he couldn't find it. Not until we were ready.'

'Not until you'd kept your side of the bargain?' Sadie suggested.

Jake's eyes were closed, his head down, but he shook his head. 'Not until I met with her…she needed to make sure…make sure I would open it…she needed me broken…'

Sadie understood. 'She knew you couldn't stand by and let another city sink. Just like I knew.'

'She was…counting on my guilt…'

'Funnily enough, I really wasn't sure you'd care,' Vincent said.

Sadie ignored him. 'And that's why Vincent came here that night. He wanted us to find him so he could lead us to the relic. Because he knew the Minotaur was waiting.'

'Waiting to take me,' Jake said. 'And the demon…'

Vincent turned to face him, the gun pointed at Jake's heart. 'The thing is, I understood Lysandra. I understood how much she needed this. That's why I helped her. I know what you think, but it wasn't just for glory, for power. It was because I understood.'

'But it's all over,' Sadie said. 'Lysandra's dead. There is no war. There's no point in killing anyone else.'

For a moment, the gun dipped in Vincent's hand. He glanced sideways at Sadie, never quite taking his eyes off Jake. 'You've wrecked everything. Wrecked me. What am I now? Just a traitor. A fool who picked the losing side.' His teeth set, fingers tightening again around the gun. 'This, this is the only revenge I have left.'

Jake opened his eyes. They had never seemed so blue, Sadie thought. For some long seconds, he stared at Vincent up the barrel of his weapon. There was no anger left, no fury. If anything, Sadie thought, it was a look of pity.

'Do it,' he said.

Sadie wasn't sure she had heard him right. What did he think he was doing?

Vincent was just as confused. He tilted his head. 'What?'

'I opened the relic. I used the demon's power. We're both traitors. Both doomed. But let Sadie go. Do one good thing.'

Oh God. Sadie felt sick. Maybe he meant it. Maybe he thought he was being noble, heroic.

'Jake,' Sadie hissed, 'shut up. Please.'

He still wasn't looking at her. 'I have always wondered what it felt like to face death. Now I know.'

Sadie was crying openly now, spluttering salt and snot and steam. 'Jake, please, shut up.'

Jake smirked. 'And, you know what, Vincent, you'll never understand that. You think you understood Lysandra? All you recognised was yourself. We don't belong in the heavens. This is all that matters, here. We were meant to live with our feet on the ground. To know what it was like to be human.' He looked at Sadie. 'Well—I know. After all these years, I know.'

Vincent was shaking with anger, his teeth grinding. He held the gun to the bridge of Jake's nose.

Jake was perfectly calm. He waited some long seconds, then allowed himself a chuckle. 'You won't do it.

I'll tell you why.'

A muscle twitched in Vincent's jaw. 'Why?'

'You're too scared. I've looked after you too long.'

Vincent's eyes bulged with new outrage. 'Looked after me?'

'But that isn't why. Ask my dog why.'

'Your—'

Vincent hadn't seen Kingsley waiting at the door, and didn't see him cross the floorboards in two bounds and sink his teeth into his calf. The first thing he saw was blood and denim and slobber. Jake's left leg swept out and knocked Vincent from his feet, landing him heavily on his side. The gun fell from his hand and scudded into the skirting board. Jake tried to dive for it, but the wound in his side checked him. Vincent crawled forward, Kingsley still gripping his leg. His fingers reached for the weapon.

Sadie was too slow, too shocked. By the time she moved, Vincent had already snatched the gun and was snarling and jabbing the barrel at the dog.

A shot went off and everyone stopped, holding on to the moment, worried what would come next.

In the doorway, a policeman with a red moustache had his gun pointed at the ceiling. 'Okay,' he grunted. 'At least one of you is under arrest.'

~

Tom's phone rang in the other room. Lifting it from the dining table, he saw Sadie's face peering from the screen. He realised that that sick feeling in his gut—he was never sure if it was terror or excitement—had gone. Two days ago he would have been doing nothing but waiting for this call. Today, her face was a surprise. He only felt happy. Comfortable.

'Yeah? It's been, what, an hour?'

'Tom, it's Jake.'

Okay, that troubled his gut. Just a little. Just for a moment. There were voices in the background.

'Sadie's here, at Ocean Street. She needs you.'

He took his mum's keys without asking and drove too fast along the beach road. Sunburned pedestrians jumped clear at the zebra crossing. There was a police car and an ambulance parked out the front of Jake's place, lights flashing about the veranda.

Sadie was upstairs, sitting on the edge of a bed. A young paramedic sat beside her, with a hand on her shoulder. Sadie was in shock, she said, it was perfectly natural.

'I'm completely fine,' Sadie muttered. She was pale, her cheeks waxy. The last few days had caught up with her, all at once. Maybe there wasn't any need to be strong now. Her gaze kept returning to the blood on the floorboards. There was no sign of Jake.

'Come on.' Tom held out his hand, and pulled her

up. 'I'm taking you home.'

'Leave me, I'm fine. I'm good. I'm fine. It's all good.'

Tom wrapped an arm around her. 'Shut up Sades.'

She let him lead her downstairs. Her head pressed against his chest. He helped her into his mother's car and drove her home in silence.

It was a lot more than nothing, he thought, to be needed.

27
THE NEXT LIFE

Two nights later, Sadie woke to find Jake, outside under the fig tree. There was no fruit left, just a few green carcasses split open among dry leaves. Kingsley poked among them with his rumpled nose.

Sadie tucked her nightie into a pair of jeans and pulled on her boots. Opening the back door, she found the night still and warm.

'You've made a quick recovery. I'm guessing Agatha's okay, then?' she asked, sitting down on her window ledge. She was happy to see him, she knew that, so why didn't she feel happy?

Jake nodded, smoothing down the front of his T-shirt. 'I'm a miracle of medical science.'

'She should open her own clinic. She'd make a mint from the Botox set.'

'I wonder if that might draw unhealthy attention, somehow.'

They both smiled into a silence that moved in like a

sudden cold current.

'The police are still all over the house,' Jake said. 'Plastic tape everywhere. I'm keeping out of their way.'

'And I thought you'd come because you wanted to see me.'

'I do want to see you.'

There was another silence. Sadie traced a figure eight in the soil with the toe of her boot. She wanted to say she missed him. That she woke up needing to talk to him.

It was strange, this distance between them. Had it been danger that had brought them close? In peace, in quiet, was there nothing to be said?

'I guess the demon is still out there, off the coast somewhere.'

Jake nodded. 'It's gone home.'

Sadie bit her lip. 'So you're good to go.'

Jake straightened up. 'You know I'm leaving?'

'That's why you're here, isn't it? To break the news gently?'

Her smirk confused him. 'Sadie, this always had to happen. I used the demon's power. The Gods will be furious.'

'But they weren't! There wasn't a war. They got rid of that wave, the clouds. You said they'd forgiven us.'

'They've forgiven you, not me. I did a deal with a forbidden creature. They're never going to forgive me for that.'

'What are they going to do to you?'

'I don't know. But I'm not going to hang around and wait.' He took her hand. 'You could come with me. We'll go out into the world, have new adventures. That's what you've always wanted, isn't it?'

In the moonlight, it seemed a pale offer, one neither of them expected her to consider. Leaving was all she had wanted to do for as long as she could remember. Now, closer than ever to the horizon, she knew she wasn't ready.

'It's funny,' she said, 'the demon offered me everything I'd always wanted. But in the end, it was easy to turn it down. I used to think there was nothing here for me. But there is. Everything is here. Not always, but for now, yes.'

Jake understood, taking back his hand. Sadie almost wished he hadn't. She wanted to reach forward and grab it.

'You'll have to keep the dog,' he said, suddenly businesslike. 'And the house. It's all in your name, of course. There are other things in that old place, things that will need to be looked after.' He met her eye. 'Dangerous things, Sadie, things people will be looking for. I wouldn't trust anyone else to keep them safe.'

'Yeah. I don't know. I can't see Grandpa ever agreeing to that.'

Jake didn't argue. He took a step backwards, already halfway gone.

'I'll find you,' he said. 'When you're ready.'

Sadie nodded. She watched him ruffle Kingsley's ears and massage his jowls. Then the only noise he made came from dry leaves beneath his sneakers, as he walked off alone.

Ida didn't say anything about the dog, not immediately. Still, she came back from the supermarket with six tins of dog food and a wicker basket. Stan didn't say anything either—just shook his head and went out into the garden.

That night, there was a knock on Sadie's door and Stan came in without waiting. He didn't say anything, not straightaway, and Sadie worried he was about to start shouting. Instead, he handed her the picture frame he was holding.

She had seen the photo before, in a different frame. It took her a while to remember where. By then, she had found not one but two faces in the uniformed line-up. There, named in a neat script at the bottom of the photograph, was S. R. Greene. And, there beside him, grinning for the camera, was a young J. L. Freeman.

'You knew Mr Freeman,' Sadie murmured. 'During the war.'

'Same squadron,' Stan nodded. 'He was a right bastard. Thought we were making a mistake fighting the Germans, thought we should be giving them a helping hand. No fan of the Jews, or the Gypsies. He used to call me Red, not for my hair colour. Then, one day his plane went down. Crashed in some village. We all thought he was dead, but he wasn't. He came back. Except he came back a different man. A better man. He became the best friend I ever had.' Stan frowned. 'But one night, when we were out drinking, towards the end of the war, he told me what he was.'

Sadie laughed, astonished. 'And you believed him?'

'It was wartime. I'd seen far stranger things than Gods and monsters.'

'But you didn't approve? Of what he was, I mean.'

'How could I? Men all over the world were laying down their lives for what they thought was right. He made a mockery of all that, jumping from body to body like some bloody flea. If death meant nothing, life meant nothing either.' His bottom lip jutted. 'We fell out. I never spoke to him again.'

'You didn't know he was here?'

'I'd told him I was planning on emigrating, after the war. Told him about Perth. Somewhere safe, the other side of the world. I never dreamed he'd come. Then I heard that name, right next to yours. And I saw this, in that house. The same picture, up in that study of his.'

Sadie remembered now—her grandfather's creased face peering into one of the picture frames that first afternoon at Ocean Street. She felt a brief pang of sadness for

Jacob, for her grandpa; these two lost friends, kept apart. Had Jake known?

'I heard you,' Stan said, 'in the garden last night.'

'Oh.' Sadie wondered how embarrassed she should be.

'You want us to move into that old house of his.'

'I think I do, yeah.'

Stan nodded, saying nothing.

'We saved the world, Grandpa,' Sadie said. 'Him and me, the whole world.' She paused. 'I just know it's the right thing to do.'

Stan's lips parted, then sealed. He patted her knee, stood up, and left the room.

On the last night of the school holidays, Sadie, Tom and her cousins ate pizza on the first floor veranda of One Ocean Street, while the sun set behind Rottnest Island. Tired from a day's packing and unpacking, they argued over a game of *Monopoly* until Margot called, wondering what had happened to her daughters.

'She's always calling now,' Kim grumbled. 'Seriously, it's driving me mental.'

'I'll give you a lift,' Tom said, tidying the game away.

Leaving, he ruffled Sadie's hair and she slapped at his thigh, not bothering to get up. Soon, she watched his car pull away from the kerb below, then turn right at Marine

Parade and drive off into the still night.

There was no one around. The town was fixed in amber streetlight like an ancient photograph.

No, Sadie realised, there was someone. A dark figure stood on the bike path, right by the edge of the dunes. For a moment, she thought it was Jake. But as he moved out of the shadows, Sadie realised she was wrong. The tips of the beast's horns glistened in the streetlight. He was staring straight at her, that much was certain, and, sure that he had been seen, he tossed his head back and bellowed.

The roar echoed along the town's empty streets, a sudden, solitary note of excitement. Lights flicked on in darkened windows and faces pressed to the glass, hoping to catch a look. It was too late, the figure had already turned and fled down the dunes, into the black water. Sadie suspected he wouldn't go far, that cutting his chain had sparked some new loyalty in the beast.

Stan appeared in the doorway. 'Sadie?'

'It's nothing, Grandpa, just the sea.'

Her grandfather nodded, relieved. He smiled.

As his footsteps retreated up the hallway, Sadie took herself off to bed. Settling into the mattress, she adjusted the old mug on her bedside table. The perfect rose swung around to look at her, keeping watch as she drifted into sleep.

ACKNOWLEDGEMENTS

I would like to thank everyone at Text Publishing for being so welcoming and encouraging. And for creating the Text Prize, without which this book would never have been written.

I'd like to thank my editor Jane Pearson for finding all the best bits and the missing parts. I worry I'll now always be dependent on her insight, guidance, patience, praise and ruthlessness.

I'd like to thank Natalie Book for her generous notes and valued opinions.

I'd like to thank Jason Andrews for building, rebuilding and managing my website.

I'd like to thank everyone who downloaded my podcasts and made me think I might have an audience.

I'd like to thank my mum for buying me a notebook when I was eight and writing 'author' on the cover.

I'd like to thank my dad for not worrying too much that I never took to finding a real job.

Mostly, I'd like to thank my wife Milly for not laughing all those years ago when I made plans to be a penniless writer. Or maybe she did laugh. But for supporting me, encouraging me and never trying to stop me, I thank her.